Wesleyan Methodist Church and Jacob's Ladder, Falmouth

THE IMPROBABLE STORY OF ORION GOSS

VICKY WOODCRAFT

INDIGO DREAMS PUBLISHING

First Edition: The Improbable Story Of Orion Goss

First published in Great Britain in 2012 by:
Indigo Dreams Publishing Ltd
132 Hinckley Road
Stoney Stanton
Leics
LE9 4LN
www.indigodreams.co.uk

ISBN 978–1–907401–89–3

British Library Cataloguing in Publication Data. A CIP record for this book can be obtained from the British Library.

Designed and typeset in Minion Pro by Indigo Dreams.
Cover design by Ronnie Goodyer at Indigo Dreams
Cover photo 'Moonlight on Gyllyngvase' copyright The Francis Frith Collection
Two further images courtesy of Andrew Campbell, Imagedelivery, Falmouth
Printed and bound in Great Britain by: The Russell Press Ltd.
www.russellpress.com on FSC paper and board sourced from sustainable forests.

MIX
Paper from
responsible sources
FSC® C021423

NOTE

The artists Henry Scott Tuke and Charles Napier Hemy lived, worked and sailed in the Falmouth area in the late Nineteenth and early Twentieth centuries.

Orion Goss, his family and friends are imaginary characters and no resemblance is intended to any real persons, alive or dead.

The following story is entirely fictional.

To George, of course. For his (almost) unending patience.

ACKNOWLEDGEMENTS

The following publications, among others, have been useful in researching the background to this story.

All About Gardening by Harry Roberts. Ward Lock and Co, 1913.

A Brief History of Thyme and other herbs by Miranda Seymour. John Murray, 2002.

Catching the Light. The Art and Life of Henry Scott Tuke by Catherine Wallace, Atelier Books. 2008.

Cornwall, A History by Philip Payton. Cornwall Editions Limited 1996 and 2004.

Henry Scott Tuke With Brush and Sail. David Crabb. 2009.

Henry Scott Tuke: Under Canvas by D Wainwright and K Dinn. Serema Press, 1989.

Everyday Fashions of the 20th Century by Avril Lansdell. Shire Publications. 1999.

Falmouth in Old Photographs – Collected by Peter Gilson. Alan Sutton Publishing. 1990.

Home Along Falmouth and Penryn by David Mudd. Bossiney Books. 1980

Images of Bygone Falmouth by Nicola Darling–Finan. Breedon Books. 2001.

Master of the Sea: Charles Napier Hemy RA, RWS by Margaret Powell. Alison Hodge, 2004.

The Gardener's Folklore by Margaret Baker. David and Charles. 1977

The Levelling Sea by Philip Marsden. Harper Press 2011.

Working Life in Britain 1900–1950 by Janice Anderson. Futura 2007.

Works by Tuke and Hemy can be seen in many galleries but especially:

Falmouth Art Gallery, Municipal Buildings, The Moor, Falmouth, Cornwall.TR11 2RT www.falmouthartgallery.com

Royal Cornwall Museum, River Street, Truro, Cornwall. TR1 2SJ www.royalcornwallmuseum.org.uk

The National Museum of Gardening, Trevarno Manor, Helston, Cornwall. http://www.trevarno.co.uk holds a fascinating collection of early gardening tools and memorabilia.

THE IMPROBABLE STORY OF ORION GOSS

Chapter 1

It was lucky for him the red runners grew so tall, the leaves were so abundant and the beans hung in such dense clusters. Leaving his basket, he could run the full length of the pathway, completely invisible from the top of the gardens that sloped steeply downwards towards him, and although he'd be for it if Mr Cyril caught him leaving the beans half-picked he didn't know what else to do. Not with the artist standing there by the top gate.

He was afraid of the artist. He had heard – hadn't they all? – too many stories about him.

He had a boat that he used as a studio from which he painted pictures of the ships in the harbour or out in the bay and he had, it was said, helped to build the town's reputation as a home of artists. Some even said there was something called 'The Falmouth School', which wasn't the same as the board school Orion had attended but meant a group of painters all working in the same place. He didn't know about that but he did know that the artist could often be seen over on Swanpool Beach or one of the coves around Pennance Point, his easel set up on the shingle, painting boys in boats or bathing or diving from the rocks... Painting them, often, in the buff.

They boasted about it, the boys – Harry, Johnny, Bert, Joseph and Charlie, who was – or so he said – the artist's studio assistant. Whatever that meant. They were his boys, they said. They went out with him on his boat and were given food and ale while the artist's friends drank wine and talked about art and poetry and life. He paid them – Johnny, who was his favourite before he went off to fight the Boers, even had a silk scarf that had belonged to the artist himself – but mainly he made them feel special. Their pictures, he had told them, would hang in collections all over England, even in the Royal Academy in Piccadilly. Whatever that might be.

The first time the artist came to the market garden – a month ago it would have been – he hadn't known who he was. Just saw this man in dark trousers, fisherman's jersey and peaked hat wandering along the path between the broad beans and the runners, pausing every so often to bend forwards and peer more closely at the flowers where they were starting to set.

Mr Cyril didn't mind customers wandering about – said it was good for business – but he liked them kept an eye on. Especially someone like this fellow, who might just have come off a ship in dock – in which case he almost certainly couldn't be trusted. And, apart from himself and Mr Cyril, who didn't like to be disturbed at this time of day, there was only Jacka who couldn't speak – leastways, he never did – so that, even though he knew all there was to know about veg, he was little use for dealing with customers.

So he had given up on his broccoli drills, wiped his hands on his sacking apron and hurried up the gardens.

"C'n I 'elp you, Sir?" he'd asked, because Mr Cyril was particular about politeness, even though it seemed from a distance that this wasn't a gent. But then, as the man turned and stood to his full height, he saw that he was mistaken. Dressed for boating he might be, but this was definitely a gentleman. His chin was carefully shaved. His thick, dark moustache, was neatly trimmed and his hair, also thick and dark but peppered in a distinguished fashion with grey, had been expertly barbered.

It was a strong face, he noticed, with arched brows above dark eyes that had a strange look in them, as though they could see right into Orion's head and read what he was thinking. And confident. This was a man who kept servants. A man used to being taken notice of.

"I was looking for rhubarb," he said. Surprisingly. "I very much enjoy a rhubarb tart and as I was passing…" He shrugged his shoulders as if the whole business of finding himself in a market garden was in some way amusing. "Do you have any?"

They had plenty. Most of the morning they'd spent pulling stalks and binding them with twine into the neat bundles which lay on the table by the entrance.

"They're up 'ere," he told him and the gentleman walked beside him up the steep path, commenting as he went on the progress of the kidney beans, enquiring if they had dug any new season's potatoes. When he dared look the dark eyes were fixed so intently on him that it was hard not to stumble in his heavy, soil-caked boots and a relief to see Mr Cyril appear from his after-dinner nap behind the glass house and come hastily forward with his toad-faced smile.

"This young man's been looking after me very well." The gentleman broke in on Mr Cyril's explanations of how he'd been busy checking the sea-kale. "But I would like to buy some rhubarb. And some new season's potatoes, if you have them. I've been meaning to call in before. The name's Tuke. Henry Tuke. I have a house out at Swanpool. You may know it."

Mr Cyril, more toad-like than ever, assured him that he did and, if he would like his order delivered it would be no trouble. He could deliver weekly, if Mr Tuke... The man nodded, briefly, as if he was no longer interested.

"Thank you Mr ..." he said, waited as Mr Cyril gave his name and then turned, brows lowered over his dark eyes. "And your son's name?"

"Oh, 'e 'ant my son Sir. Oh no, no. Not at all. This 'ere's Goss," Mr Cyril assured him. "Orion Goss."

The artist nodded and looked down his long, straight nose, the slight smile on his lips not entirely hidden by his moustache.

"Is he indeed?" he said, feeling in his pocket for his money. "Is he indeed?"

"'E's all right. You don' need bother 'bout 'im. 'E don' touch you nor nothin'."

His friend Will said this but his friend Will wasn't entirely to be trusted. Being quite willing to go round the back of the Queens Arms with any old seaman off the docks who was willing to pay. Will'd be happy enough to have the artist staring at him in the altogether for two or three pence. Probably for a penny, if the truth be known. Most things would be better than some sweaty seaman panting away down there, breathing out stale beer and pilchards. But Orion wasn't Will. He'd had offers, plenty of them, and he'd done the same thing, always. Got himself out of the way. Quick.

Easily done dealing with a tipsy sailor late at night when you knew the opes and alleyways better than he did. Not so easy with a gentleman customer in the market garden in broad daylight.

The artist had been back twice since that first time. Once a week, in fact, although not always at the same time or Orion would have made certain to be out of the way. The first time he was planting out lettuces in the south border and hadn't seen him until it was too late because the cold frames were in the way. The second time he was picking spinach for the Falmouth Hotel's evening order, hard at it because it was already late and the cart was ready to go.

Each time he had wanted to talk, the artist. Wasn't it back-breaking work, he'd asked, bending over such tiny plants? And what did they do to discourage slugs? He'd tried to grow lettuces out at Pennance where he lived but slugs had eaten his entire crop.

He didn't enjoy spinach, he'd confided on the second visit, although his doctor had told him it was good for the blood.

On both occasions Mr Cyril had been nearby – the second time he was waiting with the cart and called out to Orion to get a bloody move on before he noticed the artist. But the third time – late afternoon – Mr Cyril was out with Jacka on the hotel round and Orion was on his own.

He was working in the salad bed again, since he needed to be near the top of the garden in case of customers, tying the leaves of the Cos lettuces that were almost ready for cutting.

"Hard at it again, I see."

He walked quietly, the artist, almost as if he might have been creeping up on him. And when he spoke in his deep voice only a couple of yards away it startled Orion so much that he almost fell forward onto the lettuces.

"Steady there lad! I didn't frighten you did I?" The artist put out a hand – almost as rough as Orion's but ingrained with paint rather than soil – to take hold of his elbow and steady him. "On your own, are you?" and he glanced along the path.

He was, of course, on his own but now the artichokes were almost up to six foot it wasn't possible to see over the whole garden and it was worth risking it.

"I think Mr C... Mr Rowse's down bottom end Sir. Would 'ee like me go get 'im for 'ee?" A lie – and the artist shook his head, smiling down at him with his dark eyes as if he knew it.

"I'm sure you can serve me just as well. I want a few raspberries if you have them. My housekeeper makes excellent cream and I'm particularly fond of raspberries."

He talked all the way along the path. About the fineness of the day; the splendid blue of the sky. About the deliciousness of his housekeeper's clotted cream and how she liked to make pies or puddings whereas he preferred fresh fruit.

"How about you, lad? Do you enjoy raspberries?" He stopped suddenly in his tracks, turning his deep eyes full onto Orion so that he too had to stop and stood, staring down at his boots in embarrassment. His left lace had broken again, he noticed.

"Well?" The artist looked amused. "Surely it's not a difficult question?"

"No Sir. I mean, yes. I do. When Mr Rowse do let me take some 'ome."

"Of course." The artist frowned slightly, as if a thought had occurred to him. "Do you have a garden at home?"

"No Sir." He wished he'd stop asking such questions. "I mean, we've got a yard but we don't grow nothin'."

"We don't grow nothing."

The man spoke quietly, as if he didn't intend to be heard, then continued along the path. Orion followed. Now he'd noticed the broken boot lace it was hard not to stumble.

The artist bought three fourpenny boxes of raspberries and a bunch of radishes, paying for them with a half crown piece. As Orion started to wrap them in newspaper, he pushed one of the boxes away from the others.

"That's for you, lad," he told him. "A treat for your tea."

And picking up the badly–made parcel he turned away.

Chapter 2

His ma was pleased with the raspberries when he arrived home.

"Now that is a treat!" she said, taking her hands out of the bowl into which she was peeling potatoes and putting down the knife. "I must be sure and thank Mr Cyril."

Which was just what he did not want her doing and he watched her mouth fall open in horror as he explained that Mr Cyril hadn't exactly given them to him.

"Orion! You've never stole them!" she exclaimed, her swollen, red fingers dripping potato water onto the table. "Whatever would your fa…!" But Orion, who did not want his father brought into this, didn't let her finish.

"Course I din't," and now he wished he'd eaten the wretched raspberries on the way home. "A customer give 'em me."

"What customer?"

The fingers still dripped and his mother, behind them, stared, sharp–eyed. She had a round face, Ida Goss, with heavy jowls and eyes that had once been deepest blue – like a summer sky, one of her more poetic suitors had once told her – but age and heavy work had coarsened her skin and the deep blue of her eyes had paled and become, with the threading of broken veins in the whites, so much less distinctive. It didn't stop them flashing with anger, when she suspected something.

"Orion!" She tightened her lips so that the stiff black hairs about her chin and upper lip bristled like the fur on the neck of an angry cat. "Answer me!"

"No–one." He stared down at the table, marked from the cuts of many knives and stained, in spite of Ida's constant scrubbing, from years of preparing food. And then, hearing the angry intake of his mother's breath that might still, sixteen though he was, precede a good hiding, "A gentleman customer. Mr Tuke."

"That artist!"

For Ida Goss knew all about artists. Dirty-minded idlers at

17

best, making pictures of brazen hussies who should know better in the altogether – and not only drawing and painting them neither. Oh no! And Falmouth was full of them, wandering about with their paints and easels. Too many by far!

"What's 'e doing, giving you presents?" She banged her hand on the table with a force that would have hurt a more fragile woman. "Eh?"

"Nothing. 'E said I was polite an' I served 'im proper, tha's all. E's a gentleman and gentlemen like for you to be polite."

This was a direct quotation from Mr Cyril but Mrs Goss wasn't to know. In any case, she was still suspicious.

"Well I don' like it." She reached back into the bowl for her half–peeled potato. "I've 'eard stories 'bout 'e."

So had Orion but he wasn't going to tell his mother that. Instead he sneaked back into the yard to look at his vegetable patch.

For all he was supposed to be honest – it was one reason Mr Cyril had taken him on – he had lied to the artist when he told him he didn't have a garden. He wasn't even sure why he had done it. There was no reason, after all, for the man not to know. Except that he would have known something about him then, and Orion didn't want him knowing anything about him. For some reason he didn't understand he was frightened by those dark and searching eyes, as though they might have some sort of power over him, and it seemed best to keep things secret when he could.

In any case they didn't really go in for gardens in Quarry Place. Back yards were for hanging washing and for setting out the tub and mangle on dry days to create more room in the tiny back sculleries and, backing onto the steep, grey sides of the old quarry as they did, very little sunshine ever got into them. Some folks kept chickens and the neighbours three doors up kept a pig in a straw-littered enclosure – and didn't the rest of them know it on hot days! – but most yards were given over to the washing and

18

any rubbish that overflowed from the house.

The Gosses' yard had been no different – just the lean-to privy against the back wall of the house, the wood pile and a small, stone-slabbed area – but once Orion had started work at the market garden he had seen its possibilities.

It had been hard work prising up the slabs from the far side of the yard and clearing the ground underneath which was solidly compacted and full of stones but he had learned from Mr Cyril about improving the soil and, mocked by his brother Alfred, had wheeled up loads of seaweed from the harbour. He had even started a muck heap with his mother's vegetable peelings, straw that fell from carts delivering to shops nearby and dung from the horses that drew the carts.

His mother had complained – especially about the dung – but he'd persisted and now, two years later, his small patch, which at least caught the late afternoon sun, yielded a crop of beetroot, cabbages and runner beans as well as a few Sweet Williams and marigolds with which he hoped he might cheer her.

(He didn't succeed in this. Mrs Goss had never been a particularly cheerful person and marriage to Mr Goss, who abandoned her when Orion was a baby, had not sweetened her temper. He went on trying nevertheless.)

His mother finished the potatoes.

"You want these 'ere peelings?" she yelled. Then, "Don't you come trailing that muck in!" as Orion came to the door, scooped out the peelings for his heap and threw the water onto his beans.

Half an hour later, leaving his boots outside, he brought in a handful of beans and a bunch of Sweet Williams – the deep crimson ones he liked best. Filling a jar with water he set them on the window ledge where they caught the light and gave out a scent as powerful as their colour, brightening, for him, if not for his mother, the gloom of the kitchen.

He wondered sometimes if he wouldn't rather work with flowers. Most of the big houses and hotels around Falmouth employed gardeners and the Rosehill Gardens, across the wall from Mr Cyril's market garden, were famous for their rare and exotic plants, brought back by sea captains coming into port from distant parts of the world for the Fox family, who, among their many interests, had a thriving shipping business and owned the gardens. It would be a wonderful thing to work there but there was no hope of that for the Foxes were Quakers and Orion's mother, a staunch Methodist, disapproved of Quakers and would never have allowed her son to work for one.

It had been hot in the yard, the evening sunshine caught between the houses and the steep wall of the quarry, but in the kitchen it was hotter still. His mother had opened out the range in order to boil the potatoes on the top and cook the lardy cake in the oven to the side and her face, as she stood cleaning mackerel at the sink, glowed a livid crimson and shone with sweat.

"For 'eavens sake what 'ee go bringing in they beans for?" she demanded. "I've enough to do without stringing them. Alfred'll be 'ome any minute and I'm be'ind as it is."

Alfred was Orion's elder brother. Twenty to his sixteen. A swarthy, hefty man with strong arms and broad shoulders who worked, when he was working, on the pleasure boats that took visitors across the bay and up the Helford River.

Orion didn't like Alfred. Never had. All his life he had been that much larger and so much of a bully, taking pleasure, when Orion was small, in lifting him by his shoulders to hold him pinioned against the wall or gripping his arms and twisting them agonizingly behind his back while he bellowed and begged to be set free. Even now he could never be sure, when Alfred stared across at him with his strangely hooded eyes, that he wasn't planning something equally as painful.

The two boys who came between Alfred and Orion had died within days of each other of diphtheria not long after Orion's birth, at which point Mrs Goss had seemed to lose interest in her entire family, although she tended to take Alfred's side in arguments. Perhaps, Orion sometimes thought, she was afraid of him too, strong woman that she was. Alfred was, people said, very like his father and there were plenty of tough men in Falmouth who were wary of Percy Goss who was well known for his short temper and violent tendencies.

Leaving the beans, Orion went upstairs to the room he and Alfred shared and lay down. The only window overlooked the quarry wall so that there was little enough light even on a fine July evening. Alfred's bed against the other wall, the curtained alcove where they hung their few clothes and the black wooden wash stand with the enamel basin set into the top were little more than familiar shadows as he gave in to the pleasant sensation of allowing his eye lids to droop and close. The last thing he was conscious of as he drifted asleep was the deep, gentle-toned voice of the artist.

"That's for you, lad," he said. "A treat for your tea."

For some reason the memory didn't alarm him now.

He woke, it could have been minutes or an hour later, to Alfred's burly arms pressing into his shoulders.

"Ge-ed out of it yer idle oaf!" He pummelled Orion with a force that pressed him, through the thin, horsehair mattress, into the wooden frame of the bed. "Ged yerself…"

Orion, used to violent wakenings, rolled sideways off the bed and belted out of the room and down the steep stairway. Alfred, who also resembled his father in his liking for strong ale, must have been in the Prince of Wales or the Seven Stars as he came home from the quay and was in a quarrelsome temper. It was best to keep out of his way.

Downstairs was full of the smell of frying mackerel from the black and spitting pan on the range. Next to it was a small saucepan which Mrs Goss, face redder than ever, stirred vigorously with a wooden spoon. Milk, Orion saw, yellowed with butter and she was stirring in flour to made a hasty pudding. On the table was a buttered earthenware pudding dish and next to it

21

the cinnamon jar.

It was his mother's fallback dish – a mix of milk and flour and butter, sugared and seasoned with spices. A favourite of Alfred's, although Orion somehow doubted he would be down to eat it.

"Wha' 'bout they raspberries?"

He was still drowsy from his sudden wakening or he would have had more sense.

Mrs Goss flung down her wooden spoon with a suddenness that should no longer have shocked him, so that it bounced on the flagstones then skittered across to lie against the bucket underneath the sink.

"Raspberries!" She turned as if she would fling him down too. "'Ave I got nothing else to think of? I've had all I can take of your poxy raspberries!"

Snatching it off the table, she flung the little box after the spoon and across the floor, sending the small fruits bouncing and rolling until they were stopped by the channels between the flagstones, the legs of the table or in the dark angle between the floor and the wall. As Orion stepped forwards, too late, to prevent her, he caught one rolling fruit under his bare foot, felt it squash coldly against his skin, saw the red juice spatter outwards as if he had killed a particularly juicy insect and felt something squash and spatter inside his soul.

Chapter 3

The end of the beans. Cabbages now. Main Crops reaching into a bright blue sky, then the Hardy Greens, later and lower but still affording some cover, but then the onions, drooping now, their growth practically finished, the stems that had not naturally fallen over bent down, only last week, by himself and Mr Cyril and now giving no cover at all. They said you shouldn't plant onions near beans but Mr Cyril said this was nonsense. His onion bed had always been here at the bottom of the garden and they'd always done well. And so had the beans. Still Orion wished now that Mr Cyril had heeded the warning. As it was he had several yards of almost open ground between him and the potting shed.

Crouching by the last of the Hardy Greens, breathing in the strong, damp smell of the earth and leaves where he'd not long watered, blood pounding against his ears, he peered up the gardens. Past the carrots and the leeks. Over the peas, clambering about their tangled, twiggy sticks. Over the open ground where the early potatoes had long been harvested. Beyond the currant bushes and up towards the apples, espaliered against the upper wall, fruit already gleaming in the sunlight.

Where the artist stood, squinting against its brightness…

"Hallo there, boy!"

A loud, deep-throated cry, as if he were shouting across the water. As though Orion might be one of the boys on his boat. And, as he called out, the artist raised his arm, waved and started to stride down the garden path.

There was a caterpillar, right in front of him, chewing its peaceful way through the leaf of the nearest cabbage, already frilled around the edges. A velvety green creature with faint white lines along its sides, a fringe of fragile hairs on its skin, slight, mottled blotches on its lower parts. Seen this close it looked almost beautiful, even if it was one of Mr Cyril's worst enemies. He would like to remain here, crouching among the damp,

23

strong–smelling leaves, watching the caterpillar as it munched and looped its way along the edge. He would like to be the caterpillar, with nothing more to worry about than its next mouthful…

"You deaf, Orion Goss?"

Heavy boots, crunching against the stones of the path and then the question. Not angry, which might actually be preferable, but kind.

"A fine one you are to leave in charge if you don't hear a customer when he calls."

"No Sir."

Perhaps his answer made no sense but from down here, staring upwards, past the black trousers, the jacket – the artist was smartly dressed this afternoon – to that thick, dark moustache and those dark, smiling eyes, it was hard to make sense of anything. Except that a hand was reaching towards him, held out, presumably, to help him up.

"I was looking out for caterpillars, Sir. They d'eat the cabbages."

Avoiding the hand, he scrambled to his feet, mercifully without stumbling. Then, remembering, reached down to take the munching caterpillar from its leaf and held it between his thumb and forefinger. He felt guilty now, as if he had betrayed a friend.

"I'm sure they do, Orion Goss. I'm sure they do." The artist looked amused. "And what will you do with it?"

"Put 'im in salt water Sir. There's a bucket in the shed."

He could feel the creature, soft and mobile, wriggling against his skin. Mr Cyril would have squashed him between his fingers or under his boot but he could never bring himself to do that, even though, as Mr Cyril had often told him, death by salt water took far longer.

"You'd better fetch it then hadn't you?" the artist suggested and, as Orion nodded, "Better to have brought it with you when

24

you started, surely?"

He glanced back along the path, where he must have seen Orion's basket, half full of beans, but made no comment.

He was not a bad man, Henry Scott Tuke. He was certainly good looking, with his thick dark hair, his dark, yearning eyes and his thick and full moustache. Dressed in his fisherman's sweater and sailing cap, he was a familiar figure around Falmouth in those early years of the Twentieth century for, as well as being a well-regarded, even famous, artist, he was also Rear Commodore of the Falmouth Sailing Club, a keen yachtsman and a formidable racing skipper in his rater Red Heart.

He had converted a boat into a floating studio from which he painted the ships that came into harbour and the small boats that sailed there, often living on board in the summer months, entertaining his friends among Falmouth's gentry. Like most of the artists in the area he drew and painted local people too. Boys mainly, those they called 'quay scamps', who fished and swam and played around the Customs House Quay. Young working boys whose naked bodies he painted in all their splendour. Observing the strength and beauty of their young limbs, the eagerness or thoughtfulness in their young eyes, the effects of the sunlight on their young skin.

He would like to have painted this boy too but he was a sensitive man and it was obvious that the lad was, for some reason, nervous of him. It's all right, he would like to have told him. You have nothing to fear from me. I simply enjoy the company of young men. One or two of them I have even loved but my intentions are quite pure. (The word made him smile – nor was he even sure that it was completely accurate.) I would simply like to paint your round, attractive, very Cornish face, your wide-set, extraordinarily deep, green eyes, your hair curling forward in its tufted fringe. I would be happy to paint you as you are now, in your tough gardening trousers and your heavy and

25

rather torn brown jersey. I would not mind if you refused, as some have, to remove your clothes, although what I would like most of all would be to paint your naked body. To capture the sheen of sunlight against your youthful flesh. To reproduce on canvas the musculature of those strong, young limbs…

"Did you enjoy the raspberries?" he asked instead, as the boy came back along the path. "I certainly enjoyed mine."

Orion felt his face burn red. His mother had thrown the raspberries onto the kitchen floor, he remembered. Some of them had squashed, all were covered in dust and a few had rolled away under the sink, to be eaten, perhaps, by mice.

"Yes sir," he said.

It was wrong to tell lies; Minister said this over and over in Chapel and Orion tried to follow his words. On the other hand he was also supposed to honour his father and mother and, although honouring his father was a step further than he was likely to go, he tried his best with his mother and admitting to the gentleman that she had thrown away his gift was not the way to go about this.

"You don't sound very certain."

The artist smiled, showing strong white teeth below his fine moustache. His dark eyes shone as though this was all a great joke.

Orion was not good at jokes.

"They was lovely raspberries, Sir," he said carefully. "I give 'em to me ma."

"I see."

Orion wasn't sure what he saw but at least the artist didn't sound angry.

"So you didn't eat them yourself?"

"No Sir." This was certainly the truth.

The artist reached into the pocket of his trousers.

"In that case, Orion, you must have another treat. And this time you must keep it for yourself."

And pulling a shilling piece from his pocket, he tossed it onto the ground, turning away and striding off up the pathway before Orion could refuse to take it. Up by the gate he paused by the old wooden table where vegetables were set out for customers to examine. When Mr Cyril came in from his round he was studying a bundle of carrots as if he had only just arrived.

Chapter 4

Mr Cyril often said he didn't know why he kept on two great louts in winter time when there was so little for them to do. Which was unfair since Orion and Jacka were kept hard at it, digging trenches for next season's crops, hauling loads of stinking seaweed from the beach, piling up the dead leaves to rot, replacing the edging tiles around the beds... Even now, November, when the ground was too cloggy to work, there was plenty to keep them busy and today Jacka was helping Mr Cyril repair the broken frames in the far glass house while Orion was in the bottom shed cleaning flower pots.

It was a painful job. His hands, soaked in cold water from the rain–water barrel, were red raw and his knuckles were swollen like beets as he scrubbed at the clay pots. It was important to get off every bit of earth so no pests could get a hold but it was hard work, especially when the pots were cracked and the soil had got itself embedded, but at least he was inside. Outside, the gardens had disappeared in the murk of a sea mist and the great bell from St Antony Head on the far side of the harbour mouth boomed out every few seconds, just as it was doing when he woke this morning and, so it seemed, in his dreams before that.

And inside his shed, if it wasn't exactly warm, it was peaceful; just the sound of his own breathing and the scratch of his rough brush against the clay pots, enclosed by the distant mourning of the bell. Outside, through dirty glass made still more opaque by ancient spiders' webs, there was nothing to see but billowing banks of mist and, looming in the distance, the vague, dark shadows that were the garden walls and he felt content in his isolation.

Except that he needed a piss; had done for some time but the thought of going outside had helped him ignore the need as he concentrated on getting rid of the dried-in dirt. Now he could hold on no longer and, clutching an old sack around his shoulders, he shoved open the door and hurried round the far side of the shed.

The mist was thick and drenching, folding itself around him and finding its way under the sacking to slither in cold dribbles down his back as he jigged from foot to foot, fumbling with swollen fingers at his trouser buttons. Forcing them open at last, he let out the yellow stream to splash, steaming in the cold air, against the side of the shed and relaxed into the relief of emptiness as it joined the rain water pouring into the slate–edged gutter below.

Mr Cyril didn't allow this. There was an earth privy at the far end of the gardens that he and Jacka were meant to use and when the weather was good or there were customers around or Mr Cyril was nearby that was where they went. Not in the wet though. Or when there was no-one to see.

Which was when he heard someone calling his name.

"Orion! Orion Goss! Are you there boy?"

A voice he hadn't heard for months and at first he thought it must be Mr Cyril. That he might, from the glass house at the top of the garden, have spotted him through the mist... In which case – Mr Cyril had a nasty temper and you could never be sure of him – he might easily dismiss him.

For a moment it was a relief to realise that it was the artist.

He came striding down the gardens, head covered in a fisherman's sou' wester and wearing a thick dark jacket, canvas trousers and heavy sea boots. His thick moustache, in spite of the sou' wester, dripped with water and his cheeks were wet and red from the cold.

"What a day!" he shouted. "You can taste the salt in the rain and just smell that iodine! You should see the waves over at Swanpool, boy. Crashing against the rocks, tearing at the pebbles on the beach, dragging them back with them. I've tramped all round the cliff path this morning. It's so glorious I didn't want to stop."

"No sir."

Struggling to hold his sacking over his shoulder, it was hard to understand what the man was on about. Except he must be soft in the head. Walking round cliffs in the rain when he didn't have to!

"So boy, what do you do on a day like this? No catching caterpillars today eh?"

So he remembered, after all this time. Although it was a daft question. As if there'd be caterpillars in November!

"No sir. I've been cleaning flower pots."

"Not out here, surely?"

"No sir. In the shed."

"I see."

It was hard to tell; the mist banked between them and it was hard to see much at all but it seemed as if something in the artist's eyes had altered. As if they had got suddenly darker. Or perhaps it was just the way he was looking at him. Whatever it was, they seemed to pierce through him in a way that made Orion feel as awkward and stupid as he had when he got a question wrong at school.

And then the wind flung an even thicker bank of drizzle at them, drenching Orion's hair and face which were already quite wet enough, and the artist shook his head so that the water flew off his sou' wester in a ring of sparkling droplets.

"So…" He put out a hand towards the door latch. "Let's see what you've been doing then."

"No!"

Without even realising, Orion moved towards the door as if to bar the way. So many reasons in his head that it wasn't possible to speak any of them. Just no. It wasn't possible. The man, the artist, must not come inside the shed.

"You can't go in there."

"Why ever not boy?" The eyes were still dark. The lips, pink and naked below the dark moustache, smiled but it was not an entirely pleasant smile. "Got secrets in there have you?"

"No sir. Just flower pots. But it's not allowed. Mr Cyril don't like it. Not customers going in."

"Mr Cyril don't like it."

The artist spoke quietly, repeating the words as he had, Orion remembered, once before.

"No sir."

He was frightened now. Shivering – but that might just be from the rain which had soaked through the sack and his jacket and had reached the old shirt he wore under that. His stomach fluttered as if it might be full of moths and it was difficult even to speak because his throat didn't seem to be working properly.

But he was determined. The artist was not coming into his shed.

Perhaps it was because he'd had his John Thomas out only just before he'd arrived and, even now, couldn't be completely sure his buttons were all safely fastened.

Perhaps that was what made him feel so awkward. As if the artist might have seen – or guessed – what he'd been doing.

Or perhaps it was just because the shed was his favourite place. The only place, it seemed to him, where he could be private. Mr Cyril, tough though he was, never came down this far in foul weather and Jacka, because he never spoke, seemed not to matter.

Whatever the reason and even though it seemed as if he might make the artist – a gentleman and a customer – angry with him, his mind was made up.

"It's not allowed," he repeated and, since it was rude to stare a gentleman and a customer in the face, stared down instead at the muddy pathway and his soaked–through boots.

The warning bell boomed out above the whirling mist. A sudden gust of wind tussled at the bare branches of the elm tree on the far side of the wall, spinning a waterfall of drops around their heads.

31

"It's not allowed," the artist repeated in that slow, quiet way of his. Then, in a completely different tone and making Orion jump in surprise, "Sprouts!" he said. "I fancy some Brussels sprouts for my dinner. Do you have any?"

And followed him up the garden to where the stalks were stacked under the stone slab table that jutted from the upper wall.

Chapter 5

He's a poor specimen of a man, Henry tells himself as he strides off along Woodlane, clutching his two sticks of Brussels sprouts wrapped in sheets of newspaper which will have disintegrated long before he reaches his home in Swanpool. And Mrs Fouracre, his housekeeper, will not thank him for them either. Although she accommodates herself as best she can to the ways of her eccentric master, she has made it clear on numerous occasions that she prefers him to leave the purchasing of food to herself. She doesn't know what he's thinking of, she has told him, trailing round that old market garden picking up fruit and veg she doesn't want, when her brother can bring all they need in the cart from his farm. Giving him, as she speaks, one of what he privately calls 'her looks'. The kind that make him feel uncomfortably as though she knows exactly what he has been thinking of – and that it was not fruit and veg.

And he has tried, he tells himself. All summer he has been in Falmouth and all summer – since the end of July at least – he has kept away from Mr Rowse's garden and the boy, Orion Goss. Which should, he also tells himself, have been easy. He has been, as always, extremely busy. Apart from his painting – he is working on a large oil of six boys in and around a rowing boat, for which he has not yet found a title – he has been sailing, racing his rater, Red Heart, in almost all the local regattas and most of Falmouth Sailing Club's races. He has swum every morning. He has bicycled regularly around the narrow country lanes and every weekend and almost every evening he has visited or entertained friends – he has many friends and is a popular guest and host.

In fact life, at this point, is especially good to Henry – Harry to his friends – Tuke. He is, in these early years of the Twentieth Century, producing better work than ever before and leads a life as happy as one might reasonably expect. He has no wife, of course, and at forty two might be expected to be suitably married, but he has a wide – and varied – set of friends in Falmouth, in London; even abroad.

For Henry is a sociable man who makes friends easily and enjoys the company of local urchins as much as that of educated people like the Foxes and other leaders of Falmouth's intellectual life or the aristocratic bon viveurs he meets in London. He may have long left behind him the Quaker beliefs with which he grew up but he has never lost the certainty that all men and women are of equal value, although some have been given better chances in life than others.

Most of his friends, it has to be said, are men and he is most at ease in their company but he has female friends as well and one in particular whom he might have married, except that he has probably already hesitated too long and this is not really something that he regrets. He enjoys visiting his married friends and appreciates the comfort a wife can bring to a home, but as he walks home afterwards he is generally glad to be doing so alone.

All of which should have sent him healthily exhausted to bed at night and yet... And yet when he lies in his bed, especially on these early winter nights when the sea mists rising above the cliffs outside his window send a damp chill through his bed coverings, it is hard to rid himself of the picture of the young apprentice gardener with his sturdy limbs, his guarded, watchful, deep green eyes and puzzled, uncertain expression.

It will be hard too, he can feel this already, to forget the nervous obstinacy of his refusal to allow Henry into his shed, a refusal which is worrying him perhaps more than it should. What did the boy imagine, he wonders, he wanted to do with him in there? And a worm of discomfort curls in his entrails as he remembers his own determination. What made him, he asks himself, press the poor boy so hard? Why did his mild curiosity to see inside the battered little building – he is, after all, an artist: odd places interest him – become such an imperative? Why, when it was obvious that the boy was afraid – either of himself or his surly employer – did he not let the matter drop?

And try as he might he cannot rid himself of the suspicion that what he really wanted was the pleasure of being, just for a few moments, in a confined space with this nervous boy. To smell the damp warmth of his rough clothes and tousled hair. To see, close by, the honest, grimy, work–hardened hands. To touch...

But no. This is not what he does, he tells himself, striding out faster than ever. He draws. He paints. He appreciates. But he does not touch.

This last summer, he admits now, has tested his resolve and, as he turns down the steep incline past the gloomily dripping trees the Falmouth Burial Ground, he remembers the effort of concentration on his as yet unnamed painting. Thinks of Bert, Harry, Charlie who, with Mrs Fouracre's sons, acted as his models – getting stiff and cold in the process, even on the hotter days. Remembers the joy of capturing the muscular curves of their slender bodies, the shimmer of golden light on their bare flesh, the roguish innocence of their young faces... But as part of his composition. The boat, its oars, the rocks, and, above all, the jewelled effect of the sparkling, green and golden water are as important. This is not to be simply a painting of naked boys – two of them are in any case not naked: 'Lucky buggers,' Harry has said – it is a painting of the effects of sunlight and they are simply part of it. And Henry has always respected their privacy. Is always careful not to watch them as they dress or undress and never, ever, touches them.

There are men who do. Even men he knows and numbers among his friends, both in Falmouth and in London. But he is not one of them. Which is why he kept away, for almost four months, from the market garden. Because he felt himself becoming... the word that comes to mind is 'entranced', with this boy Orion, as he has never been before.

Which is why, night after night, he found himself giving up

on sleep, creeping from the house and clambering down to the little cove below his garden to dive into the sea. Where he felt, after the first shock, the comfort of the silken chill which folded itself about his limbs as he swam out across the tiny bay, silent except for his own movements and the occasional wail of a gull, circling, white across a dark blue sky, or the faint mutterings of the water birds on the pond beyond the beach.

Only then could he feel free from the claustrophobia of the house and his discomfiting thoughts. Free and once more – there is no other word for it – healthy.

Perhaps he thinks now as he strides along the pathway beside a pool of waterfowl, thick with reeds and overhung with willows, his face and moustache drenched from the thickly gusting drizzle, he is actually mad. The thought amuses, rather than frightening or disgusting, him for he comes from a family of doctors and knows something about insanity. His great, great grandfather, William Tuke, established The Retreat, a humane habitation in York for those afflicted with mental disorders, at a time when the treatment of such people was generally far from humane. His father was a leading authority on mental disorders, publishing several books on the subject, including The Influence of the Mind on the Body, and often discussing his ideas at home so that Henry is quite familiar with them and knows that those who differ from most other people are not necessarily insane.

His energies, he realises, are unusual; perhaps they might even be termed abnormal. And perhaps his feelings for the boys he loves to paint are abnormal too, although he has never really thought this, until now, when he has to acknowledge that his longing to see again the rough, awkward market garden boy cannot be considered entirely natural.

Which is why he has gone to such pains to repress it.

Repressed it until today and he smiles grimly, blinking his eyes in an attempt to keep out the drizzle which is turning to rain. Today, even after his brisk and bracing walk around the headland, he has been unable to keep himself away. Today, in spite of all his resolutions, he has given in.

Thank goodness, he tells himself, he will be off to London at the end of the month. He is working on another painting now – has been for some weeks – of three raters in a full breeze with Bert White and Harry Cleave, in white hats and jerseys against a grey green sea and himself, he intends, at the helm of Red Heart, which he has kept late on the water for the purpose. But the weather has been too bad for him to continue painting on board his studio boat, the Pie Box, and he has had to admit defeat. Besides, it is time for his winter visit to London, to see his mother and sister and his many friends and enjoy the thrill of the winter season in the metropolis. The painting, which is proving at the moment somewhat disappointing, will have to wait until next spring for completion.

Is this the reason, or is there another, he wonders, for the dark depression that folds itself more thickly round him than the now unrelenting rain? Pulling his sou-wester low over his eyes he loses patience with the sticks of chilly sprouts, their leaves choked with scraps of disintegrating newspaper, and before they can slip completely from his grasp, he flings them angrily in the direction of the rain torn pond. Somewhere among the reeds a disturbed duck quacks in unseen protest.

Chapter 6

January was a poor month in the market garden. There were plenty of onions plaited into straws, boxes of potatoes and swedes piled up in the upper shed, a few heads of Brussels sprouts and some winter cabbage but little else.

Plenty of work to be done nevertheless, especially in the damp, mild Cornish winter where frosts were rare and, this year, had not come at all. Orion and Jacka planted rows of early peas and broad beans in the sheltered area below the south facing wall and Mr Cyril sowed leeks and carrots and caulis under glass. The new season's onions and cabbages were already showing and every afternoon it was Orion's task to hoe between the rows but it was poor work and he was glad when the light faded at around four and he could go home.

Which, on this particular afternoon, was empty, although two pasties were laid out for himself and Alfred on the wire tray on the kitchen table and the room was filled with the meaty scent of their cooking. Ignoring them, Orion went out into the yard where, even this early, a few daffodils were already in bloom and there were buds on the fat stems between the polyanthus leaves. Picking three of the fullest flowering daffs he took them carefully indoors.

The little house was quiet in a way it rarely was. In the kitchen the pump at the side of the stone sink dripped as it always did, the water splash-splashing with regularity against the stone. In the front room the clock Grandpa Goss had bought some fifty years before tocked gently with the regular swing of its short pendulum. On the road outside a horse clopped slowly past, the wheels of the heavy laden cart squealing in protest, and a woman called to the carter who shouted back, then lashed his switch at the horse's backside so that he picked up speed with a sudden grating against the stones.

Orion stood still, enjoying the peace and the knowledge that, for a few hours, he had it to himself since, tonight being pay night, Alfred would be drinking until midnight and his mother would have walked across town for her weekly visit to her friend Bea Rogers.

Bea, like Ida, was a Redruth girl, forced, like Ida, by the shortage of local eligible young men to look further afield when, with the collapse of copper mining in the 1860s and, in the 1870s, the decline of tin, young men left the once mineral-wealthy Camborne-Redruth area in their hundreds to seek work in the mines of California, Peru, Bolivia, South Africa…even Australia.

Some came back but most stayed and many did well for themselves, often sending for their wives or girls to come out and join them. But Ida and Bea had heard stories of the rough life in the distant, strange–sounding mining districts of Moonta in South Australia or Grass Valley in California. The terrible 'lung disease' in South Africa, caused by the fine quartz dust when digging for gold. The violent quarrels between the Cornish 'Cousin Jacks' and other miners – Irish, Italians, Finns and Croats – also seeking escape from starvation and the chance to make a fortune.

Nor did the thought of travelling for weeks in the overcrowded, disease-ridden hold of a ship to some unknown place on the other side of the world appeal to either Bea or to Ida, who had, in any case, waited in vain for a letter from the one man she felt might have been worth the risk. Instead the girls settled for two young men working in the newly built dry docks that were bringing prosperity to Falmouth on the South coast and who came to Redruth one Sunday to give a sacred concert at the Wesley Methodist Church they both attended.

Orion found it hard to imagine his coarse–spoken, heavy-drinking father – or even the rather less coarse Uncle Joe, who was Aunty Bea's husband – taking part in a sacred concert but it was a fact that both had fine baritone voices, even if they exercised them more often in the public house than in chapel.

And both men had jobs with prospects in the thriving dockyard even if, in Percy Goss's case, these had never been realised.

Aunty Bea – she was not a real aunt but Orion had always called her this – had been bedridden for years. He had no idea – perhaps no-one had – what was wrong but she spent her life in the bedroom of the house in Railway Terrace, on the far side of town, where, propped against pillows in her high bed, she watched from one side of her window the comings and goings at the dock gates and from the other side the trains steaming out from Falmouth station across the railway bridge. All week she looked forward to Ida's Friday evening visits when they would sit gossiping, usually bemoaning the way their lives had turned out, although neither, in all probability, had ever had great hopes or expectations that they would be much better.

And Orion, at home in Quarry Place, had the house to himself.

Shutting the bedroom door, he poured the morning's leftover washing water from its enamel jug into an old jam jar and stood his small bunch of daffodils in it. Gently he moved the golden heads into an arrangement that pleased him and then, pausing first to listen for noises from downstairs rather than next door, he took out from under his bed a small sketch pad and a piece of charcoal.

All this he did in semi-darkness, as if fearing someone might see him, but now he lit the candle in its saucer on the edge of the wash stand so that a blue and then a golden glow sent a diminishing halo of light around that part of the room. Then, reaching for his sketch pad, he perched himself on the side of the bed, facing his jar of daffodils…

He had not intended at first to spend the artist's shilling. He had hidden it, instead, under a pile of flower pots and hoped to forget about it, which, for several months, he had done, until, remembering one Sunday in chapel, it had occurred to him, uncomfortably, that he should give it to the Overseas Mission.

But before the next Sunday came he had paused one afternoon on his way home outside one of the shops that, with so many artists in the town, kept a stock of art supplies. Which was when he saw pads of sketching paper on sale for one shilling and three pence and knew what he wanted to do with his unexpected windfall.

The following Saturday, taking the shilling from under the flower pots and adding a sixpence from his small savings, he went back to the shop.

He felt quite nervous about going in. He was in his work-clothes and it would not have surprised him if the young man with the very long, white fingers and the longer-than-normal hair who stood behind the counter had thrown him straight out again. It was even remotely possible that the artist might be there or that he might come in and trap him with those strange, half-humorous questions which he never knew how to answer.

The shop smelt of a mixture of dust and new paper and another, acrid, smell he couldn't recognise. It was also quite dark, although the back window overlooked the harbour where the water was brilliant blue in the winter sunshine and a flotilla of small sailing boats whirled in the wind.

The young man was occupied in serving a woman and a small girl and Orion heard the words 'sketching pad' and saw him bring out first one and then another for them to consider. The largest cost five shillings and the next in size, three shillings and sixpence. He did not even bother to show them the one Orion wanted – the only one he could possibly afford – but, when they had decided on the five shilling one, started to extol the wonders of what he called 'pastels', which looked to Orion like the coloured chalks his teacher had used at school.

When they had completed their purchase and it had been wrapped, it was easy to point to the pad he had seen in the window.

"One of they one and thruppeny pads," he said. "And three

penn'orth of charcoal."

The young man served him without comment and made no attempt to sell him anything else. He was perfectly civil, however, and Orion left the shop with his small parcel, feeling as though he had passed some sort of test.

This was, he felt sure, the right thing to do with the artist's money. Not that he would ever tell him but drawing had been one of the few lessons – perhaps the only one – that he had enjoyed at school when a visiting master came once a week to teach the boys drawing while the girls did sewing.

He was a shabby, bad tempered man with long and greasy hair, whose breath smelled of ale – a smell Orion easily recognised – who set them exercises before settling into the teacher's chair and dozing off. The exercises were dull enough and usually involved copying pictures of leaves or animals or buildings from a sheet fastened to the blackboard but occasionally they were given a still life arrangement, generally an apple, a large curved shell, a couple of books and the bust of Queen Victoria which normally sat on top of the bookcase behind the teacher's desk, which most of the class found impossible to copy. Orion, however, enjoyed these lessons, although it did sometimes occur to him that it would be better if Mr Trevithick actually offered them more help, especially with difficult things, like the queen's headdress. But on the whole the copying was easy. Easier, certainly, than writing and now in the quiet of his bedroom, his lower lip folded across his upper lip in concentration, he tried his best to transfer onto his pad of paper the delicate outlines of his jar of flowers.

Chapter 7

March now and many weeks since he had last seen the artist. Orion and Jacka were busy sowing their second crops of onions and cabbages as well as broccoli, beetroot, peas, kale, spinach, turnips... The leeks and broad beans sown last November were coming up well, the tomato and lettuce seedlings were filling out in the glasshouse and Mr Cyril had started the celery and marrows under the cloches. Only that morning Orion had finished double–digging the runner bean beds and tomorrow he and Jacka would have the foul job of digging in the fish manure which would have a good six weeks to work in before they did the planting. For now he was hoeing between the early carrots and the rows of parsley they'd sown between them to discourage carrot fly.

And, once again, the artist arrived when he was on his own.

Mr Cyril and Jacka were out with the cart, delivering to the hotels which, with Easter less than two weeks off, were starting to fill with visitors and Orion almost wondered if Mr Tuke might have planned it this way. Perhaps he knew when Mr Cyril did his rounds. Or perhaps he had happened to see the horse and cart...

"Hullo there Orion. 'Ow you doin boy?" He assumed a mock Cornish accent that caused Orion to wonder if he might be laughing at him.

"Awright," he said, sulkily. "Sir."

"That's good." And perhaps he noticed Orion's wariness because he changed back to his normal voice. "I'm glad to hear that. And Mr Rowse? How is he?"

"'E's awright too Sir. Thank you."

"Good!" The dark eyes beamed below their dark brows as if this was excellent news. "Very good." Then, "Look at that," he said suddenly, pointing behind Orion. "Look! There!" And, placing a hand on Orion's shoulder, he turned him to face the wall with the thick crops of navel wort growing from its crevices.

"See! There!" The hand clutched at him so that he stood, stock still, hardly able to breathe and with no idea what he was meant to be looking at, until a small house–sparrow flitted between the round, fleshy leaves of the thickest outcrop and disappeared into the wall.

A sparrow! A dull, dumpy, brown and grey sparrow! That was all and there was nothing special about them. Except they were nuisances and he and Jacka had to cover the peas with netting to keep them out, which made the picking that much harder.

"Isn't that glorious!" The hand was still there and there was nothing glorious about that. "Look at that delicate, pale plumage. And that little speckled bib!"

He was whispering now, his mouth so close to Orion's ear that he could feel the warmth of his breath; the bristles of that thick moustache tickling against his flesh. And then, as the little bird, unbothered by humans – not surprising as Orion and Jacka tossed their pasty crusts onto the paths every lunch time – paused, its tiny claws clenched around an old nail sticking out of the wall, he saw what the artist meant.

For the little bird, a common-as-muck sparrow, was beautiful. The soft, grey feather cap on its head merged into a speckled, chestnut brown and then into a fluffy ball of greyish white, broken by the bib of black and grey feathers that the artist had noticed. The sharp, dark beak that opened occasionally to let out its familiar chirping gleamed like a cherished tool and the tiny eyes, set back among dark feathers like patches, glinted as the little creature turned its head onto one side as if it might be waiting to see what happened next.

"Just keep looking at him." The artist's hand was still on Orion's shoulder, he could still feel the warmth of his breathing but somehow it no longer mattered. "See those delicate patterns? The way the plumage lies in that scallop design? Those greys and browns? What a glorious little masterpiece he is."

And then, as the bird bobbed its head and took off from its

perch, fluttering down to pluck some invisible bug from one of the sprouting cabbages, the artist stood suddenly back, letting go of Orion's shoulder as if it had grown spikes.

"You see boy…" He sounded flustered. As if he might be talking for the sake of talking. As if he were covering his embarrassment, although it was hard to imagine a gentleman like Mr Tuke feeling embarrassed. "You see boy… you must always look closely at things. Observe them carefully. Don't ever imagine you know what something looks like until you've really studied it. That's the secret of art…"

He paused, turned away and stood staring around the garden, the neat rows of sprouting vegetables rising up towards the glass houses and cold frames, the espaliered apple and pear trees spread out against the surrounding walls, their branches already covered with the fresh new leaves of spring.

"See," he turned back to smile at Orion, who stood helplessly waiting. And then he pointed towards the shed – Orion's shed at the bottom of the garden, a haphazard pile of wooden boxes piled up against it from which he and Jacka had spent half the week planting out kale and cabbage seedlings. "See the beauty of that." He pointed a finger that was, Orion couldn't help but notice, almost as grubby as his own. "See the shades and shapes of those boxes against the darkness of the shed. The way the sunlight strikes the window and lights up the dirt and the cobwebs on the glass…" Orion shifted awkwardly. Wondering if this might be some sort of complaint. And then the artist stopped talking. Breathed heavily inwards and then, turning back to Orion, beamed at him, his dark eyes shining so brightly that it was hard not to smile back.

"You've a fine shaped face boy." He stared intently up and down as if he might be looking straight through his cotton shirt and his thick woollen trousers to his bare body. "A fine physique, altogether. Muscular shoulders – from all that digging I suppose."

Orion said nothing. He wasn't entirely sure what a physique was. Nor was he sure he wanted to. It had been warm work, hoeing, and he had pushed up his shirt sleeves but now, seeing the artist looking at his sunburnt arms, their hairs already turning to gold, he felt awkward. One hand, without his realising, tugged at a frayed cuff as if to pull it back down towards his wrist.

"My friends and I are always looking for models." The artist turned away, looking up the garden, perhaps at the lines of growth he had been admiring or perhaps he was checking that they were still alone. The breeze blew against his hair and he put up a hand to tidy it. "We would pay you for your time, of course."

"No thank you sir. I mean, I don' 'ave no time." He spoke so quickly that the words tumbled over themselves and he wasn't sure the artist would have heard him properly. "I don't 'ave no time," he repeated firmly so that this time the words came out much louder than he intended. Almost as if he were shouting.

It seemed the moment to take up his hoe again. It didn't seem as though the artist was here to buy potatoes or a string of last year's shallots and Mr Cyril would be angry if he got back and found the weeds still growing between the carrots.

"Not even at weekends? Sundays perhaps?"

"No! I d'go chapel Sunday."

"Oh yes, I suppose so." For a moment he seemed to forget what he was asking. "So you're a Methodist?"

"Yes sir."

"Ah well." The artist's eyes took on a far away look. "I forget these things. I no longer believe, you see. I was raised a Quaker but I've long moved away from any sort of religious observance."

He sounded almost sad.

"Like Mr Fox Sir?"

"Eh? Oh I see. Yes, a Quaker like Mr Fox. All the Mr Foxes," he added, smiling. "But how would you know about them?"

"The gardens Sir. I do dearly like to see the gardens."

"Of course. I should have known. I shall have to tell Mr Fox. He'll be glad to know you enjoy them."

"Don' do that!" The thought of two gentlemen talking about him was terrifying. "I mean... I'm no-one, Sir. I don' matter 't'all."

Once again the artist turned his dark eyes on him and this time they were very serious.

"Oh yes you do, Orion Goss," he said. "You matter a great deal. Everyone matters." And then, as a cloud crossed the sun and the garden darkened, "I must go. I have friends expected to dinner and I should go home and get changed."

Which left Orion wondering why he had troubled to call in at the garden, when it seemed he had no intention of buying anything.

Chapter 8

His mother was out when he got home that evening. Her employer, Mrs Trembath, who lived up Kimberley Park Road in one of the fine houses opposite the park – not far from Quarry Place in distance but some miles in social standing – was also expecting guests and Ida Goss, as her cook–housekeeper, having spent most of the day preparing the meal, was needed to serve it into the hands of the house–maid who would be waiting at table.

Alfred, who was home unusually early for him, was rooting about noisily in the pantry, emerging, as Orion came into the kitchen, with a hunk of bread and a jar of pickled onions.

"Ma not 'ome?"

He didn't even know why he asked – except that the sight of Alfred, especially Alfred with a bread knife in his hand, always made him feel nervous. Their mother had been complaining most of yesterday evening about being expected to work late, with very little expectation of extra money at the end of the week, and had told the boys they would have to fend for themselves.

"Do it look like she is?" Alfred thumped the bread onto the table, carved himself a rough chunk and stuffed half of it in his mouth. "An' don' you go puttin' yer filthy paws on that neither." He spat crumbs onto the table as he spoke and picked up the onion jar. "I'm off down Seven Stars. Meetin' a young lady!"

Leering, he unscrewed the jar, tossed two onions into his mouth and went out crunching them. She couldn't be much of a young lady, Orion thought, if she was prepared to get anywhere near Alfred, but he kept his thoughts to himself.

Everyone, it seemed, was doing things tonight. Mrs Trembath was expecting guests, the artist was giving a dinner party, even Alfred was meeting a young lady, who, perhaps, did not object to the smell of pickled onions. Only he, Orion, had nothing to occupy him.

Lying on his bed with a piece of bread and a slice of cheese,

Orion thought about the artist. Who would be changed by now – into evening dress, he supposed. The sort of dress he had seen gentlemen wearing who dined at the hotels on Falmouth's sea front that he had sometimes passed – dark trousers and tail coats, high collars and white bow ties. Some he had seen with silk top hats and carrying canes but the artist, being at home, would have no need of these... He imagined him all the same, his glossy, dark hair and thick moustache neatly kempt, shoes gleaming with polish, and his long-fingered hands scrubbed clean of paint and charcoal.

And this elegant man, this gentleman, had said that he, Orion, had a fine–shaped face and a fine physique, whatever that meant. That he would like him to model for him...

Which he would never do. Not like Bert and Charlie and Harry and the rest of them.

And yet... And yet it had felt...'comfortable' might be the word to describe the feeling of standing beside the artist as they watched the sparrow... What had he called him? A glorious little masterpiece! And he was right. And he, Orion, had seen that, as they stood together, the bristles of the artist's moustache almost touching his ear, his hand resting on his shoulder. The little bird was a masterpiece and he, Orion, had understood what he had meant. This artist. This gentleman.

The shadow of the quarry covered the window and, with it, the small, shabby room and Orion, with no guests to entertain or young lady to meet, felt himself drift into a gentle, comfortable sleep where the artist, tall, dark and handsome, handed a vast jar of pickled onions around a white-naped table surrounded by foxes in resplendent evening dress.

Weeks passed. Two, three... Orion was never sure since his days tended to be the same but he was kept busy with his hoe amongst the fast–growing crops of vegetables and herbs and they were bringing on tray–loads of seedlings ready, so Mr Cyril hoped, for some bumper crops. The weather was good for growing – warm; hot on many days but also wet, with fine showers of rain most afternoons which saved them most of the trouble of watering and filled the water butts against the dry days that were bound to follow.

It was raining the afternoon the artist reappeared. Not enough to matter and Orion had not even bothered with his cap as he followed Jacka along the rows, dropping tomato seedlings into the hole made by his dibber. It was perfect weather for this, although they would follow on with the watering can when they'd finished planting out, to give the small plants what even Mr Cyril said should be a 'grand start.'

And it was Jacka who spotted him first, the artist. Standing to ease his back for a few moments he glanced up the garden, then nudged Orion with the quiet grunting sound that was the nearest he ever came to speech as the tall figure in his dark sailing garb came striding down the path.

"Orion!" he exclaimed. "And Mr…?"

He held out his hand towards Jacka, who stared at it as if he had never seen one before and bent back to his dibber.

"'E's Jacka." Who must have, Orion supposed, a surname but he had never known what it was. "'E don' speak." And the two of them watched as Jacka continued marking out his holes, a regular foot apart – not that they ever measured the distance, or needed to do so – towards the end of the row. When he finished he gave another grunt and a curt nod in Orion's direction and set off back towards the potting shed with his scuttling, hunch-backed walk.

Orion glanced at the artist who appeared to be about to smile and then to change his mind. His lips, below his moustache, which glistened black with tiny beads of moisture, tightened and his dark eyes gleamed with amusement. A sudden gust of wind blew rain into Orion's face and he put up his hand to wipe it, forgetting the seedling tomato he was still holding.

"Now your face is all muddy." The artist was smiling properly now and Orion reached up to his face again. "No. Don't do that boy! Here, wait a moment…" And rooting in the pocket of his trousers he pulled out a handkerchief, clean and white although screwed up rather than folded, as if he had thrust it carelessly away. "Hold still." And to Orion's consternation he rubbed the cloth gently against his cheek, bringing it away damp and smeared with brown. "That's better – just a bit…" and, seeing the look on the boy's face, he handed him the cloth. "Just a patch, right on your cheek bone."

And, as Orion scrubbed frantically in what he hoped was the right place, the artist looked down at the box of tomato seedlings and the row of unfilled holes. Then,

"There he is again," he exclaimed. "Our little friend," as a sparrow – it might well have been the same one – fluttered down onto the disturbed earth and started to peck. But this time they were both, for some reason, feeling too discomfited to do more than stare blankly at it without speaking.

"Right." The artist took back his by now distinctly grubby kerchief and thrust it into his pocket. "I should be going. I just called in for…" he looked around as if for inspiration, "a few spring greens. This will be my last visit for a while," he added. "I'm off to London again in a couple of days. To see to my work for the Summer Exhibition. It's varnishing day next week – not that my paintings can be varnished; the paint will still be wet but it's my last chance to make any alterations."

He spoke as if to himself and he might as well have done so since his words made no sense to Orion who bent to drop his tomato seedling into its hole and then picked up another. Only the artist's final words meant anything to him.

"I'll be in London for the next three months," he said. "I have a couple of portraits to paint. I shan't be back in Falmouth until July." He held out his hand towards Orion. "I'll see you in the summer, Orion Goss. Perhaps in the mean time you might like to consider my offer. Remember? About allowing me to paint you?"

Orion paused, still bent over. Apart from the Minister when he had called at the house when his Grandfather Goss had died, he couldn't remember a gentleman ever offering to shake his hand – and the Minister, to be honest, wasn't much of a gentleman. Swapping hands with the seedling, he rubbed the right one on the seat of his trousers and held it out.

"Until the summer." The artist grasped his hand firmly, smiling down at him. "Au revoir Orion."

"Yes sir. Good bye sir."

As the artist strode away up the garden he pulled out of his pocket a sailing cap and put it onto his head, covering his dark, wet hair, although the rain had, in fact, very nearly stopped.

Goodbye little garden sparrow he said but there was no–one close enough to hear him.

Just for a moment Orion felt sorry to see him go. Which was strange when he had felt so flustered when the artist rubbed the soft cloth of his handkerchief against his face.

Turning to his tomatoes, he wondered why this should be.

Perhaps because the artist treated him as if he was a friend, talking to him in a way no–one had ever talked to him before. He wasn't sure, in fact, that anyone had ever really talked to him at all. Not even his friends – and he had few enough of these – since their communication consisted generally of plans for fishing trips, for drinking beer or getting their way with a girl. Followed by the bragging, about the amount caught or drunk or the willingness of the girl to be 'had'. Mostly incoherent and, almost always, inaccurate and of little or no interest.

Adults on the whole gave him orders. In the garden Mr Cyril instructed him in his tasks. In Chapel the Minister told him how he must lead his life; mostly by insisting that he avoid most of the things that might make that life worth living. At school his teachers had stated facts – which numbers added to which amounted to which other numbers, which letters put together formed which words, which kings and queens had ruled England and what battles they had won…

And Jacka, of course, said nothing at all. Which, it often seemed to Orion, was preferable.

Certainly no other conversation he remembered had given any of the pleasure that, now he was gone, he seemed to have had from his two last brief meetings with the artist and suddenly the thought of not seeing him for three months seemed upsetting. He watched as the artist, in his seaman's cap and jacket, reached the top of the garden and, without turning, waved his hand behind him and disappeared though the arched gateway. He did not even look at the table to check for spring greens, Orion noticed.

The sun came out sharply through the clouds, striking the rain-soaked leaves so that they shone as if polished, and a second sparrow flitted down from their wall, hopping about with its mate in the damp earth, pecking for grubs and worms.

Orion watched them. Noted the brown staining above their eyes; the fluffy dumpiness of their round bodies; the way their wings folded in against them like neatly furled umbrellas. Mr Tuke – he tried the name in his head like a nice secret – was quite right; there was so much to see in quite ordinary things when you really looked at them.

And that, he had told him last time he visited, was the secret of art. The secret that Mr Trevithick had never bothered to tell him – but then, no-one had ever told him, Orion, a secret before. He wasn't important enough for that. Except that Mr Tuke had said he was. Or at least that he mattered, which must mean the same thing.

And now he was going away to London for three months. And what in the world, he wondered, was a 'varnishing day'?

Chapter 9

Has he, Henry wonders as he strides along the high pavement above Woodlane, gone too far? His hand, deep in his trouser pocket, fondles the damp handkerchief, smeared with mud from the boy's still downy cheek and he remembers the startled look in his wide, blue eyes, the way he turned away to stare down at his muddy boots and the row of little plants, already wilting in spite of the rain.

And he is a fool, he tells himself. What does it matter if a boy who works in a market garden has mud on his face? And why could he, Henry, not control himself sufficiently to ignore the smear on his healthy, young cheek?

He is an utter fool, as his friend Charles Fox would certainly tell him. Except that he will not tell Charles – although for reasons that he does not entirely understand.

The trees that line the pavement are still dripping but the sun has broken through, steam rises from the wet roadway and there is more blue sky than cloud – enough, as Mrs Fouracre would say, for a pair of sailor man's trousers. And he is off, in two days time, to London where he is confident that his two latest paintings – now titled The Run Home and Ruby, Gold and Malachite – will have prominent placings in the summer exhibition of the Royal Academy.

His paintings are generally, after all, admired by both the public and his fellow artists, especially his studies of boys bathing or lying, relaxed and naked, on the beach or on board ship. He is a master, it is said, of the lines of the body, of the play of light on naked flesh, of conveying the unselfconscious beauty of young men's limbs and these are also the painting which give him the most pleasure, although not everyone, of course, is entirely happy about them.

For London is still reeling from the shock of the trial of Oscar Wilde, whom Henry has met and with whom he has friends in common, and there are always comments, he is well aware, on his subject matter. His August Blue, for example, which hangs in the national collection of British Art now housed in the fine new Tate Gallery beside the Thames, has drawn comments, some from fellow Royal Academicians. Painting naked boys – obviously real boys, engaging in natural boyish activities such as swimming and diving, as distinct from naked boys disguised as characters from mythology – is considered by some to be a bold, if not foolhardy, enterprise. One could hardly hang such a painting, more than one lady has told him, in one's drawing room.

Fortunately the President and Council of the Academy, who have purchased August Blue under the terms of the Chantrey Bequest do not, it appears, agree with them but Henry is aware that many do.

It doesn't worry him – or, if it does, he doesn't allow it to show – and certainly none of his models have ever complained that he has taken liberties. Not that some of them – Falmouth is, after all, a thriving port filled with lonely seamen whose needs are not always met by the equally thriving population of female prostitutes – would mind if he did; provided they were paid for their services.

But not Orion Goss and, as he strides down Hangman's Hill towards Swanpool in the clean brightness of the sudden sunshine, Henry's mind veers reluctantly away from the anticipation of yet more professional success. For it seems to him that he has, up to now, been making progress. That the boy has been more at ease with him than at this time last year, when he did everything he could to avoid him among the cabbages or beans. He is still nervous of him, of course, still awkward in his company, but slowly, slowly, like the distrustful fox cub Henry and his brother spent weeks, one summer when they were boys, enticing to eat from their hands, he has been starting to relax in his company.

But as he sits in the corner of his First Class carriage two mornings later, as the little branch line train pulls out of Falmouth station with a great deal of self–important chuffing and letting out of sparks, Henry feels a sense of what he can only describe as disappointment.

It is a dreary day – grey sky meeting a grey sea and both rendered close to invisible by the thick sea mist that overhangs the town, drenching the face, the hair, the clothes and even the boots. Not a day to regret leaving the chance of a morning swim or an afternoon sail and as the train emerges from a cutting he can see, between dripping pines, the grey curtain that obscures his final glimpse of Falmouth bay and the bleak outline of the fine house of one of his friends spoilt by the long, dark streaks of moisture that stain its stuccoed walls.

And, ahead of him, after he has changed onto the main line at Truro, overseeing the transfer of his trunk and his carefully-packaged – and still-damp – paintings from the guard's van, lies a six hour journey and then the pleasures of London. Time to spend with his mother and his sister, to renew friendships, visit galleries and theatres and, most of all, to enjoy the plaudits of the public and his peers at the Summer Exhibition.

It will be a busy, happy and productive time and, much as he loves Falmouth, he has never regretted these weeks away.

Until this year.

This year, for reasons from which his critical mind veers away, is different. This year he does not want to leave.

Chapter 10

He looked forward all week to this time – Orion, for whom, up to a few months ago, days generally merged to one, with little excitement to be gained even from his Saturday half holiday.

Now, on nights when he couldn't sleep for Alfred across the room, tanked up with beer, grunting and snoring, occasionally letting off wind to add to the sour stench of the piss in the chamber pot, he would actually count the hours until Friday evening.

It was summer now and daylight, this far West and in spite of the overhanging quarry wall, stayed on until ten or later so that he no longer needed to light a candle to see his sketches. Not that he felt he was making much progress with them.

In spite of Mr Tuke's words – about really studying something before he tried to draw it – he didn't feel that his flower drawings were any more like the flowers he was copying than when he first started and it was hard to think what else he could draw, limited as he was to his bedroom and the view from the bedroom window. No proper artist, he knew, would make pictures of dull, everyday things like beds and wash stands and the lean to, tin–roofed privy in the back yard.

If he only dared to take his sketchbook outdoors, up into Kimberly Park for example, with its tall trees and rare and unusual plants, which he had often seen young ladies sketching, he might have done better but this was not something he could imagine himself doing. Too many people walked in the park and he would feel foolish and self–conscious. The children who played there would mock his feeble efforts. And he was bound to be seen by people who knew him and would comment to his mother or worse, Alfred.

He ventured back, nevertheless, into the little shop in the High Street to purchase from the long-haired young man a set of pencils – B, 2B and 3B – with which he hoped it would be easier to convey lines and shading and improve his pictures. He had foregone several evenings in The Greyhound with Will and his other mates in order to afford these but that didn't matter. He didn't have much in common with Will or the others, he'd begun to feel.

"If you're interested in sketching, there's some books you might like," the young man suggested when he went back to the shop for another sketch pad. It was a wet evening and Orion was his only customer – perhaps the only one he would get before closing – and he directed him to the shelves in an alcove towards the back of the shop, turning up the gas so that Orion could see the books more easily.

Not that he dared touch them. It was quite obvious that these were not books he could afford. One look at the bindings was enough to tell him that. In any case books were not something that he – or his family – went in for. They had a bible, of course, and a Methodist Hymn Book, and on the table in the front room were three books that Ida Goss had brought from her home in Redruth for she had been quick at school and had, before her marriage, enjoyed a good story. 'The Wide, Wide World' one was called and Orion had looked in it once but the few lines he had read were very dull and of no interest to him.

"No thanks," he said. Adding, because the young man was friendly and because he could see, now that there was more light, a vivid, unhealthy–looking spot on his chin which, for some reason, made it easier to hold a conversation with him, "I don' really 'ave no money. I'm just a labourer, you see, over to Mr Rouses' market garden. I don' earn much."

"Nor me," the long-haired young man said gloomily. "I get eight shillings a week." Which was only sixpence more than Orion and, now he dared look properly at the shop assistant, he saw that he had outgrown his trousers which showed his thin ankles in their thin, dark socks, that his card shirt cuffs hung down below his jacket sleeves and that the edges of his jacket lapels were worn in places to the threads.

Then he realised he was staring and that staring was rude.

"Must be better in 'ere than outside in all weathers," he said. "Drier," he added, when the young man said nothing and although he realised, even as he spoke, how much, even when it rained, he would miss the smell of earth and roots and growing plants and the feel of the breeze off the sea.

The bell over the shop door gave its fussy, jangling sound but it was only the post man with the evening post. The young man went over to take the small bundle of letters and the conversation, Orion felt, was over but,

"If you're keen on art…" He placed the post on the counter, "there's talks at the Polytechnic Hall up Church Street. Some of them are very interesting. There's one next Friday on the Impressionists."

This was not a word Orion knew but he often passed the Polytechnic Society hall and when he looked at the bill board outside the next evening he saw that the 'Lecture, Illustrated by Lantern Slides' cost one shilling and sixpence for the first six rows, reducing to sixpence – 'three pence for minors' – at the back of the hall.

He hurried home on Friday evening, gave himself an all–over wash in the kitchen sink – bath night was Saturday and there was no time to heat water on the range so he made do with cold – and changed into his white shirt and Sunday suit. It was fortunate the lecture was on a Friday and he hoped to be home before his mother who would be annoyed about the shirt, which she washed and ironed every Monday, ready for chapel the following Sunday. Then he buffed up his Sunday shoes, sleeked down his hair with water, took the pasty she had left out for him and hurried off towards town, biting into it as he went.

"Chapel do, is it Orion? Or got a young lady, 'ave 'ee?" old Jos Tregenna called out from his perch on the wall opposite the

Market Hall and he knew he must tell him something or he would be the more likely to mention it to his mother. In any case, knowing he was bound to be asked, he already had his story ready.

"Meetin' a customer, with Mr Rowse," he said. Jos was unlikely to meet Mr Cyril and if he told his mother it was worth the risk because she rarely saw him either.

He gave the same answer to Mrs Barnicoat, to Suzy Eva and to Tom Proud, who all saw him on his way up Church Street and saw no reason not to ask where he was going –'dressed up like a dog's dinner,' as Tom put it – and it was such a relief to arrive at the hall that he hurried inside without even thinking to be nervous, in spite of the smartly dressed ladies and gentlemen crowding up the steps. The gentleman in evening dress who sat at a small table just inside the entrance paused for a fraction of a second as he mumbled his request for 'a thrupenny,' but took his money and gave him a pasteboard ticket in return.

"Up the stairs, young man. Anywhere in the back three rows," he told him in a friendly enough tone of voice.

The room was broad and imposing with windows high up in the walls and Orion found a seat in the farthest corner at the back from which he could watch the hall filling with ladies and gentlemen. For Falmouth might be a dock and fishing port but there were plenty of gentry and the hotels attracted a smart clientele, many staying several weeks for the sea bathing and cliff walks as well as such social and cultural events as this.

Many of the ladies wore impressively sized hats on their elaborately piled-up hair and were escorted by gentlemen in frock coats and striped evening trousers but not all were so formally dressed. Some ladies wore dresses which were daringly looser and more flowing in style and there were two not far in front of him, who wore plain, dark skirts and high-collared blouses with ties and caps that looked almost manly. They must be 'artistic', perhaps even 'Bohemian' and Orion felt excited and quite proud to be in such unusual company. Some of the younger men wore blazers and flannels and one wore a long fisherman's jersey over dark canvas trousers that looked, even from a distance, to be stained and spattered with paint and Orion, in his Sunday suit, began to think he might have been less conspicuous if he had worn his ordinary working clothes.

On the whole, however, he was enjoying himself. He felt quite safe in his corner as people strolled in, greeting acquaintances and looking around the room before deciding where to sit and gradually even the back rows began to fill, mostly with the more 'artistic'-looking types, although Orion recognised his long-haired friend from the art supplies shop with another dark-suited young man who was a clerk in the Trustee Savings Bank just down the street.

He was less certain whether he enjoyed the talk itself and was still uncertain when he came away as to why the painters the speaker mentioned were called 'Impressionists.' He was also unsure of the speaker's name, since he was introduced by an elderly gentleman, apparently a prominent member of the Cornwall Polytechnic Society, who spoke in a low, rather quavering voice, but it was thrilling to find himself in the same room as a man who had been fortunate enough, he told them, to attend the exhibition in the Hanover Gallery in Bond Street, London, where the Impressionist painters Monet, Sisley, Renoir and Pissarro had shown their work.

It had been, he said, a revelation. These men had broken away from the restraints of form. According to Monet, in fact, there was no such thing as form apart from light and one must learn to look at light in order to find form. Monet himself painted, the speaker told them, the atmosphere which lay between the viewer and the object and therein lay his genius…

Orion listened, attempted to write notes in the small book he had brought with him – but he had never been much of a writer – and gaped in incomprehension. In front of him members of the audience nodded in agreement – although one elderly man with crimson cheeks and white side whiskers occasionally snorted and once said 'Shame' quite loudly and causing loud whispers of 'Hush' – and the speaker moved on to the artist Pissarro, who dispensed, he said, with outline and succeeded in capturing the passing moment in gleams of colour.

At this point he asked for the lights to be extinguished and a man at the back of the central aisle projected onto a screen a picture of a woman in a field which was like nothing Orion had ever seen. There were trees, undeniably, and a wall and the roofs and chimneys of houses above it. And in the space which occupied about a third of the painting was the figure of a girl with a bucket in each hand.

But none of these outlines were definite. Nothing was painted with the exactness Orion had always tried to achieve and which he had assumed was the point of art. All was vague, almost haphazard and yet... and yet he felt, as he stared across the rows of dark heads in front of him, as if he were in that field. As if the girl, whose face was a pale blur and who had no visible hands or feet, was actually walking towards him.

How in the world, he wondered, as another picture – a street scene this time and the figures, the horses, carts and carriages, were just blobs and lines of paint and yet he could feel that they were moving – did the man, Pizz–whatever his name was, achieve this?

And where did this leave him, Orion, and his drawings of daffodils?

"I do hope you enjoyed the evening. Such an inspiring speaker, don't you think?"

The talk and the lantern slide were over, the gas lights were turned up and the audience, with much conversation and scraping of chairs, were making their way out. Orion, from his back corner, was one of the last to leave and felt quite alarmed when a lady standing at the top of the stairs addressed him. She was very tall and appeared even taller because she wore a deep blue, floor–length dress, and held her head very high on the longest, whitest neck Orion had ever seen. She wore a broad–brimmed, dark blue hat trimmed with black ostrich feathers which seemed to reach even higher and yet she was smiling at him in a friendly enough manner.

"Yes, Ma'am," he said. Agreement seeming the only possible response. "But I din' understand everything 'e said," he couldn't help adding. The tall lady laughed, a low–pitched laugh in contrast to her general upwardness, and said that it was honest of him to say so.

"But I do hope you'll come again. We're so keen to attract the widest possible audience for our events."

Orion stumbled down the steps with no idea what she meant by this – except that she seemed to mean to be welcoming.

It is an entire new world, he thinks now, as he sets out his pastels – he has saved up to buy a set of these from the long–haired young man – whose name, he now knows, is Cyril and who appears to have developed more spots than ever, perhaps from spending so much time indoors – on his most precious evening of the week. For he has been to two more lectures on the Impressionists and he now knows not only who they were but, more or less, what were their ideas of art.

They experimented, he knows now. They refused to be restricted by classical views of art and they painted – often in the open air – people and landscapes as they saw them and not in what Mr Hemy, last week's speaker, called 'an idealized form'. Nor, Mr Hemy said, were they concerned with a meticulous finish but applied their paint with swift and spontaneous brush strokes in order to capture the impression of the moment.

Orion's notebook is crammed with his notes – and with the words and phrases he has not understood – and he has ventured further than the Polytechnic Hall and joined the Passmore

Edwards Free Lending Library.

He had never been inside before, although it was only a few minutes walk from his home, being one of the buildings on the Moor, near the Town Hall, which he had never entered either, and it took all his courage to venture up the steps and under the portico into the dark, imposing entrance lobby where a polished oak staircase led to an upper gallery, heavy–framed portraits of stern men looked forbiddingly down from the walls and Orion's thick boots scraped and echoed against the floor.

Someone, he was sure, must come out and tell him he had no right to be there – possibly the large woman behind the counter just inside the inner doors to the library, who wore tortoiseshell spectacles, had her hair drawn back angrily from her face and stared at Orion as if he was a tradesman come to the wrong entrance.

Although she was, in fact, less terrifying than her appearance, merely explaining that he must complete an application and get it signed by someone who would 'vouch for his decency and honesty.'

"A minister of the church, perhaps," she suggested helpfully and Orion took the form to chapel the following Sunday and asked the Minister to sign it for him. "I d'want to read the books," he explained when he asked why he wanted to join the public library and, although the Reverend Ogden still seemed suspicious of his motives he could obviously think of no good reason why he should not sign.

All of which is behind him now and he feels almost at home at the dark wood desks in the Reference library which he uses regularly, sometimes to consult a dictionary for the meaning of some word he has heard in the Polytechnic Hall and sometimes to read about great painters of the past and to look at the prints of their paintings.

And now, Friday evening, he prepares himself, with his sketchpad, his B, 2B and 3B pencils and his new pastels, for his evening's work. For attendance at the three lectures has given him the answer to at least one of his problems.

He can draw, he has learnt, whatever he wants to draw. Or – more importantly – whatever is on hand. And having seen the lantern slides of the painter Cezanne's still life paintings of apples and jars and books and brushes, he is preparing an arrangement of his own.

He has brought upstairs one of his mother's stone preserving jars, her copy of The Methodist Hymn Book, an onion filched from Mr Cyril and a bunch of nasturtiums from his own garden and it takes him some time to arrange them to his satisfaction on top of the wash stand. Then, settling back onto the edge of his bed and clutching his sketch book, he starts…

Chapter 11

June 1902 and Henry returns to Falmouth earlier than usual.

London is all very well and he enjoys his visits; it suits his sociable nature to meet friends for dinner or the theatre or to visit one of the select and slightly unusual clubs of which he is a member. There is an energy about the place that invigorates him, old friends to see, as well as his mother and sister, new friends to make and money to be made too from the portraits he is commissioned to paint and for which he is much in demand.

This year he has also visited the new gallery, recently opened in Whitechapel and already attracting interest in that very Jewish area of the city. And there has been, as always, the pleasure of the summer show at the Royal Academy where both 'The Run Home' and 'Ruby, Gold and Malachite' have been much praised and prominently hung, viewed by, among many hundreds, the famous actress Lily Langtry and her escort, the Prince of Wales.

How, with such success and activity, can he not have enjoyed himself?

And yet he has longed for Falmouth, where, in this remote area and mild climate, he can paint in the clear light and freedom of the open air. Where he can sail Red Heart. Where he can swim, every morning, before breakfast, in the sea…

Which is why he has not, this year, followed his usual pattern and remained in London until July. And on this first morning after his return, following his morning dip in the clear, cool water below his house, he is eagerly looking forward to seeing his boys again. Charlie, who has been looking after his boat, which he is also looking forward to seeing again, Bert and cheeky, accident-prone Harry…

And Orion. Bashful, rough–hewn, beautiful Orion. Who cannot be termed one of his boys because he is still so obviously nervous around him, but is perhaps – although this is not something Henry is prepared to admit – the main reason for his early return.

How he would love, he has thought in these past weeks, to see Orion without his working shirt, his corduroy breeches, his heavy, mud encrusted boots. How he would love to see him rejoice in his naked beauty, freed from those ugly working clothes to slide from one element, air, into another, water. How glorious it would be to paint that joyous moment!

Henry whistles to himself as he strides along the path at Swanpool, beams at a pretty nursemaid with a baby carriage and shouts a cheery greeting to an old man driving an over-laden donkey along the road. On such a morning and with so much to look forward to, it is impossible to do otherwise. He has friends to meet. Work to do. And all the infinite possibilities of six months by the sea...

It was hard work, planting out winter greens on a baking morning when the sun was already high and the seedlings he had set out in their long rows already drooped miserably in the parched soil. But Mr Cyril hated to see bare earth and this patch, halfway up the garden, where Jacka had removed the stumps of the old cabbages, had been a reproach to him over the last three hot, dry days. Get them in this morning boy, he had told Orion first thing. Water them in well and they'll do.

But first there had been lettuces to pick and carrots to pull and bunch and Mr Cyril had called Jacka away to dig beets and now Orion's back ached from bending, his skirt prickling so uncomfortably against his skin that he would have liked to take it off but this was something Mr Cyril would not allow. Not with ladies calling into the gardens. Even when he was working at the very bottom of the garden he must be fully and decently clothed.

Pausing to ease his back, he looked up the gardens to where Mr Cyril was selling strawberries to a young girl. She was a pretty girl – even from a distance he could see that. She wore a white muslin dress, a straw hat with flowers on the brim and her long, brown hair fell loose over her shoulders so that she looked, next to Mr Cyril in his brown jacket and sacking apron, like a princess in a fairy tale.

He wasn't sure about girls. His friends, Will for example, were always boasting about their exploits, most of which Orion found hard to believe, but, having no experience himself, how would he know?

There was Cassie Oliver, of course, who lived three houses up the road and hung around outside doing what his ma called 'making eyes' at him but she was two years younger than him and smelt of fish. And there was a young lady at chapel who had caught his eye but he had always been too nervous to approach her, in her sober Sunday outfit and demure hat. Especially when she was carrying her prayer books.

And the young women, like this one in her pretty white muslin, who called at the garden, were customers and out of his range.

One day, he supposed, when he was older, it would be different but it was hard to know how. Or, for that matter, why.

He bent over his seedlings again, pressing into the dry earth with his dibber, dropping in the little roots, tidying in the soil then moving a hand's span along the row. As he pushed his hand across his forehead to stop the sweat running into his eyes he knew he would be leaving brown smears but there was nothing he could do about that.

Reaching for the watering can he glanced back up the garden where Mr Cyril and the young lady stood, still talking, in the shade of the wall. A man, as he watched, came through the arched entrance-way. A tall man, hatless, in spite of the heat, with dark brown hair and wearing a seaman's canvas jacket over an open-necked shirt…

He hasn't forgotten the artist. On the contrary, he thinks about him a great deal. Every time he takes out his sketch book and pencils, in fact. Look closely at things, he told him, all those weeks ago. Observe them carefully. Don't imagine you know what something looks like until you've really studied it.

And, for these last three months, he has been trying to do exactly this. To examine the objects – the pots and apples and plants that he has been sketching in his room on his precious Friday evenings and those other things that he has moved on to sketching in other places and at other times.

The lectures at the Polytechnic Hall have helped. Not always, he has to admit, and his notebook is still crammed with words he has later decided he must have misheard because they make no sense. But he has understood some things without needing to make notes.

The speaker on Cézanne, for example. What he said made perfect sense – even if Orion had no idea how to spell the artist's name and had to consult Cyril, with whom he is now quite friendly, before he could even look him up in the library. Now he knows a great deal about him and has seen pictures of his painstaking studies of fruit and jars and books. And all the time he remembers how he and Mr Tuke watched the sparrow together. How he saw for the first time, and only because Mr Tuke pointed it out to him, the delicate pattern of the plumage, the little speckled bib, the differing shades of grey and brown...

No, he has not forgotten about him. Far from it. It is just that calendars have no place in Orion's life. Certain days are significant – he looks forward now to his Friday evenings and his Saturday afternoon holiday and contemplates with some gloom the prospect of chapel on Sunday – but otherwise the passage of time is marked by the changes within the garden and he thinks in terms of seasons and weather but not of dates. And so, when the artist said he would see him in July the words had no great meaning. He would be gone 'some time' he thought and nothing more.

And so, when he at last recognises the bare-headed, dark-haired man, it is a surprise – and for a moment he is not sure whether it is a pleasant or an unpleasant one.

Meanwhile, at the top of the garden, the scene shifts. Mr Cyril steps back from the table and moves his hand to where his forelock would be if he still had any hair on that part of his head. The young lady glances round at the artist, who raises his hand to where his hat would be if he had been wearing one and gives a shout of laughter which Orion hears, even at such a distance.

He stands up, brushes the dry earth from his trousers and picks up the box that holds the seedlings. It is too hot, he tells himself, to plant out any more this morning. They must wait until the cooler air of the early evening. Waving the watering can over those he has just planted he hurries back to the shed, dumps the seedlings and picks up a basket. Then, without looking up the garden again, he makes his way across to the red runners.

It is one of the pleasanter jobs, picking beans, and customers want any amount when they are in season. Pushing in amongst the tall poles with their thick growth of leaves he breathes in their sour scent and sets about hunting out the longest, fullest stalks.

"Orion Goss!" It is ten minutes since he moved in amongst the beans and his basket is almost full. "Is that you hiding in the beans?"

The artist stands smiling on the pathway. The sunlight gleams on his dark hair and he puts up a hand to push back a stray lock from his forehead.

"Not 'iding Sir. Pickin' beans."

"Excellent! You can pick some for me! I told Mr Rowse I'd collect them for myself since he's occupied with customers."

And Mr Cyril is indeed occupied with customers. Three women crowd around his table, among them Mrs Cowling, owner of Harbour View Guest House and well known for her fussy ways.

Orion emerges with his basket from the shelter of the beans.

"Will these be enough sir? I can easy pick 'ee some more if you wants."

"No, those will do fine. They look magnificent. So…" The artist steps back, squinting against the sun. "What have you been doing, while I've been away?"

"Nothing sir. I been 'ere most days. Working."

"I can see that." The artist stops looking at him and stares round the garden. "So much growth! Those beans! Those magnificent cabbages. Those lettuces. My God! And apricots! Surely not?"

"Tidn' just me Sir. Mr Cyril, Mr Rowse, that is, and Jacka. They d'do a great deal of the work." As always, the artist's enthusiasm alarms him. "I'll get something to wrap these in, Sir."

He does not expect the artist to follow him but he has forgotten what he is like. After the brilliance of the sunlight it takes time for his eyes to adjust to the darkness inside the shed and as he comes out with a sheet of newspaper Mr Tuke is waiting by the door.

"So, have you thought about what I said last time we met?" He fixes him with his dark, smiling eyes. "I'm back for the whole summer now. Why don't you come out with me on my boat? Or come to Newporth beach with the boys? You may know them. Bertie and Harry and…"

"No sir."

Orion doesn't mean he doesn't know them for, of course, he does. He is distantly related, through his father, to Bert White and Harry Cleave goes, if rarely, to the same chapel.

"I don' 'ave no time," he says firmly. Which is what he said last time.

"Surely you get holidays? And Sundays? Surely you don't have to be in chapel all day?"

Orion blinks, surprised that he has remembered that he is a Methodist.

"No sir. Just the mornings. But…"

"So you could come out in the afternoon!" The artist slaps his hand against his thigh as though a problem has been resolved.

"What do you say? This Sunday! Come out with us on the boat. Come down to the quay after chapel. I'll send Charlie ashore to row you out."

He beams, eyes bright with pleasure, teeth gleaming white behind the darkness of his moustache.

"I can't Sir!" Terrified – this is a gentleman and a customer and he is supposed to do what a gentleman and a customer asks – Orion looks up the garden for help but Mr Cyril is still occupied with Mrs Cowling and Jacka – not that he would be much help – is nowhere in sight. "Don' ask me Sir." He speaks in a whisper, almost as if he does not want the man to hear. "Please don' ask me no more."

He stares downwards – dry earth and his own, heavy-toed boots, white from scuffing – biting his lower lip. Please God, make him go away, he begs. Please make him go away and not come back and I'll be your humble and devoted servant for ever and ever. Amen.

"Oh Orion." The voice has changed. So much that he can hardly believe it is the same man. "I didn't mean to frighten you."

He speaks quietly, haltingly even, with none of his usual ebullience, and when Orion dares look up it is hard to be certain against the brightness of the sun but it appears almost as if there are tears in his eyes. But this can't possibly be so. Not a gentleman like Mr Tuke, who is educated and is friends with important men like the various Mr Foxes and has paintings hanging in galleries in London.

"I'm not a pederast, Orion, if that's what you think. I promise you that. If that's what you've heard… Is that what you've heard?"

It is hard to look at him and even harder to look away when he fixes him with his dark, almost black, eyes as if he is begging to be believed, and even though Orion has no idea what he is talking about. He shakes his head. Whatever a pedder–whatever he said might be, this is not what anyone has said to him.

"I'm an artist, Orion. I like to draw and paint young men. Draw and paint them! That's all. You must have seen paintings… Pictures of women without their clothes on. Artists have always drawn from life. How else can we capture the reality of the body? Certainly not when it's covered with clothes. And that's what I try to do in my work. Capture the reality of the body. The truth and beauty of the naked flesh. Especially in the sunlight and especially by the sea where the light is so clear and pure… You don't understand a word I'm saying do you?"

His voice changes from impassioned to hopeless, he lowers his arms, which he has been waving, as if to illustrate the truth and beauty, the sunlight, the sea… and Orion shakes his head. He understands about the pictures of naked women. He has seen them in books and at one of the lectures at the Polytechnic Hall they were shown lantern slides of naked women bathers – as fat as his mum they were and the speaker explained that the artist wanted to show women as they really were and not in an idealised form…

But that was women. He has never seen pictures of naked men.

"What I'm trying to tell you… " The artist's face is scarlet and there are tiny bubbles of sweat on his forehead, although this is hardly surprising, in the heat of the day and when he is not wearing a hat, "is… I wouldn't hurt you, Orion. I wouldn't touch you. I promise. I would like to paint you but there would be no need for you to remove your clothes. I did a painting of Jack Rolling on the Lily a few years back. One of my finest works. You should see it. He has all his clothes on. Even his cap!"

"You should 'ave a cap on Sir, this 'ot weather." Orion picks up on the one thing he understands. "You'll get sun stroke, standing out like that."

And the artist lets out a shout of laughter so loud that Mr Cyril and his customers turn and stare down the garden to see what is happening.

Chapter 12

"'E's all right. 'E don' touch you nor nothing."

That was what his friend Will had said all that time ago and perhaps he should believe him. Will was, after all, more likely to boast that the great artist had touched him than that he hadn't. And surely a man like Mr Tuke wouldn't tell lies?

As he went about his work the next few days, pulling and bunching carrots with Jacka, hoeing between the rows, picking the ever–heavier crop of beans, supporting the shooting tomato plants with stakes, pulling out the side shoots from amongst the pungent leaves… as he went about all these tasks he found himself looking out for him. Mr Tuke. Looking up when he heard a man's voice at the top of the garden. Hoping, when Mr Cyril and Jacka were out on their rounds, that he might call in as he did back in the spring. When he was frightened by him, he had to remember. By his noise and general boisterousness and the feeling of uncertainty about what he might say, or do, next.

Now, for some reason he could not possibly explain to himself, everything was different. Dating from that moment when he squinted into the sunshine and saw, or thought he saw, the tears in the artist's eyes. Certainly when he heard the tears in his voice.

Since then he had wanted, more than he could remember wanting anything, to see him again, although it was impossible to understand why this should be so.

Henry, meanwhile, is busy. Cannot remember a time when he has been busier. After his early morning dip in the cool, unspoilt water of the cove beneath his cottage and Mrs Fouracre's hearty breakfast of bacon and eggs, hog's pudding and several cups of strong tea, he is ready for his day's work. Some days he works on his new painting, using young Georgie Fouracre and Bert White as his models, sprawled on the sand in Sunny Cove. On others he cycles or walks across the town to the Customs House Quay where he rows out to the glass–topped boat the locals call the Piebox, because this is what it resembles, from where he sketches and paints other boats, boatmen and harbour scenes. Sometimes he doesn't even pause to eat, and, sometimes, in this glorious weather, stays aboard all night, sleeping under the stars.

This bohemian way of life can lead to problems – for example he can hardly appear in a lady's dining room in his sailing garb and, handsome and concerned with his appearance as he is, would not in any case wish to do so. And so he has been known, before arriving in a front hall in immaculate evening dress, to deposit his clothes for the next day's work tied in a handkerchief and hidden under a bush outside the door – the sort of behaviour that delights most people, who enjoy both his company and his eccentricity, although his older friend, the artist Charles Hemy, is not so easily amused.

But then he is often worried by Henry – Hemy, who spent three years as a Dominican monk, who built his house right next to the Catholic church, goes regularly to mass and has a tendency to wander the house at night, praying in his Dominican habit...

Why, he has often wondered, must Henry spend so much of his time in the company of young men and boys? And so much time with other, rather older, men whose morals are, to say the least, dubious? Those who call themselves Uranians, who celebrate the love of adolescent boys as the purest, most enduring form of love, a sentiment which causes Charles's naturally severe features to arrange themselves into their grimmest expression.

And why, he also asks himself, if he must paint the naked male form, can Henry not at least conform to convention and choose biblical or mythological subjects for his pictures?

But that is not real life, Henry has told him; he cannot arouse the same passions painting angels and satyrs. And Charles, frowning, turns back to his own work – he too has a boat from where he makes his detailed sketches of ships and boat, fish and gulls and every aspect of life in the harbour and around the Carrick Roads – and thinks that the arousal of passions is exactly the problem.

How much better it would be for Henry if he had a wife, as he has himself – a pleasant, sensible woman who has given him ten children. Henry is a good-looking man, after all. There are plenty of girls who would be delighted to marry him.

Visiting Henry's studio, surrounded by studies of Bert White – who is a marine apprentice at the Docks but often fakes accidents in order to model for him – that are the preliminaries to his latest work, Charles pulls at his thick white moustache and shakes his head. The boy's body, toughened by his work, is undoubtedly an attractive one and he can only hope....

But he does not dare voice his hopes – or fears – even inside his own head.

And Henry, who likes and admires the older man, as a friend and an artist, would be saddened to know of them. For he is no pederast. As he assured Orion on the morning after his return from London. Orion, the good chapel boy, whose nervous beauty haunted him, even while he was away, and whom he now finds impossible to forget.

Nor can he forget the look – a look of fear, almost of terror – that he observed in those wide, sea-green eyes below the grimy forehead that same morning.

What people think has never bothered him before. With friends like the now shamefully imprisoned Oscar, the lustful Sir Robert Gower and one or two Falmouth men about whom rumours have long circulated, although most have never been substantiated, people are bound to have ideas about Henry himself and he has always felt that they are free to do so. But not Orion. He does not want Orion to be afraid of him. To think of him as a sodomite. Nor, although for very different reasons, Charles...

Meanwhile he concentrates on his work, forcing himself to

stay away from the temptations of Mr Rowse's market garden. In a glorious Cornish summer he concentrates on the effects of sunlight – on flesh and supple young limbs, on the sea, on masts and spars, on ropes and sails – spends day after day and some nights as well, aboard ship and then, coming ashore one evening for supplies, he calls into the little art shop in High street and comes face to face… with Orion.

At first it seems too unlikely to be true and, having come down two steps from the sunlit street into the much darker shop, he imagines his eyes must be deceiving him. But they are not. Standing at the counter in his working clothes and heavy boots and in conversation with Cyril, is Orion Goss. They are examining a box of water colours and, for a moment, neither of them notices him. Then Cyril, whom Henry knows well but he would never want to paint that bony, pasty face so liberally decorated with red pustules, looks up.

"I'm sorry, Mr Tuke. I din' see you there. What can I get you Sir?" he asks but Henry, who has forgotten completely what he came in for, can only gape speechlessly.

"Paper," he says eventually. "A ream. My usual weight." For he always needs paper. And then, recovering some of his composure, "This is a surprise, Orion. Are you a friend of Cyril's?"

For even spotty, unattractive Cyril must, presumably, have friends.

"No sir. That is, yes," the boy stutters unhelpfully, pauses, stares down at his boots and then seems to make up his mind. "I'm a customer," he says firmly. "I do come 'ere to buy stuff," he adds, as if the statement requires definition.

"Do you indeed?" The answer surprises Henry still more but he is in command of himself by now. "Well, well. And what 'stuff' do you buy?"

"Paper, sir." Cyril, who has been watching with some interest, decides to join in. "And sketching pencils. And brushes. I was just showing 'im this new water colour…"

"It's way too costly," Orion interrupts, puce with embarrassment.

Henry, to whom the cost of this, quite small, box would be nothing, would love to buy it for him but knows this is impossible and that the boy is too guileless to be making hints.

"I didn't know you painted," he says instead.

"I don't. Not really. I do draw really but…"

"I see. Well… That's excellent. I'm very pleased to hear it. Have the paper sent round as usual, will you Cyril?" Henry pulls a ten shilling note from his pocket. "You must show me some of your sketches sometime," he tells Orion, as Cyril counts out his change and then, turning abruptly, goes out of the shop.

Halfway up Church Street he remembers that what he really wanted was linseed oil and, although he dares not turn back, he smiles, partly in amusement at his own confusion but mostly in pleasure at what has just happened.

The gods, perhaps even God, although he is not sure that, in spite of his Quaker upbringing, he still believes in Him, appear to have tossed a present into his lap. The boy, his boy, has admitted to sketching. Can it be possible that this, rather than the purchasing of fruit and vegetables, is the way to his heart?

Chapter 13

The tomatoes kept on coming and Orion and Jacka were kept busy picking and staking as the plants bowed towards the earth with ever–ripening fruit. The peas were also doing well and still had to be protected by networks of string with paper ribbons tied to them for demand was always high; indeed Mr Cyril had just set off with six boxes for the hotels and guest houses.

Although it was not so hot today, which was something to be thankful for. A haze over the water blew inshore during the afternoon bringing cool weather for the first time for weeks so that Orion pulled down his shirt sleeves as he set off, via the cabbage patch, for the peas. Mr Cyril was worried about flea beetles and he paused to check the cabbage leaves for the tiny, round, tell–tale holes that would mean another dusting with derris powder. As he straightened up he saw the familiar figure in the dark jacket and seaman's cap appear through the archway.

"Good day Orion. Not so hot, eh?" he called as he strode down the steep pathway. "No good for sailing though. Or for painting. Too misty."

"Yes sir."

He'd been expecting him ever since the meeting in the art shop. The artist. Mr Tuke. Had been looking forward to it, perhaps – but he wasn't sure about this. What he had said that last time he came to the gardens had been so confusing. Almost frightening. All those words about not touching him; about not painting him without his clothes on; about not wanting to frighten him… No-one, especially no adult and even more especially no gentleman, had ever spoke to him in that way and when he dared to remember it in bed at night, it made him feel… he wasn't sure how it made him feel since he had never felt that way before either; nor was he even sure whether it was pleasant or unpleasant.

And then there was the meeting in Cyril's shop. When he had

admitted his interest in sketching…

Since when he has brought some of his pictures to the market garden where they lie, wrapped in a piece of old sacking, behind the potting table.

"Ah peas! I must take some home with me. And some carrots, if you have any. And tomatoes."

The artist, Mr Tuke, stops on the path and stares around him.

"Where's our good Mr Rowse this afternoon? Out on his rounds?"

"Yes sir."

"Excellent! You can serve me. But first of all…" He pulls his cap from his head and rubs a hand through his hair, "you must show me your work."

"My work sir?" He stares, uncertainly, at the cabbages.

"Yes boy. Your drawings. You told me last week that you're an artist."

"No Sir. Nothing like that. I d' like to draw, tha's all."

"Then you're an artist, Orion. If you draw you are an artist. So! Do you have anything to show me?"

The potting shed seems much smaller inside than when he is here with Jacka – but then Jacka is small himself, skinny and silent and easily overlooked – and, on this misty day, it feels very warm and damp in here. Muggy, Mr Cyril would say. It smells too – of damp wood and damp earth and the old tar with which the boards are treated.

And of something else which he identifies eventually as a salty tang from the thick hair of the artist, of Mr Tuke, as he bends forward to look at the drawings which Orion has spread out nervously along the work bench.

There are six of them, still life compositions – he has learnt that this is what they are called – drawn in his bedroom at home. His mother's pudding basin with a potato and two carrots. A bunch of Sweet Williams with an onion and some beans. The enamel water jug filled with May blossom. There is the corner of the wash stand against the window frame and, beyond that, the yard wall. There is the end of Alfred's untidy bed, the blanket pulled back across the quilt. And there is the old, paint–scarred chair with Orion's work jacket hooked over the back.

And, compared to paintings he has seen in books in the library or the Art Gallery in Grove Place or in lantern slides at the Polytechnic Hall, they are nothing, he can see this now. Dull, pointless drawings of dull, pointless things. Only the flowers have any beauty and, without colour, there is little of that.

Mr Tuke looks in silence. Picks up one drawing – the corner of the wash stand – and holds it to what little light comes through the grimy window, obscured by webs and the salty residue of years of sea mist. Puts it down and picks up the drawing of the bed...

"Interesting." He speaks quietly, as if to himself. "Fascinating, in fact." He turns to Orion. "And not at all what I expected. Why... why did you draw these?"

His hand hovers above the pictures of the bed, the wash stand, the chair with the hanging jacket, as he stares intently into his face. And Orion, uncomfortable in this small space, looks down at the floor. Dry earth. Broken pieces of clay pot. A few scuttling ants. Dead bits of weed. Old grass cuttings. The crusts from Jacka's dinner–time pasty, which will be gone by morning when the mice have been...

"Because they was there, Sir. I c'n only draw what's there," he mutters, not daring to look up.

Beside him the artist is silent. Except that he can hear his breathing and there is something frightening in this – being so close to someone that he can hear his breath.

"I see."

"I c'n only draw in the bedroom. When there's no–one else 'ome."

"I see."

But it is obvious he does not.

For how can Henry, an established artist from a secure, if not wealthy, background, who can paint where and whenever he likes… How can he understand Orion's problems, who shares a bedroom with his brother in a small cottage, where no-one must know what he does? How can he possibly understand?

Meanwhile he goes on looking at the drawings. Which are crude; it is obvious the lad hardly knows how to hold a pencil, let alone how to deal with the more complex problems of balance and perspective. He draws, head on, what he sees and the results are, inevitably, childlike and yet – Henry returns to the drawing of the wash stand, the window frame and, beyond that, the stone wall – so truthful.

There are marks on the side of the wash–stand – they are where Alfred catches the blade of his razor when he shaves, as he generally does, carelessly, but Henry is not to know this. There are shaded areas along the window frame which – and Henry does realise this – are mould. And in one place the view of the stone wall is blurred because – and again this is something Henry recognises – the window glass is damp.

Such honesty is the mark of a true artist and Henry, who has been a punctilious examiner of life drawing in South Kensington, is used to spotting where talent does, or does not, exist.

"I know they ain't no good…"

He has been so busy with his thoughts that he has forgotten Orion, waiting patiently for his verdict! And now, as he tries out the words inside his head that will express his feelings, he sees the boy put out his hand to the latch and pull open the shed door.

"Wait Orion! That's not what I meant. They are… they are fascinating! You need help, of course. Some lessons in perspective. Some… where are you going?"

The door has sunk on its hinges and scrapes on the earth floor but Orion jerks it open and is thrusting his way out.

"I got work to do. Sir. An' you wanted peas."

"Yes, but not…"

"An' carrots. An' tomatoes."

And Henry watches as he treads his way firmly back along the path and then across to the pea patch where he picks up his basket and starts to pick.

Chapter 14

"I direct my words particularly on this glorious morning to the young men present with us."

Orion felt his shoulders droop as the visiting minister paused to stare around the crowded chapel, picking out individually with his passionate, far too bright, blue eyes, each of the young men seated on the benches around the building. Ministers, visiting or otherwise, were always, or so it seemed, directing their words particularly to him. Even when they didn't announce it, as this one had, it still felt as if it was on him that the clear, all–seeing gaze fell as the preacher pronounced the punishments awaiting those who rejected Christ Jesus and failed to walk in His way.

"I shall tell you the story of Spencer Thornton," the minister continued – his name was Tompkins and his visit had been much anticipated – and Orion felt his shoulders, and his heart, droop further still. He had no expectation of pleasure from anyone with such a name – and he was right.

Spencer Thornton was, apparently, the most pious of young men and never ashamed – why should he be? – of his piety and, for almost an hour, the congregation were told how he had influenced for the better not only his schoolfellows but even his teachers, so that they were led to turn away from the vain pursuits in which they had engaged before to read their bibles instead. Even his landlady was converted by the pious efforts of her young lodger and when he met an old man who was a stranger to the light and refused, even when sick, to allow Spencer Thornton into his house, he went back twenty one days in succession until the old man gave in and allowed him inside to pray with him.

Orion stared upwards into the high roof space and felt sorry for the poor, old man.

The chapel was built in against the cliff that rose up on the south side of the Moor, and the stone mullioned windows on the other sides excluded much of the sun – perhaps this had been the intention of the builders, who may not have wanted the congregation to be reminded of the world outside – but now, on this 'glorious day' as the minister had called it, a thin beam of light had worked its way through topmost panes of one window to fall in a pale gold puddle on the flagstones below the pulpit.

Bugger Spencer Thornton, Orion thought. Interfering busy body. Why couldn't he just leave people alone? And bugger Mr Tompkins, who wanted him to lead a life that was just as miserable. Bugger, in fact, the lot of them…

"Isn't this the nobility of life, the purity of purpose, which we all seek?" the minister was asking, oblivious of Orion's thoughts. "In which case we must not be afraid of reproach or ridicule. We must, like Spencer Thornton, delight in fulfilling the law of the Lord and our lives will shine with the beauty of our devotion. For life," he declaimed loudly, this being one of his favourite topics, "is uncertain and we may, at any moment, be removed from all that we love and value most…"

Orion twisted resentfully on the wooden bench. It seemed to him unlikely that he would die at any moment but, if death was so close, it seemed worse than ever to be wasting his few precious hours of freedom and sunshine shut into this gloomy place.

The congregation were on their feet now and leafing their way through the hymn books as the organ growled into voice. And then,

'Death comes in unexpected forms,
At unexpected hours;
To–morrow we may never see,
To–day alone is ours,'

they sang, the strong Cornish voices echoing to the roof beams and on, through four more, doom–laden verses until Orion suddenly knew that he could take no more. Closing his hymn book, not even conscious that he had made up his mind to action and without looking at his mother, the minister or any of the congregation, he edged his way along the row and out into the chapel lobby.

"Are 'ee all right boy? Feeling badly are 'ee?"

Mr Hoskin, the door–keeper, had followed him out; a tall man whose broad shoulders and hefty arms belonged more properly to the leather jerkin he wore when he was delivering sacks of coal and not to the Sunday suit he must have worn for the past twenty years, since a time when he had been that much thinner. The thought raced through Orion's mind and not for the first time, that he was there not so much to let in latecomers as to prevent sinners like himself from escaping and, about to say his head ached, he stopped himself. It was bad enough leaving halfway through the service without being forced to lie about it.

"I gotta go see someone," he said instead and turned out into the sunlight.

On the Moor, the fine open space at the bottom of Killigrew Street, bordered on three sides by the granite building that housed the mayor's parlour and the public library, the Town Hall and the Wesley Methodist Church from which Orion had just emerged, people were strolling in the sunshine. Godless people, no doubt, although they looked harmless enough, the ladies in their broad hats and summer muslins, the gentlemen in Sunday suits, many of them visitors to the town, on their way to view the harbour or to walk in the Kimberley Gardens with their shady trees and fish–filled ponds.

And what, he wondered as he hurried past its gates, was so wrong about that? Why shouldn't he too, Orion, who had worked hard all week, enjoy a holiday?

Chapter 15

Sunday afternoon and Henry is not, for once, on his boat, although this was what he had intended. Instead he is entertaining guests at Pennance Cottage, members of a house party at Marlborough House, where he played bridge on Friday night, who expressed an interest in visiting his studio and whom, ever sociable, he invited to join him for lunch.

They have eaten early so that Mrs Fouracre can have her afternoon off and she has roasted a leg of lamb, with potatoes, suet pudding, cabbage and mint sauce, which have been followed by rice pudding and a treacle tart and custard. Heavy fare for a hot summer's day and Henry's guests – two ladies and three gentlemen – are chatting increasingly drowsily now on the seats he has set out under sun shades on the lawn. One of the gentlemen is, in fact, already asleep.

Henry, who is not a sleeper – or even a sitter – paces restlessly. It seems impolite, when his guests are so somnolent, to suggest they join him for a walk; in any case they would almost certainly insist that it is too hot and it would be unpardonably rude to stride off, as he longs to do, up the track towards Stack Point, leaving them without their host. It would be even ruder – and it is in any case too soon after lunch – to go swimming, although the sea looks enticingly cool, and so he paces, stooping occasionally to pull at the withered bloom of a day lily, and watching the progress across the bay of one of the three–masted barques he loves so much.

The light shimmers off the surface of the water and below the cliff three boys are laughing and splashing in a dinghy. Henry wonders if he knows any of them but does not, as he would have done this time last year, put up his telescope for a closer look. Instead, making up his mind, he turns his back on his guests – but people know and, to an extent, love his eccentricity – and sets off up the garden away from the house.

It is the better part of two miles from the Moor to Swanpool. Up the long drag of Killigrew Hill, along Western Terrace with its fine, gentlemen's houses, then downhill into Swanvale, past Marlborough House, built by Captain Bull, one time skipper of the 'Duke of Marlborough', one of the Packet ships that sailed from Falmouth, carrying the mail and other, more lucrative, commodities across the empire. A particularly fine house and Captain Bull's descendent, May, one of his dozing lunch guests, is a close friend of Henry Tuke's and might have been closer still, were he a different sort of man.

Orion notes as he passes the deep red rhododendron still in bloom and continues past the farm until it reaches Swanpool, where ducks and moorhens poke around marshy reed beds or paddle across the sunlit water along with the white and black swans which give the place its name, taking care to avoid the model yachts being sailed, mainly, by boys and their fathers.

At the far end, across the roadway which divides the pool from the sea, is a small, shingle beach and behind it the chimney stack and waste tip of an abandoned lead mine and a scrubby area where three traps are parked, their ponies grazing nearby. On the beach families are enjoying their day of rest – women hold flimsy parasols against the sun, a group of girls, skirts bunched about their waists, splash in the shallow water, small boys attempt to swim and, out beyond the first tongue of rocks, three young men splash wildly, yelling with laughter as they attempt to row.

Orion pauses to watch, feeling the heat on this warm day and in his Sunday suit. His shirt is wet under the arms and between his shoulder blades and, infected by the holiday mood, he removes his jacket to feel the cool of the breeze against his skin as he stands staring first out to sea and then at the house on the cliff top where he knows the artist lives.

Then he sets off with some determination up the steep road

on the west side of the little bay. When he reaches a track to the left he pauses but only briefly.

Henry does not at first recognise him. Sees a young man in white shirt and dark trousers, jacket hanging from his shoulder. A young man with hair bleached almost white from the sun, face red from the heat of the day... It could almost, apart from the clothing, be Orion, he thinks, in that split second before realising,

"Orion! It *is* you!"

"'S'nice day." The boy stares down at the path. Mumbling. "Thought I'd come out and see the sea."

"Of course! An excellent idea! Well done!"

He sounds, to his own ears, like an over–hearty schoolmaster, praising a dullard pupil. Perhaps also to the boy, who continues to stare downwards, nudging at a stone with his dusty boot.

"So, you must have something to eat – and drink, on a hot day like this! My place is just along here." ('My humble abode,' is how he describes it to his friends and, compared to the grandeur of Marlborough House or the Fox residence out at Glendurgan, Pennance Cottage is indeed very humble, with no gas or running water and without the convenience of an indoor lavatory) "There's plenty of cold lamb left from lunch – and wine or beer..."

"No thank 'ee, Sir. I don' need nothing."

Bad enough to have left chapel before the end of the service without drinking beer on the Sabbath.

"But you must... Some water, at least, after your walk. We have wonderful water here. I draw it myself from the well."

"You got... company."

They have reached his garden and Orion, looking uncertainly round – Henry's eager offers are making him more nervous than ever – sees that there are seats set out on the lawn below the cottage and that there are people sitting in them.

"Good grief!"

Henry, who has forgotten his guests, strikes a hand against his forehead, Orion moves sideways, keeping Henry between him and the unknown 'company' and for some seconds they stare in silence down the garden.

Facing them on a swinging seat, two ladies recline against cushions, sheltered by a canvas canopy from the sun. One holds an open fan, downwards and motionless in what could be lifeless fingers. Opposite them a dark–trousered leg sprawls below a high–backed wicker chair. Below the chair next to it can be seen the bottom half of a leg in white trousers and one shining black shoe...

The scene swims in heat – pale dresses against bright green grass, the black leg breaking diagonally across, sunlight splintering off a glass tumbler – and, beyond the immobile, almost certainly sleeping, figures, the sea lies pale beneath the heat–haze as soaring gulls create patterns of pure white against a cobalt sky.

"We won't disturb them."

Taking Orion's arm, Henry leads him towards the back door. Inside, the kitchen smells of the heat of the stove, is dark after the sunlight and tidily organised. Plates and serving dishes are stacked on a wooden draining rack, cleaned pans on the barred shelf above the range. On the table a tray has been prepared for tea, a newly baked fruit cake on its stand and plates covered with linen napkins containing other, hidden, foodstuffs.

"Water!"

Taking a stone pitcher from the pantry Henry fills two beakers and Orion feels the cool water trickle down his parched throat.

"Wonderful, isn't it?"

Moustache gleaming with moisture, Henry holds out the pitcher and Orion, to whom the water seems nothing special, nods politely.

"After London water I appreciate this, I can tell you."

"Yes sir."

But water, surely, will not differ from place to place?

"Henry." He bends his face to his beaker and drinks again. "You must call me Henry. Harry even, It's what my friends call me. And after all, I call you Orion."

"Yes sir. Mr Tuke…"

He covers his confusion by drinking the rest of his water.

Unusually, Ida Goss was not angry with Orion for leaving chapel early – Alfred, after all, had not attended at all. Nor was Ida immune to the call of the sunshine after a hard-working week and she too had noted the incoming sunbeam. It reminded her of afternoon Sunday School long ago in the Wesley Chapel in Redruth. Of sitting on the hard, unyielding bench, legs itching under the heat of her thick black stockings, listening to the hard, unyielding words of the minister's wife.

They must give themselves to the Lord – after so many years Ida had forgotten her name but not the thin-lipped mouth which opened like a drop-down trap door to let out her homilies – forsaking all other pleasures except the joy of serving Him.

Which was, Ida knew, impossible. Not while she could see, fixed on her from across the room, the glinting, dark brown eyes of Ivan Hart with his glossy black hair, his thick black moustache and his devil-may-care grin. 'Big Hart' the lads called him and he was certainly that. Over six foot tall with muscular arms, thick with coarse, dark hairs, broad shoulders and a broad belly to match, his black hair gleaming with the solution he applied on Saturday nights for the dance at the Druid's Hall and was still there on Sunday, in spite of the minister's – and his wife's – disapproval.

He was a fine dancer, Ivan Hart, as big men often are, and loved to show off on the dance floor after a week spent digging out ore down the mine, often choosing Ida, who was slender in those days and light on her feet, as his partner. And he had gone off, of course, like so many others – and perhaps, if he had asked her, she might have followed him – to one of those strange-sounding places on the far side of the world. But he never did ask her and her last sight of him was marching among a crowd of his friends, singing their hearts out on the way to Redruth station to catch the train up country on the first stage of their journey to the townships of South Australia.

"And shall Trelawney live," they sang, as Cornishmen had sung for a hundred years, "Or shall Trelawney die, here's twenty thousand Cornish lads will know the reason why."

Every time she heard that song Ida thought of Ivan Hart and felt something move in the back of her throat. For, if he *had* written to her, if he *had* asked her to follow him and if she had dared to do so, who could say how different her life might have been?

And so Orion had Ivan Hart, of whom he had never even heard, to thank for her excuse to the Minister after the service...

"'E's worked 'ard all week," she told him. "'E 'ad some business to attend to and 'e gets little enough time to himself."

She met the minister's gaze with something that, had he been less self–important, he might have recognised as defiance; as if daring him to ask what 'business' a young market garden apprentice might have to transact on Sunday morning.

God's business, he murmured, should always come first – but Ida had already gone.

Orion seemed subdued when he eventually got home, well after ten o'clock, to find his mother back in her kitchen.

"Where did you get to, missing yer dinner?" she asked. Noticing that, whatever he had been doing, the question seemed to fluster him.

"Nowhere," he said. Then, "Met some friends. Over Swanpool," he muttered and, rejecting her offer of bread and dripping, went straight upstairs.

So, Ida Goss thought, humming, uncharacteristically, to

herself as she put out the cheese and pickles that Alfred would expect when he returned from the public house – quite soon, since they closed early Sunday nights – Orion had found himself a girl.

She just hoped she was a decent one. He was a steady boy, as well as a good–looking one, who was doing well in the market garden and would be a good catch for some girl.

Lying on his bed, Orion stared out at the small patch of sky that was visible above the quarry face. A deep, bright blue of late summer, still holding within itself the memory of the sunlit azure that had lit it all day and reminding him of all that had happened since he had walked out of the chapel and into the glorious sunlight of the Moor.

Above all, he remembered Henry. No longer Mr Tuke. No longer a gentleman, and to be feared as such, but his friend.

Who suggested, as they stood together in the gloom of his kitchen, that they should avoid his sleeping guests and go up onto the headland.

"On a day like this we'll be able to see right down the coast to the Manacles. Have you ever done that Orion? But of course you have."

And when Orion admitted that he had never done so gave him a look with those piercing, dark eyes that was both surprised and pitying.

And yet what leisure had he ever had for such pursuits? What time – or inclination – for walking cliff tops? Until this afternoon. When the two of them crept like conspirators through the garden and along the earth track towards the headland known as the Stack, after the two chimneys built fifty years before to disperse the fumes from the old arsenic works that had operated then in the fields above Henry's house.

The chimneys were long gone, one demolished, one blown down in a gale, but the brick–lined tunnels linking them to the arsenic works could still be seen in the coppices of oak and ash and the fern and bramble undergrowth, just as the decaying buildings of the works themselves were clearly visible as Orion and Henry strode uphill and then, turning their backs on the spoilt landscape, stood together on the headland.

Below them clear green water lapped gently against the rocks, to their left was the revealed expanse of Falmouth Bay and to their right, across bushes of densely–flowering yellow gorse, was the view Henry had promised him. Grass–topped headland after grass–topped headland, right down the coast to Porthoustock and the treacherous rocks known as the Manacles, and a trawler heading west, spreading her deep red sails against the breeze.

The cocoanut smell of that gorse would stay with him for ever. That thick, creamy scent above the tang of the wild garlic, while small butterflies – intensely blue and dowdier browns with streaks of orange – fluttered above the flowers and the air was loud with the humming of heavy bumble bees, the buzz of flies, the gentle rattle of a million grasshoppers. If only... he felt himself smiling at the memory. If only he could paint those scents and sounds. If only he could paint that feeling. The joy of that moment. The joy of that whole afternoon.

Chapter 16

They were busy now in the market garden from early morning, picking, hoeing, attending to pests and, as each crop finished, clearing the ground for planting out root crops and winter greens. Mr Cyril had even taken on a new lad and some of the task of training him, because of Jacka's silence and Mr Cyril's need to deal with the customers, fell to Orion.

It was a good feeling, he had to admit, introducing Ricky to the mysteries of mulching, overseeing him as he removed the last, decaying remains of pea haulms, bean stalks and cabbage stumps, showing him – as Mr Cyril had shown him three summers before – how to trap earwigs and where to find the daytime hiding places of slugs and snails. It made him realise how much he had learnt since he had been here. That he wasn't as stupid as they had always made him feel at school.

But it was not this that made the summer so wonderful. That accounted for the sense of joy with which he woke every morning. The cheerfulness with which he went about his tasks in the garden.

What made this summer different from the last and all the summers before was what happened when he left the garden when the gates shut at six and, instead of walking across the top terraces of the town towards his home, turned along Woodlane, passing, as he walked along the high pavement from which ladies and gentlemen could dismount with ease from their horses or their carriages, the fine brick or white stuccoed houses of some of Falmouth's wealthier families, and out along the road to Swanpool and Pennance where Henry would be waiting for him.

Henry has changed his habits this summer, his friends have noticed. He still goes out, most days, in the 'Piebox' where he paints harbour scenes and makes sketches of the other boats, but now he rarely spends nights or even evenings aboard. Nor – or only rarely – does he dine out with friends, some of whom live in those very houses which Orion passes in his heavy boots and drab workmen's clothes, or invite these same friends to dine with him. Now he packs away his paints most afternoons by five o'clock, rows himself ashore and then walks jauntily the mile and a half home. And now, when his boys, Bert, Harry and the others, are free from work, he rarely joins them on the beach below the headland where they used, in past years, to pose for the famous artist.

A fact which annoys them.

Henry is by no means the only artist in Falmouth and there are others who require models but none are as accomplished as Henry Tuke – apart from his friend Mr Hemy, who concentrates on the sea and ships and the fully clad seamen who work them and does not need young models. Nor are the other artists as generous in their friendship and their behaviour is often a great deal less courteous – and more demanding – so that it is no surprise that his boys miss Henry in this summer of 1902. Charlie, whom he pays to look after his boats and still comes to Pennance Cottage to help with odd jobs, even dares ask if he has done something wrong.

Of course not, Henry tells him, slapping him boisterously on the shoulders. He has simply been busy with other things – but he does not say what these 'other things' are, which is unlike a man who has always been so open with his friendships.

Others have been wondering too. His friends in Falmouth's elite society with whom he has always spent so much time. Charles Masson Fox, for example, who introduced him, a couple of years back, to the game of bridge and now finds that his friend is rarely available to make up a foursome. May Bull, another bridge fanatic and keen sailor, who has always taken pleasure in his company but now seems to see him only on regatta days. Charles Napier Hemy, whose company and that of his gentle wife and lively family, Henry has always enjoyed…

What, Charles wonders openly to Amy, is occupying Henry's

time? He hopes it is not... But Charles is a religious, not to say puritanical, man and will not voice his suspicions even to his wife. Who, as it happens, shares them, although she doesn't mention this to her husband. Anyone who is a friend of Charles Fox, who may be a Quaker, a chess player and a respectable timber merchant but whose enthusiasm for his boys' club has caused many raised eyebrows in Falmouth society, needs, in Amy's view, to be treated with at least a little caution.

Henry, meanwhile, goes his cheerful way. Arrives home by six most evenings, drives to distraction poor Mrs Fouracre his housekeeper, a discreet woman who could have answered everybody's questions, by his enquiries about supper and, at last and to her relief, goes out to his studio to wait for his pupil.

And Orion's lessons – for it is he who is the pupil – are progressing well.

Under Henry's tutelage he has learned to hold his pencil correctly, has learned where to place his subjects on the paper, is developing a sense of perspective. He is no longer restricted to pencil and charcoal but has his own set of water colours with which he is making discoveries that Henry has not taught him, although he has, perhaps, absorbed them from looking at his paintings and those in the Falmouth Art Gallery. He has learnt that he does not have to paint every detail of an object or a person, that a few strokes of the brush, an interplay of light and darkness, a sweeping movement or a gentle dabbing can indicate reality far more vividly and with more life. Above all – although he does not yet realise this – he has learnt confidence. To be bolder with the marks he sets on the paper. To dare to strive for the effect he is seeking.

It is hard now to remember how fearful he was once, that his first, tentative pencil strokes or, later, the marks of his brush, could ruin his attempt at a picture almost before he has begun. Now, as well as Henry's own works, there are, displayed around the studio amongst the paraphernalia of sailing, fishing, sports and painting he keeps there, several water colour studies by Orion himself – a vase of tall, white daisies from Henry's garden, a pile of pebbles and a small bunch of sea thrift, an unknown and abandoned piece of machinery in the old arsenic works... When he looks at these, and although it is obvious that he has nothing like Henry's talent, he feels pleased enough.

Henry himself, is working on studies of rocks and water for his latest work – Two Boys on a Beach. Remember, he has said to Orion, what I told you about observation. The sea, the sky, the clouds... all of them hold within themselves so many shades and colours, often completely unexpected ones. Like leaves. Don't let anyone tell you that leaves are green. There is green there, of course there is, but so much else, from black to white, yellows, fawns, shades of blue...

This evening he is painting water channelling between rocks, different depths of green with blues, mauves, even black, and tiny strokes of white indicating the movement of the current on what is clearly an almost windless day.

"I won't never be able to do that," he says but Henry glances across at him and shakes his head.

"You won't never need to," he says grinning. "You have your own subjects – and your own skills. Each to his own, my boy! And you've had enough for tonight I think. Come along!" He sets down his brush and stands away from his easel. "While there's some light left! Let's see how far you can get without falling off!"

For drawing and painting is not all he is teaching Orion and, washing the paint from their hands in Mrs Fouracre's kitchen, they go out to the small shed by the back door and take out Henry's bicycle and another, much newer, one.

For a few minutes, when Henry first showed this to the boy, he was afraid he might have overplayed his hand. For Orion, who had hardly received a gift in his life and never one worth more than a couple of shillings, was completely overcome at the sight of a bicycle costing fourteen guineas which Henry, beaming, insisted was to be his own.

"Never!" he said, startled and with an expression of actual fear on his face. "I can't 'ave nothing like that! Thank you," he added but turned immediately away in case his politeness might be taken as acceptance. "I can't take nothing so costly."

And it took Henry a week – and several lessons on what he insisted would be his own spare bicycle if Orion refused it – to change his mind.

He wanted a companion on his rides, he said. It was lonely cycling on his own. And the bicycle could remain in Henry's shed – even he could see the impossibility of Orion riding it home, much as he would like him to and convenient as it would be.

Eventually Orion, thrilled, as any seventeen year old, by the speed of the new acquisition and his own increasing skill, gave in and now, two or three evenings a week, the two of them cycle off together, along lanes too narrow for the new fangled motor cars Henry dislikes so much and where they are unlikely to be seen by anyone they know.

Afterwards they return, hungry, for Mrs Fouracre's cooking and then Orion walks home across the top of the town in the gathering darkness.

"Where've you been to this time?" his mother asks but increasingly without curiosity. For Alfred is courting Mabel Vigus from Lister Street and spends most of his evenings with her so that Ida no longer has to cook for her men after her long days of cooking and cleaning for Mrs Trembath in Kimberley Park Road.

They have been pleasant for her too, these warm summer evenings, sitting in her back doorway, looking out over Orion's flower bed – although this too has been neglected – with a slice of the cold pie that now lasts her two or three days. Sometimes she hints to Orion that he should 'bring the young lady 'ome one Sunday', but Orion has always insisted that there is no 'young lady', which she takes to mean that the courtship is at an uncertain stage.

Although no-one has seen him with a girl, which, in a town like Falmouth, suggests that he is being astonishingly discreet – or as Alfred has hinted, that he has something to hide. But Alfred, fortunately for Orion, is too taken with Mabel, who is pretty and flirtatious and is not going to give in to him easily, to have any attention to spare for his young brother.

Chapter 17

August – and by now all Falmouth's hotels and guest houses were full so that Mr Cyril's afternoon round took almost twice as long and the dry weather that the holiday makers enjoyed so much on the beaches and in the garden walks brought their own problems to the market garden. Jacka, Orion and Richie were kept busy early morning and late afternoon, watering the thirsty leeks and lettuces, tomatoes ripened too fast and a plague of wasps caused terrible damage to the pears. And then for several days at the beginning of the month, it rained. Heavy, relentless rain that turned the dust to mud, split the tomatoes and caused the lettuces to bolt – and Mr Cyril's temper with them.

On Thursday the Seventh Orion spent all morning picking tomatoes, discarding for mulch those that had split and rotted, and the afternoon cutting back old raspberry canes and thinning the young growth. He was drenched, although the rain had at last ceased, from the water that still dripped from the leaves.

"Will we be closed Saturday, Mr Cyril?" he dared ask, bringing a few bunches of parsley, as requested, to the top of the garden. "The 'oliday for the King's coronation."

"What 'oliday?" Mr Cyril, bending to pull out a potato box from under the table, paused to glare up at him. "Why should we be closed?"

"For the King's coronation. Like we did for the end of the war, Sir. Leastways we closed early."

He remembered the thrill of the long–awaited announcement of the Boer surrender and the signing of peace which had arrived on the evening of Sunday the First of June – his mother had been in the congregation when the Minister announced it in chapel and had come puffing home with the great news. By midday on the Monday, and although there was no official programme, most shops and houses had displayed flags or bunting in celebration and gradually, with more and more people on the streets and hundreds of school children waving flags, a holiday fever had gripped the town.

The National Anthem and other patriotic songs were sung, a bonfire was constructed on the Moor under the supervision of the Borough Surveyor and the Mayor had expressed the hope that business houses would close at four in the afternoon.

And for once even Mr Cyril, who, true Cornishman that he was, felt no great loyalty to the Crown, had been caught up with the general sense of jubilation; possibly because he had two nephews in South Africa and shared his sister's hope that they might at last return home to safety.

"Get off with you, boy," he had told Orion, just beyond four. "And don' get yourself too drunk to be in early in the morning."

"That was different," he snorted now. Red faced – although whether from anger or from bending it wasn't possible to say. "That was celebrating they bleddy Boers giving in at last, not 'aving a gambler and a wastrel being crowned king." (Mr Rowse, like many of his countrymen and the late Queen herself, had a poor opinion of the former Prince of Wales and no intention of reversing it.) "Some of us 'as work to do. If you wants an 'oliday, I suggest you 'ands over your job to someone what doesn't."

"I just thought…" It was unlike Orion to be so persistent and he surprised the both of them. "I just thought p'raps this once it'd be all right…"

"It'd be all right, boy, if we din' 'ave tomatoes rotting on the vines and no–one to pick them." Which seemed particularly unfair to Orion who had spend all morning doing exactly this. "If we din' 'ave a plague o' bleddy earwigs. If we din' 'ave…" But Orion didn't wait to hear about the other misfortunes whose absence might have allowed him a holiday for the coronation and went off to pick more tomatoes.

"Good morning Mr Rowse. How are you today? Weather's brightening, don't you think?"

Impossible now to remember how that jovial voice, ringing out over the garden and easily reaching Orion among the tomato vines, had once had the power to terrify him. Now the sound brought only pleasure – until he remembered what Henry had said the night before, when he told him he had to work on Saturday. The day of the coronation.

We'll see about that, boy, he had said. We'll see about that.

And now he was here, complimenting Mr Cyril on the plump hearts of his lettuces, enquiring if he had any black currants left – knowing full well he hadn't – expressing amazement at his tomato crop.

"You'll be shut, of course, tomorrow, for the celebrations?" He picked up one of the few pears the wasps hadn't ruined and examined it as if it were the only thing that interested him. And when Mr Cyril, bending obsequiously forward and rubbing his hands together, assured him that they would be open for customers as usual, "Good gracious," he said, putting down the pear. "But none of the shops will be open, surely? Not on an official holiday. It was very good of your employees to agree to such a thing. I hope you'll reward them well for their loyalty. Double pay at the very least, I should imagine."

Jacka, who was stacking potato boxes nearby and had nothing wrong with his hearing, even if he never spoke, jerked his head upwards at the words and glanced across at Mr Cyril. Who went on rubbing his hands together – but now there was a definite nervousness about the action – smiled his toad–smile and muttered to the effect that he didn't know… He wasn't at all sure…. Hotels still needed their deliveries…

Henry continued to look down at him, which was easy enough since he was the taller by several inches. He was unusually smartly dressed, in neatly pressed white ducks, a navy sailing blazer and the sort of yachting cap he rarely wore, with a soft white crown and a shining, black peak. There was a special lunch, he had told Orion, at Falmouth Sailing Club of which he was Vice Commodore, ahead of the national celebrations, an event that obviously warranted finer than his normal sailing wear.

"Well, I am surprised Mr Rowse," he said in an aristocratic drawl that had none of his usual affability. "I understood that all business was to be suspended by law on the occasion of the coronation." He laid particular emphasis on the word 'law'. "You surprise me indeed."

He paused, looked down the garden, noted Orion among the tomato vines, nodded briefly and turned out through the entrance, leaving the lettuces and bags of tomatoes Mr Cyril had assembled in front of him standing on the table. Leaving, also, the two ladies who had come in after him and had overheard his last words staring at Mr Cyril as if he had committed some sort of crime.

"If you two wants to take the day off I suppose you must."

Mr Cyril interrupted Orion and Richie, eating their pasties on upturned buckets outside the potting shed, and grumbled the words in their direction. Jacka, he said, was willing to come on the rounds with him, as usual, and he supposed he would have to manage.

"You can stay late this evening instead," he growled as he turned and stamped off up the garden, leaving Orion grinning with pleasure.

He sets off early next morning. Before six, while Alfred is still snoring and Ida, enjoying the rare luxury of a lie–in, drowses in her bedroom, he is downstairs and heating water for shaving.

He is going fishing, he told Ida last night – with Richie and his brother, off Antony Point where there are reports of shoals of mackerel and from where they will have a fine view of the armada of craft that has assembled out there since the announcement of the coronation, postponed from June because of the new king's ill health.

104

Ida is sorry that he will miss the service at Wesley Chapel – the combined congregations of local non-conformist churches – but is not surprised. Nor does she believe that he is going fishing, still preferring to think that there is, somewhere at the back of the story, a young lady. Which is why there are two pasties in the tin she has left on the kitchen table, and why they are carefully wrapped in the sort of white cloths she would never normally put out for a fishing trip.

The air is loud with birdsong as Orion leaves the house. Gulls, at first, wailing and wheeling in a sky from which the mist is clearing to reveal an azure blue, and then, as he reaches the wooded area along the top of the town, the sweeter calls of blackbirds and thrushes and the chirpings of sparrows already out hunting for food. The milk cart, clanking with churns, comes slowly towards him; the horse's hooves clopping hollowly on the roadway, falling silent as the boy brings jugs from doorsteps to be filled, then clopping on once more.

And then the sounds are lost as Orion turns down Bull's Avenue, his boots scraping against the loose stones which skitter noisily away in front of him. As he passes Marlborough House he sees that the gates have been festooned with swathes of evergreens, pots of scarlet begonias decorate the window ledges and flags flutter from either end of the building. In the gardens below the house Japanese lanterns hang among the bushes and lines of red, white and blue bunting criss-cross the lawn. Obviously, as in so many big houses today, there is to be a party. (He is right about this and Henry has, of course, been invited but will not be attending.)

The beach at Swanpool is empty, waves breaking against the shelving pebbles with a sparkling clarity, the foam bright white against the rocks. Out in the bay, where the mist still lies on the water, the rounded shape of Pendennis castle on its far headland is barely visible and a three-masted barque at anchor could be a ghost ship floating on a miasma.

Henry, hair glistening wet from his morning swim, waits at his gate.

"Too hot for cycling," he says, and leads him, obviously with some other plan in mind, down the narrow path to the small cove where his dinghy is tied to an overhanging thorn bush and an easel, a roll of paper, his wooden paint box and Orion's own watercolours are heaped together on the narrow beach. "Too hot for cycling," he repeats, "but perfect for painting," and taking hold of the rope he hauls the small boat closer in to the beach, instructs Orion to grasp the bow and, turning up his trousers and removing his boots, which he hangs round his neck by the laces, he wades into the shallows. "You hand me things and I'll stow them. I know how it all fits."

He stacks the paints, a cluster of brushes and a pile of paint-stained rags into the bow, balances the stern with a picnic basket, Orion's canvas bag, a rug and their boots then stows the rolled-up paper with great care alongside the oars.

"Now comes the tricky bit," and, while Orion holds hard to the dinghy amidships, he climbs aboard and sits himself in the stern. "You pass me the easel," and the little boat dips low into the water as Orion struggles to retain his hold as he heaves the easel in Henry's direction. "It's a bugger to hold square but I'm used to it. I hope you can row," Henry adds as Orion, who thinks he has left it a bit late to ask the question, clambers aboard.

It is not an easy trip. The easel, jutting in front of Henry, impedes Orion as he unships the oars and as soon as he pushes off from the shore they are caught by the currents around the rocks. Once they are through these the easel catches the breeze like a sail, threatening to overtip them as they round Stack Point, but eventually Orion pulls into the sandy cove a short distance along the coast and Henry clambers into the shallows to wade ashore holding his awkward cargo triumphantly aloft.

At almost the same moment the peace is shattered by the sound of gunfire from Pendennis Castle echoing across the bay.

One shot, and then another, another, another and another until – although neither of them has been counting – there have been twenty one and the echoes which have built up one on the other gradually die away. Orion, still aboard the dinghy, shakes his head to clear his ears of the sound and Henry, laughing, wades out to take hold of the prow and tow him ashore.

"The start of the big day. How could we have forgotten? Good old Bertie, eh?" Then, apparently forgetting his king already, "So, here we are. What d'you think, boy?"

The beached dinghy lies sideways on the sand and Henry stands, barefoot, the bottoms of his rolled trousers dark with seawater, sunlight glinting through his hair. Orion stares back at him, head reeling from the shock of the guns and too tired from his exertions to answer.

He is also afraid. For this place, Newporth Beach, he knows, is where Henry and his other gentlemen friends come to paint. Where they paint boys like Johnny Jackett, Harry Cleave, Jack Rolling, Charlie, Bert and Joseph. Paint them – for Orion has seen pictures in Henry's studio – in the buff. And so,

"Dunno, Sir."

He stands stock–still on the sand, looking anywhere but at Henry.

"Orion?" It is the first time for weeks that he has called him 'Sir'. "What is it? What's the matter?"

But the boy turns away and starts to unload the boat. His silence and his dogged concentration remind Henry of his early visits to the market garden when it was well nigh impossible to persuade him to respond.

"Is something worrying you Orion?" He takes the picnic basket from him and drops it onto the sand. And then, as the boy turns away again, "No–one else is coming, if that's what you're afraid of. Bert's taking the boys out on the boat, to see the sights in the harbour – and to go fishing. There's shoals of mackerel over by…"

107

"I know that," Orion interrupts, alarmed by the reminder of his own untruth. "What 'bout your other friends?" he asks, nervousness making him sullen. "Your gen'lemen friends?"

"Them!" Henry, understanding at last, gives one of his sudden shouts of laughter. "They only come if I invite them. And the only person I've invited today, Orion, is you. In any case there's too much else going on. Church services. Processions. The womenfolk want to be seen in their new hats and gowns. It's just you and me today, Orion, I promise. Just you and me."

Nevertheless it takes time to relax. Not until Henry has chosen his view point, set up his easel and prepared his paints. Not until he has settled Orion with a new sketch book and his paints on a low rock at the foot of the cliff. Not until he has brought out a flask of Mrs Fouracre's lemonade...

"Now, just paint!" he tells him. "Look at what you see in front of you. Mix your colours – and paint! Don't be afraid. Don't worry what it's meant to look like or what anyone might think!"

And, dipping his own brush in his jar of sea water, he washes it across the bottom third of his paper, then, in the little trough in his paint–tray, mixes blue with green, then yellow, then more blue... and Orion, safe from attention, concentrates on the rock that rises from the sand in front of him, skirted with a pool of water.

The rock is brown, and black, and green and, where the sun catches it, gold. It is grey. It is faintly blue. It is... Mixing black with brown, adding a little green, then some yellow he holds out his brush, nervously, to that point, a third of the way up the paper and third of the way across, where Henry has instructed him to place a feature of interest. Touches the paper – bright white in the sunlight and now, immediately, blemished by his mark – makes a tentative line, and then another, and then another, limiting the darkness, following the line where he will put his sand, his pool and, further out, his sea...

They work in silence. The only sounds, the tap of a brush

against the side of a jar, the gentle lip-lip of the falling tide against the sand, the breathing of the wind amongst the bushes higher up the cliff and the occasional 'pseest' of a rock pipit in flight.

An hour passes. Henry pulls a soft, white linen hat from his bag and tosses it across the sand.

"Put it on boy; you'll burn in this sun," and both remember – although neither mentions it – that day in the market garden, when Henry assured Orion that he was not a pederast. The memory hovers, nevertheless, like the shadow at the back of both their minds and Orion feels a new tension inside himself that he finds hard to understand.

Two hours pass. Henry's painting shows the sea, almost white, mirror–like, a background of rocks rising from its unbroken calmness and, in the foreground, his dinghy, beached on the sand, one oar left carelessly jutting upwards from its rowlock. Orion's painting has his rock, darker and lighter in streaks, an island within the glassy pool left by the withdrawing tide. He has caught, or hopes he has, the bright, flat surface of the water against the tiny, crumbling cliff of sand that surrounds it but the water diminishes every minute and it is so hard to tell...

"Leave it." Henry looks over his shoulder and sees his problem. "You're trying to catch a moment and by the time you do so, it's passed. Stop now, while you've got something."

This is what he loves about painting en plein air. Capturing the ephemeral – the blossom about to drop, the water, rising and falling and never the same from moment to moment, the flush of pleasure that is, at this moment, on Orion's cheek, the velvet gathering of moisture on his shadowed brow...

"I'm going for a dip."

He is hot after so long in the sun and there is a tension within his body that is hard to ignore. There is sweat below the fringe of his thick hair and between his shoulder blades. And he has been standing still for more than two hours...

Flinging down his brush, he strides across the beach and, sheltered behind the outcrop of rock, removes his shirt, trousers and, after a brief pause, his under drawers, races over the smooth sand and, with a cry of pleasure as he exchanges heat for chill, flings himself full length into the shallows. Orion wonders at the lack of inhibition that comes, he supposes, from being a gentleman. Sees jewels of water rise from the splashing limbs, sees the dark–haired head dip below the surface, the brown limbs and white feet rise above it and then Henry's beaming face, as he shakes the water from his hair, treads water and waves his arm.

"It's wonderful! Come on in!" he shouts.

Orion pauses and cannot prevent himself from looking around him – but there is no–one to see. The sea before him is empty, except for the figure of Henry now swimming purposefully away from the shore, an oil–black shag, which leaps from the water and then dives, and two barques far out on the horizon. The beach is empty and there is no way, apart from the sea, for anyone to reach it. The cliffs behind them are overgrown with scrub and bushes and who, in any case, will be walking on the cliffs today?

Slowly he replaces his brush in the water jar and, more slowly still, undoes his shirt and then his trousers. When Henry stops swimming to look back, treading water, towards the shore, he is surprised and thrilled to see him swimming, clumsily but strongly, in his direction.

Ida Goss could not remember when she'd enjoyed a day so much. After watching the gathering on the Moor – Councillors and Aldermen, Oddfellows, Rechabites and Foresters, all in their regalia, all wearing white gloves and rosettes, the police, the volunteer fire brigade, the coastguards, the Artillery Volunteers with their band and the Rifle Volunteers – ready to process to the Parish Church, she joined in the service of the combined non-conformist congregations in the Wesley Chapel, packed full almost to bursting point and raising their praises to the roof beams.

After which, herded eagerly together, they marched up the steep hill of Killigrew Street to the recreation ground where they met the Anglican contingent who had marched from the Parish Church at the far end of town. The ground was bright with bunting as Alderman Bowles read out the King's message to his people and Ida, tired as she was after the walk, felt a thrill, a feeling almost of exaltation, such as she had occasionally felt when they had a more than usually stirring preacher.

Perhaps it was patriotism. Not that she had ever thought much of the man who was now King, whose life seemed to consist of theatres, horse–racing and shooting deer. And London was over three hundred miles away and she was never likely to go there, Windsor was almost as far and those other places, like Sandringham and Balmoral, were further still. For someone like Ida, who had never been further than Truro, the goings–on in these places had no relation to her life in Cornwall.

And yet there was – perhaps it was the first time in her life she had felt this – a link. Not only was this message from the King himself, addressed to his loyal subjects, of whom she was, she supposed, one but, as Reverend Ogden had reminded them earlier, their own Mayor, who would otherwise have been reading out the message, was in London, representing their town at the coronation ceremony.

And then the combined bands struck up the first notes of the Old Hundredth and several hundred voices rose in unison into the warm air of the early afternoon:

> *All people that on earth do dwell,*
> *Sing to the Lord with cheerful voice.*
> *Him serve with fear, His praise forth tell,*
> *Come ye before Him and rejoice.*

111

The sound folded itself around Ida, growing in strength and fervour as the drums rolled, trumpets blared to a crescendo and the crowd gave themselves wholeheartedly to the music so that it felt to Ida as if she might be in the centre of a thunderstorm but without the threat and fear.

> *Oh enter then His gates with praise.*
> *Approach with joy His courts unto...*

The crowd bellowed out the words and Ida heard her own soprano rise against the baritone notes of the group of men behind her; men who had been bragging not long before how drunk they intended to get in toasting the new king but who now seemed caught up in the thrill of the moment.

> *To Father, Son and Holy Ghost,*
> *The God whom Heaven and earth adore,*
> *From men and from the angel host...*

A final crescendo of trumpets and a collective drawing-in of breath.

> *Be praise and glory evermore.*

The voices soared as if the sound might reach to heaven – or at least to London – followed by an exhausted hush and then the murmur and fluttering of adjustments to hats and shawls and corsages disturbed by the energy of the singing and a general sigh of satisfaction at having, in some small way, contributed to the occasion.

Later that afternoon Ida walked across town to sit with Bea Rogers. She had brought her sewing bag and settled herself with relief into the chair by the bedroom window, ready to share her excitement with poor Bea, whose social life consisted only of such visits and her view from the docks' gates on one side to the railway arch on the other and, just visible beyond it, the white walls of the Falmouth Hotel, decorated today with swathes of crimson, blue and white material and branches of evergreen.

And yet Bea seemed hardly to listen to her account of the gathering on the Moor, the Wesley service and the service up at the rec. Yes, she said, she had heard about that. And she had seen the sailors in their dress uniforms coming out of the docks into Bar Road. Had seen a detachment of soldiers march down from the castle, as well as the crowds of ladies and gentlemen from the hotels. And beautifully dressed too, she said they were. The gentlemen in their dress suits and top hats, one lady with a hat this wide and she drew a circle in the air around her head and described so many ostrich feathers, flowers and netting that it seemed impossible that so much could fit onto one hat, however wide, and Ida decided she must be exaggerating.

And perhaps, she thought, Bea's life was actually less restricted than her own. For when, apart from today, did she go further than the shops, the chapel and Mrs Trembath's house five minutes walk away in Kimberley Park Road? How much of her life did she spend beyond yards and kitchens – her own or her employer's? What excitement did she have in her life?

Whereas outside Bea's window seamen passed who had been to Spain and Portugal, to the West Indies, to New York and up into the cold wastes of the Baltic sea. Trains came and went across the railway bridge, to and from Truro, Exeter, Bristol and, at the far end of the line, London. Traps and carriages, even motor cars, passed between the tall gate posts of the Falmouth Hotel, carrying all manner of wealthy men and women…

Railway Cottages in their humble way overlooked the world and if poor Bea with her bad legs and frail chest was unable to take part in it neither, in any real sense, was Ida Goss.

Life, she thought resentfully, didn't seem to have a great deal to offer her – whatever the Minister might have to say about present suffering and future joy…

"Kezia brought that in lunch time."

Bea indicated the magazine that lay on the table that stood in the window with its obligatory potted fern and, on the under shelf, a copy of the Bible and the collected works of Robert Browning which, as far as Ida was aware, were moved only to be dusted. The magazine would have come from the hotel where Kezia, the niece who came in most days to cook and clean for her, worked as a chambermaid.

"Just look at they!" Pressing discontent from her mind, Ida flicked through the pages to pause at a picture of three young girls standing, apparently, in 'The Orangery at Glendale House'. "You'd need some corsets to fit into that lot."

For the girls, who stood in pleasing attitudes, heads held high to balance hats liberally charged with flowers and feathers above their luxuriantly coiled hair, wore dresses whose waists appeared to measure little more than a hand span.

Bea prattled on about the woman who had left the magazine – the Honourable Mrs Whyte "with a 'y', Kezia said. She were very fussy about that, she said, but less fussy about leaving her under garments tossed across the furniture."

"Probably no idea 'ow to look after 'erself, if the truth be known." Ida turned the page to a picture of a young woman in a dress with a frilled shawl collar and sleeves inset with blonde lace and tried to imagine herself in such an outfit. "If she's never 'ad to."

Losing patience with the idle rich, she put down the magazine, took up her work bag and brought out a pin cushion and a wad of coloured cotton hexagons, each one tacked over a paper template, probably from a magazine very like the one discarded by the Honourable Mrs Whyte. Placing two of them back to back, she started, with surprisingly small stitches for so large a woman, to sew one edge to the other, adding hexagon after hexagon until she had achieved a pattern resembling a six-petalled flower. As she worked, matching or contrasting colours whilst seeming hardly to look at them, she listened as Bea described the bonfire on the open space next to Pendennis Castle that was to be lit this evening.

"You should stay and watch. There's to be a procession from the Drill'All up to the Horn Works and it's going right past 'ere. We'll 'ave a grandstand view even if we don't see the bonfire."

"I do dearly love a bonfire." Ida's needle poised above her neatly–sewn hexagons. "Remember that time up to Carn Brea?" Her voice had a wistful tone that her children would not have recognised. "After Chapel Tea Treat? When Ivan Hart got the lads building a fire with branches and dead furze. Sparks everywhere, remember? Flo Munday screamed like she was being murdered!"

"Flo was always a fool." Bea stared, like Ida, out of the window as if their youth might still be out there if only they could locate it. "But 'e was a one, that Ivan. Whatever 'appened to 'im, I wonder?"

On the opposite pavement three young sailors marched, arm in arm, towards the sea front. In their bell bottomed trousers and broad collars they looked handsome and eager for the pleasures of the day. Two girls in white muslin dresses, shading themselves with parasols, appeared to ignore them as they stepped off the pavement to let them pass, and went on talking animatedly although Ida noticed one of them put up a hand to pat her hair self–consciously into place.

"I'll make us some tea."

She gathered her sewing together and laid it on the table. There was no point, she thought as she made her way down the narrow staircase to Bea's back kitchen, in dwelling on what might have been. Ivan Hart had gone off to Moonta and had never written. Quite possibly he was dead. And Ida had married Percy Goss and lived to regret it. There was nothing else to be said. Or thought about.

115

"How's your Orion then?"

The spare table drawn up between them, laden with the tea tray and the plate of scones and saffron cake left ready by Kezia, Bea might also have been musing on the subject of handsome young men. Childless herself, she had always had a soft spot for Orion.

"'E's going on all right." Ida lifted the heavy tea pot and poured a little into her cup to see if it had brewed. "I think 'e might be courting."

"You don' say?" Bea looked up with interest. "'Oo's the lucky maid then?"

"I don' know that." Ida felt immediately that she might have gone too far. "'E's not said nothing." Removing the tea cosy and then the lid of the pot, she gave a few, not entirely necessary, stirs. "'E's out a good deal an' 'e don't never say where."

"So you 'ant seen 'im with no-one then?"

Had Ida been less flustered she might have noticed the expression on her friend's face – a mixture of uncertainty and mild concern.

Bea Rogers, with her various visitors and a niece who worked at Falmouth's largest hotel, knew more than one might imagine about what was happening, or rumoured to be happening, in the town.

"What will you do this evening?"

The row back, the wind having dropped and the tide being with them, was easy enough and now, having carried their gear back up the steep path to the empty house – for Mrs Fouracre had taken her family to witness the celebrations – Henry and Orion were sitting together on the swing seat in the garden where the ladies, Orion remembered, sat the first time he visited.

Out in the bay pleasure steamers dressed overall and sailing boats displaying multi-coloured flags, criss-crossed the gleaming water. Nearer at hand, the beach at Swanpool was strangely quiet for a fine August afternoon, most people choosing to be in town, on the quay or the sea front or in some of the gardens which were being opened for the occasion.

"I thought I'd go see the lights down Fish Strand. And on the Moor. An' they say there's to be a bonfire up the horn works."

"We could see it from here." Henry waved an arm in the direction of the castle on its wooded peninsular on the far side of the bay.

"Ye'es."

Orion was slow to answer. Partly because, in the warmth of late afternoon and after his exertions, he felt increasingly drowsy. Partly because – in spite of his drowsiness – he could not help feeling that he wanted to be back in the town, taking part in at least some of the festivities. For there was to be a torch–lit procession, the streets would be lit with fairy lights and Chinese lanterns and there was to be a bonfire up by the castle. His friends, Will and the rest, would quite likely be up there and he wanted, quite suddenly, to be there with them.

"But you would prefer to be over there." Henry heard and understood the reluctance in his tone.

"And I," he added, "in any case am dining out."

He had neglected his friends all day. If he did not put in an appearance on this very special evening more questions might be asked than he was prepared to answer.

117

The bonfire on the horn works was lit at a quarter to ten, the flames crackling golden in the night sky and throwing off hissing showers of sparks, the sound, together with the cheers and yells of the crowd, reverberating off the walls of the old castle. It was a fine sight and Orion was glad to see it but it had been a long and confusing day and there were things he needed to think about, so that even before the flames started to die down he turned to walk back towards the town.

In any case, and in spite of his expectations, he could see no-one he knew and it began to seem quite lonely being on his own among such a cheery crowd. In The Grapes or Simmons's he would be sure to find friends to drink with – if that was what he wanted. He wasn't entirely sure about this. There were a lot of things, at this moment, he wasn't entirely sure about... Perhaps more than anything he needed to be on his own to think.

It took him some time to make his way through the crowds along Bar Road into the town which had, in the past twenty four hours, been transformed. The customs house above the quay was decorated with gas–lit stars. Fairy lights were strung from side to side across Church Street and along the front of the Polytechnic Hall, where he had attended the lectures. Shop windows showed pictures of the King and Queen surrounded by flags and rosettes and garlands of flowers and in Mr Uglow's music store every piano in the establishment – and there were many – was decorated with burning candles.

Orion gaped and dawdled, regretting, perhaps – but he was still unsure of this – that he had come so late to the celebrations, until he arrived at The Moor, where the Free Library was draped with purple and gold cloth and even the Packet Memorial column in the centre was festooned with lights. It was certainly some celebration, he thought, staring across at the Seven Stars Hotel, hung with garlands, lights and bunting, with the pictures of the King and Queen displayed above the entrance. Some celebration indeed!

"Where you bin all day, boy?"

The crowd were singing. Of course. The Cornish will always sing and on this great day, with fairy lights and Japanese lanterns lighting the Moor like a fairground, and with much ale and spirits having been consumed, nothing would hold them back. Mostly they sung hymns – suitably for a crowd overlooked by the Methodist chapel – and now they launched into 'Before Jehovah's Awful Throne' with a gusto that would, in different circumstances, have delighted Reverend Ogden.

> *Know that the Lord is God alone;*
> *He can create and He destroy...*

Several hundred voices bellowed out the words and Alfred's question broke hoarsely into the relative silence of a collective intake of breath.

His arm clutched Orion's shoulder and his breath was hot against his ear, smelling, even in air hot with alcoholic fumes, particularly sour. He had been employed, Orion remembered, for the old folks' boat trip earlier in the day and had, presumably, been drinking his payment.

"Bonfire, up castle. Wan' a drink, do 'ee?"

"I don' mean tonight." Alfred's fingers dug painfully into his flesh. "I mean all day. Since you went off, first thing. An' don' tell me no fibs about goin' with your friend Rich, 'cause I seen 'im an' 'e asked where you was an' all."

> *We'll crowd thy gates with thankful songs,*

The voices of crowd boomed in chorus.

> *High as the heavens our voices raise,*

119

Orion tried his frantic best to twist from his brother's grasp.

"Where's Mabel?" he asked, gasping for breath.

He hardly knew the girl but his mother had said that she was 'nice and ladylike,' and Alfred, drunk though he obviously was, might be better behaved if she were nearby.

"None o' your dam' business!" It was not a good question as it turned out – Mabel having told Alfred some three hours before what she thought of his arriving to meet her late and already the worse for drink. The hand gripped tighter than ever, as if he would break his shoulder bone. "Li'l inderfering toad."

Firm as a rock thy truth shall stand,
When rolling years shall cease to move.

The crowd sung on around them, their voices dying to a reverent hush as the hymn ended, then rising, almost immediately, into renewed cheers. Desperately Orion scanned their faces, although with Alfred's arm across his shoulders and the numbing pain of his fingers pressing hard into his flesh it wasn't easy. There was a group of men and women not far off – workers, decently dressed in Sunday clothes. They might even be from the Chapel, perhaps there might be someone he knew among them but there was not and the man shouldering his way through the crowd towards the Seven Stars was more Alfred's type than his…

"Arthur!" The man paused as Alfred called out, turned, showed a row of black and broken teeth and lurched towards them. "This 'ere nancy boy's said 'e'll stand us a drink." His knee made contact with Orion's back and the great hand twisted him to face in the opposite direction. "We're going down Market Strand," he growled and Orion found himself propelled towards the fairy–lit frontage of the town hall.

Nancy boy, he was thinking, as far as he could think anything with Alf's fist pressing into the small of his back. What did he mean, nancy boy?

They were halfway across the Moor by now, where the crowd were thickest, around the Packet Memorial. Where perhaps, among all these people intent on celebrating, it might be possible to wriggle himself free and run...

"Sorry sir. Din' mean to knock you." Alfred sounded almost polite as he lurched against a decent looking man in a dark suit and bowler hat. "Boy 'ere's taken a drop too much."

And the decent looking man put out his hand to make a gangway in the press of bodies as Alfred and Arthur hoisted Orion off his feet and sent him lurching forwards, almost onto his face.

"Tha's it, boy!" Alfred dealt him another wallop in a back. "'Ome to bed now."

And home to bed would have suited Orion well enough but was obviously not what Alfred had in mind. Nor, although that was the general direction in which they were heading, was Market Strand, and amid the confusion filling his head as he struggled to stay upright, struggled to pull himself away from that bruising fist, struggled to understand what was happening to him, he began to realise where they were actually going...

Towards the Wesley Chapel it seemed at first. Or the steep flight of granite steps beside it, known as Jacob's Ladder. Or into the narrow opening between the two, down which, it was obvious from the stench, plenty had already found their way in the past few hours; where even now a bloke was pissing against the chapel wall in the relative darkness beyond the lights.

Help me, Orion thought. For God's sake help me. But, jammed as he was, between Alfred and his friend, both gripping so tight that his bones felt they were about to shatter, what was the point? And in any case when he tried to force words between his parched lips all that came was a sob.

The chapel was built close in against the rock face. Between the granite wall of the building and the granite wall of rock was a space of not much more than a foot and Orion felt the flesh tear on his cheek as Alfred sent him sprawling to the ground, hitting the chapel wall as he fell, to lie, breathless and terrified, the hot blood running down his face. Behind him he could hear Alfred's gasping breath – or perhaps it was Arthur's; he had no way of knowing. Beyond them, and muffled by the bulk of the building, the crowd were still singing.

> *My eyes have seen the glory of the coming of the Lord.*
> *He is trampling out the vintage where the grapes of wrath are stored;*
> *He hath loosed the fatal lightning of His terrible swift sword...*

A clumsy but powerful kick landed in the small of Orion's back, followed by another and then another, which caught against his thigh as he flinched sideways, followed by a thud as a heavy boot caught against the rock face and a howl from Alfred.

"Bugger'n! I've broke me bleddy foot," he roared as the crowd on the Moor built an altar in the evening dews and damps, vicious blows landed on Orion's back and legs and head and the day went marching on...

"Nancy boy," he heard again, through a mist of scorching pain. "Filthy li'l pervert." Followed by the thud of a boot against the side of his head, an agonising crack and then a moment of giddy comprehension before the light, mercifully, went out.

> *In the beauty of the lilies, Christ was born across the sea,*

The background voices that Orion could no longer hear sang lower, sopranos rising above the gentle boom of bass and baritones like a well–rehearsed choir.

> *With a glory in His bosom that transfigures you and me.*
>
> *As He died to make men holy,"*– the deeper tones swelled powerfully –
>
> *Let us die to make men free, while God is marching on.*

The sound echoed around the Moor as Alfred delivered a final vicious kick at his brother's huddled body and turned away, lurching against his friend, towards the glowing lights of the Seven Stars.

Chapter 19

He was on the ground, mouth full of dirt, his head pressed against something cold and damp and hard. The chapel wall, of course, and as he tried to spit out some of the dirt, the giddiness swept over him again and it seemed easier, much easier, to just give up and go on lying there.

Except that it hurt. In his chest. His back. His legs. His throat... When he coughed the pain scorched, red hot, through his ribs. When he tried to lift himself his legs folded under him. When he reached out an arm to pull himself upwards pain tore across his shoulders and the groan that came out of him might have come from a wounded animal.

And such cold! Seeping from the rock. From the granite wall of the chapel. From the ground below him. Such cold that he was shaking with it – or perhaps it was from something else. How could he know when his head was filled with swirling banks of fog?

What time was it? Another impossibility. It seemed to be dark but the darkness might just be inside him. Surely there had been people before? And noise? Through the drifting fog he remembered singing. Mine eyes have seen the glory... His truth is marching... As He died to make men free...

Now nothing. No singing. No voices. No oaths. No thud of heavy boots.

Standing upright was torment. Not that 'upright' was the word, as he crouched, one hand clutching the side of the cliff. And so much pain that he hardly noticed when the barbs of an overhanging bramble clawed at the raw wounds across his face.

But he must move. One foot agonizingly in front of the other. Ignore the pain in his bruised thighs. Ignore the swollen ankle, throbbing inside his tight-laced boot. Try not to move his chest. Try, God Almighty, not to cough! Dragging himself, pitifully slowly, around the edge of the chapel, along the narrow gap between the wall and the rise of Jacob's Ladder, out onto the pavement and the empty Moor.

Fairy lights, no longer glittering, hung from their thick, dark cables. Flags fluttered listlessly, leached of colour in the pale light of a waning moon. Many of the flowers decorating shop fronts had lost their heads and as he started his painful stagger up Killigrew Street he trod on the fallen blooms of dozens of blue hydrangeas, their crushed petals already browning on the paving stones.

He met no-one. It was too late even for the last of the revellers but too early for the milkman or street cleaners as he dragged himself uphill with no clear idea where he was going except that he could not, for some reason, go home.

"Can I help you?"

But the voice did not sound particularly helpful and the face, as he twisted to look upwards, was alarming. Stern, dark eyes below heavy brows in an austere and bony face, the lips obscured by a thick moustache, iron grey like the flowing hair with its central parting. More disturbing still, the man wore a thick, dark robe reaching to his ankles and tied by a length of rope at the waist...

Charles Napier Hemy, Falmouth's Royal Academician, an older and an even more successful artist than his friend Henry, had joined the Dominican Order at the age of nineteen and spent two years in a monastery in Lyon before accepting that it was not his vocation to be a monk. He had never, however, lost his faith, building his Falmouth house, Churchfield, on land adjacent to the Catholic Church on Killigrew Street, attending mass daily and often wandering around his home at night in prayer and wearing the old Dominican habit in which he felt most comfortable. Which was how he was dressed when, hearing a noise in the street, he went outside to investigate.

An animal, he thought at first, peering from his front

125

doorway in the faint light of early morning. Then saw that it was in fact a young man, slumped forwards on the pavement and in the act of vomiting. No doubt the worse for drink after the excesses of the coronation celebrations and the sides of Charles' mouth turned sternly downwards. He was, however, a Christian and not entirely unsympathetic to the weaknesses of his fellow men and this young fellow did appear, as he crossed the road and came closer, to be in a bad way.

"Can I help you?" he asked and was horrified to see, as the young man looked up at him, the bruising across his forehead, the dirt–filled scrapes across his cheeks and the sunken dimness of his eyes which, almost immediately, rolled upwards and then closed.

The room in which his eyes eventually flickered open was filled with sunlight. The walls and wainscots were painted white, the ceiling was finely plastered and embossed with decorative patterns, the tall windows hung with white muslin and even with his limited view Orion could see that it was the most beautiful room he had ever been in. Nor had he ever felt such smooth, fine linen against his skin and, if it were not for the sour taste in his mouth and the aching in his chest and head, he might have imagined that he had died and gone to heaven.

But no heaven, surely, would contain this sort of pain. According to Reverend Ogden it was a place of eternal rejoicing, where God's balm wiped away all pain and suffering. Nor had he made any mention of muslin curtains or ornamental plasterwork. Nor, for that matter, beds.

The lady who came into the room as he was considering all this had a rounded, gentle face and wore a long, heavy dress in dark grey which rustled as she moved.

Was he feeling better, she asked. Would he like something to drink? Some lemonade perhaps? And when he nodded as best he could from under so many, unaccustomed bedclothes, poured some into a glass from a flask beside his bed.

"Can you lift your head?"

And when he tried and fell back, wincing at the pain, she reached, very gently, to lift him by the shoulders, holding the glass to his lips as he drank.

"Lie back now," she told him, "and rest. Doctor Ellis will be here soon."

"But…"

But Doctor Ellis, he would have said if his voice were working, was far too costly. Orion had seen his house, up Kimberley Park Road, not far from the house where his mother worked. A three storey, double-fronted house above a steep pathway, with a shining brass plate on the side gateway that led to his surgery at the back.

He knew the house and he knew Doctor Ellis, who wore a frock coat and top hat and had a more than passing resemblance to the new king, but he was not his doctor. Families like the Gosses could not afford to consult men like Doctor Ellis and relied, if they were ill, on Mr Hosking the chemist in Market Street who dispensed remedies for most ailments and, if they didn't always work, well neither did the medicines Doctor Ellis so expensively prescribed. The kind-faced lady, however, seemed not to hear his croak of protest but went quietly out of the room and downstairs to her husband's studio.

"Is the boy well?"

Charles Hemy stood in front of his easel, brush in hand. He had been early to Mass, as he did every day, and now, and although it was Sunday, stood contemplating a seascape. A white-sailed dinghy, the result of many weeks' meticulous sketchings, skidded below a grey sky across a turbulent, deep green sea. Two youths sprawled across the decks, reaching for ropes and Charles, brush laden with black, leaned forwards to paint more shadows on the jagged rock they had just avoided.

"Not well," his wife told him, "but he's awake. I shall be glad when Doctor Ellis has been."

Charles, his attention still on his painting, grunted.

"He'll be busy, no doubt, with the results of yesterday's over–indulgence. There'll be plenty of sore heads and dyspepsia this morning."

"Well this boy has more than a sore head. I hope he comes soon."

"Did you find out who he is?"

The artist dipped his brush in water, shook it, and applied the wash to his rock.

"He can hardly speak, poor lad. His mother must be frantic with worry. I wish I did know."

But her husband, dissatisfied with something, bent further forward over his painting and made no comment. Amy, who could not count the nights she had laid awake fretting when any of her six sons were out late, turned towards the conservatory that opened off the studio and went on worrying. Wakened in the early hours by her husband anxious not to disturb the household, she had heated water and wiped away with soft, damp lint the worst of the dried blood around the boy's face. It had been obvious, even through the cuts, the swellings and the bruises, that he was handsome. Perhaps even beautiful.

"He'll live. He's been badly knocked about – broken ribs, a great deal of cuts and bruising and a sprained wrist and ankle – but on the whole he was lucky. He has a thick skull, otherwise there might well have been some damage to the brain. I can have him moved to the hospital…"

Doctor Ellis waited for Amy to agree to this obvious end to her inconvenience but masked his surprise when she said she would prefer to nurse him herself. In that case, he said, he would have some ointments made up for the bruises and she should put iodine on the cuts and scratches. He had bandaged the lad's ribs and wrist and ankle and there was little else to be done, provided his temperature remained stable.

Amy promised to check it regularly and settled herself comfortably in the guest bedroom with her sewing. Sunday lunch, she had already decided, could be eaten without her. It was the least she could do on behalf of the boy's absent mother.

Doctor Ellis went downstairs, collected his gloves and hat from the hall table and replaced them with his bill. Charles, coming out of the studio, glanced at it, wondered why doctors, like horse-dealers – not that this was his line of country – seemed always to charge in guineas, and reached into his pocket.

He preferred always to pay bills on presentation.

"His name's Goss, by the way," Doctor Ellis informed him, accepting his fee. "Orion Goss. Lives down in Quarry Place. Shall I send one of my boys to tell his mother? She works for one of my neighbours. A decent woman, I believe."

Charles, frowning, seemed about to speak, then nodded slightly and turned away.

After lunch, and without saying anything to Amy, he sent one of his sons to order a pony and trap from the livery stables.

He was not at all sure whether Henry would be at home. With no religious beliefs and therefore no obligations, Sundays was one of the days he often chose to go painting at Sunny Cove or round at Newporth and the ex-Dominican monk had no intention of seeking him there. If Henry could not be found at Pennance Cottage he would leave a message.

Meanwhile his youngest daughter was eager enough to leave the improving book that was supposed to occupy her this Sunday afternoon and take her turn at driving the staid little pony that was brought round to the house. They were taking a message to Uncle Henry, her father told her before reverting to one of the austere silences from which his family had learned not to disturb him and as the pony clip-clopped along Western Terrace and then down the rough track towards Marlborough House she gave her attention to her unexpected treat.

Charles meanwhile was regretting the impulse that had caused him to act the Good Samaritan. Obviously he wished the lad no harm but doubtless little would have come to him had he been left for an early workman to find. Now he had him in bed in his guest bedroom with Amy to fuss over him – and Henry was going to have to be told.

"You will be careful. You won't do...anything..."

But he had stopped at that point. Having no idea what manner of activity he was warning his friend against. And Henry, with whom he had been selecting paintings for display in Falmouth's annual art exhibition at the gallery they had helped to found, had given one of his carefree guffaws.

"You worry too much, old boy. Now, what about this one?" And he offered for scrutiny a gloomy watercolour of low tide at Fish Strand Quay from a local amateur painter.

But he had become quieter, Charles remembered, and rather more reticent, although he had spent the previous half hour enthusing noisily about his new protégé, the lad from the market garden whom he was teaching to draw and paint. He came every evening after work, he said, to spend time in the studio. Unless they went cycling. Henry had bought him a bicycle and on fine evenings they would cycle out along the coast or around the lanes...

It was at this point that Charles had warned his friend to be careful...

He had worried about the conversation afterwards. And remembered the lad's name, because it was an unusual one.

He dismounted at the bottom of Swanpool Hill, leading the pony up the steep, curved slope to the lane which led to Pennance Cottage. There he suggested to his daughter that she should stay with the trap whilst he went in to see if Henry was at home and she, recognising the suggestion as an order, did as she was told.

And Henry, unusually for a Sunday, was at home.

Even more unusually for such a sociable man, he was on his own and Charles found him, pacing around the garden, moodily slashing dead heads off a display of crimson dahlias.

"What in the world brings you out here, old man?" he demanded. "It's good to see you," he added but it was obvious that he was not his usual ebullient self. The smile with which he greeted his friend left his face almost immediately, he did not suggest tea or a glass of wine and it seemed as though his attention were elsewhere.

"I've got some rather worrying news for you." There was no point in putting off the moment. "Your young friend. The one you were telling me about the other day. Is his name Goss? Orion Goss."

"Of course! Yes. Why?" Certainly Charles had his attention now. "Has something happened…?" Gripping his friend by the arm, Henry pumped it, quite painfully up and down. "What is it, Charles? Tell me, for heavens sake!"

"It's all right Henry. Do please calm down." Not given to such outbursts himself, Charles was easily startled. "He's in our guest bedroom and Amy's looking after him. Doctor Ellis saw him this morning and says there's no danger. He's got some broken ribs and…"

In his confusion he had started at the wrong end of the story.

"Broken ribs! How? What happened to him? And how the blue blazes did he end up in your…? Tell me Charles! I don't understand!"

Chapter 20

Ida Goss had no suspicion that anything had happened to Orion until Doctor Ellis's boy banged on her door not long after she had returned from chapel.

After such an exciting day she had fallen into a deep sleep the moment she got into bed the previous night and was not even woken by the noise of Alfred falling drunkenly up the stairs. She woke late the following morning and, hurrying to get ready for chapel, assumed that her sons were sleeping late as well.

Now, confronted with the news that Orion was lying injured in the large house called Churchfield, next door to the Catholic church and owned by the strange Mr Hemy whose imposing, even fearsome, figure she had occasionally seen crossing the Moor, she was alarmed and confused. How could her son have got into such a place? And what did the boy mean when he said that he was injured?

"He 'ad an accident but you can go see 'im, Missus." The boy had no more idea of the answers than she did and, seeing little prospect of a tip, wanted to get home for his dinner. "Like I said, 'e's up Churchfield."

But Ida, in spite of her concern, was not at all sure about this. Churchfield was a big house. Bigger than Mrs Trembath's or any other house she had worked in.

And Mr Hemy was a Catholic.

For a moment, standing in her doorway, staring helplessly after the disappearing boy, she wondered if her son was being held prisoner. She remembered stories in Sunday School about the Jesuits, who were also Catholics, and the terrible tortures they had inflicted on their enemies. Perhaps Orion had in some way fallen foul of this Mr Hemy? Was it he who had caused his injuries? There had been, she remembered, rumours about him walking about at night wearing monk's clothing – a young girl who had gone there as house parlour maid had been frightened out of her wits, meeting him on the stairs one early morning and thinking she was seeing a ghost. Obviously there was something not quite right about the man.

Hurrying up the stairs, almost falling in her haste over her Sunday skirt, she called out for Alfred but when she stumbled into the bedroom his bed was empty and there was no sign of him other than the stench of the brim–full chamber pot next to the wash stand and the good trousers he had been instructed to wear for yesterday's boat trip lying rumpled on the floor and unaccountably stained with mud.

It was several hours before she summoned up the courage to walk the short distance up Killigrew Hill and turn in by the Catholic church to stand staring at the house next door. It was a splendid house – not more than twenty years old, three stories high with a fine slate roof sweeping across its twin gables and surrounded by a garden filled with shrubs and trees. About a dozen windows faced onto the road from which, or so it seemed to Ida, any number of people could be watching her.

Somewhere inside this house and for no reason that she could imagine, her Orion lay injured and, although Doctor Ellis's boy had said she could visit him, she was far too fearful to walk up to the front door and ring the bell. Instead she turned slowly – and still nervously – towards the back of the house.

She tapped on the back door, quietly at first and then more loudly but received no reply, Sunday lunch being long finished and the servants having gone out to enjoy their free afternoon. The silence, apart from the insistent shrilling of a wren, began to seem more and more sinister and when she looked up and noticed that one of the upper windows had bars on the inside she began to wonder if she should go down the road to the newly opened Police Station and ask for their help.

"Oh my dear! I thought I heard something. Have you been there long?"

The lady who opened the door wore a grey dress, trimmed with elegant braiding and was quite obviously not a servant.

"Are you the boy's mother?" she asked, when Ida, overcome with confusion, did not answer, and, as she remained silent, drew her into the house. "I'm so glad you're here my dear. Come along in."

She leads her up the back stairs, along a broad and airy corridor and then into the room where Orion lies in bed. A beautiful room, Ida has to notice, in spite of everything, and certainly not a prison. So light, with white muslin curtains, pale blue carpet, chairs with velvet coverings and beautiful paintings of sea scenes, so that Ida does not, at first, look closely at her son, who lies against white linen, under a counterpane whose blue matches the blue of the carpet. Except that the linen of the pillow cases is stained reddish–brown with the dried blood that must have come from the cuts on his face and yellow from the iodine with which they have been treated. Except that her son's arm, resting on top of the counterpane, has transferred to it some of the dirt that seems to be engrained into his bruised and scraped skin…

"Orion! Whatever 'appened? Who done this to you?"

For Ida has witnessed plenty of fights and beatings. Drunken disputes in the street or on the Moor on a Saturday night. Fights between sailors and local youths, generally over a maid or some insult, real or imagined. She knows well enough what the results look like and it is obvious that Orion, far from meeting with an accident, has come off worst in some sort of brawl.

His face is so swollen that his eyes have almost vanished, the purple of his bruises merging with the yellow staining of the iodine that covers the cuts and scrapes across his cheeks. The bruises on his arm are broad and violent and when he attempts to raise himself from his pillow it obviously hurts.

"Oo done it?" Ida demands again. "My gor, I'll go down police station this minute an'…"

"Don' do that!" The sound is little more than a croak between swollen lips, the lower one painfully torn at one side so that she can see a loose flap of drying, white skin. "I know 'oo done it."

"You sit down, my dear. I'll fetch you a cup of tea."

Amy Hemy, sensing that there is more to be said – and that she might prefer not to hear it – touches Mrs Goss gently on the shoulder and moves a chair closer to the bed. Then she goes quietly out of the room and down to her sitting room where she has the materials for making her afternoon tea on a little spirit stove.

"'Oo was it then?" Mrs Goss leaned across the bed. "'Oo done it – and what for? Was it 'bout a maid?" She has, after all, suspected for some time that Orion has been courting. Supposing some other lad is after the same girl? Or supposing she is no maid at all but some man's wife? Orion's good looks, she has sometimes thought, may not be entirely a blessing. "'Ave you been up to something' you din' ought?"

"No, ma. There in't no maid…" Orion is worn out, confused and in pain but he is quite sure of this. Of this and of the fact that his mother must not go to the police. "It were Alf an' one of 'is pals. I don' know why. You'll 'ave to ask 'im that."

And then, as Ida Goss sits back, dumbfounded, in her narrow chair, they hear heavy footsteps on the stairs. Taking them, from the sound, two… even three steps at a time.

"Orion! Where the blue blazes are you?" The steps clatter on the landing, a door crashes open, there is an exclamation, a slam, the footsteps come closer and this time it is the door at which they are both staring which is flung noisily open and Henry Tuke, wild-eyed, hair and jacket in total disorder, who plunges through it.

"Orion! " he exclaims, not even noticing the bulk of Ida Goss in her black Sunday dress at his bedside. "My poor boy! What have they done to you?"

Chapter 21

The easiest thing would be to close his eyes and let himself slide back into sleep. The sort of sleep he had slept for most of the day, from the time the round faced lady with the kind eyes had finished anointing his cuts with iodine so that they stung like a million nettles to the moment when his mother was unaccountably standing over him. A deep, sound sleep in which the rosemary–scent of the bed linen mingled with the acrid tang of the iodine and his bruised limbs relaxed into a mattress softer than any he had ever known. A sleep in which the fear and confusion of the past hours seemed to unknot themselves so that he woke feeling almost calm.

Not any more.

How could he… how could anyone feel calm with Henry bursting into the room like a mad man and his mother, her face a mix of fear and horror, leaning across the bed to clutch painfully at his hand, as if she feared that Henry might be about to drag him away? It was an immense relief when the white–haired gentleman with the thick, dark eyebrows, who had brought him into the house – but had, thank goodness, changed his black robe for a suit and cravat – hurried into the room behind Henry, followed closely by the kind–eyed lady.

"Harry! Please! Calm down." The man placed a hand on his shoulder and spoke severely and with such force that Henry, apparently about to launch himself across the bed, stood stock–still, although still breathing heavily, in the middle of the room. "Have some self control, for heaven's sake man."

"Mrs er… Goss." The kind–eyed lady came forward in the brief silence that followed. "May I introduce my husband, Mr Charles Hemy, and this is our friend Mr Henry Tuke. I was about to bring you a tray of tea but perhaps it might be better for your son if we all went to my sitting room and allowed him to rest. Doctor Ellis was confident he will make a complete recovery but he said it was most important he should be kept calm."

(Amy Hemy was inventing here but assumed, quite reasonably, that it would not be good for the boy to have Henry snorting hysterically about the room, terrifying still further his already terrified mama.)

Nobody argued with her although Henry recovered himself sufficiently to step forward and hold out his hand to Mrs Goss who, in her confusion, for this was a gentleman but he was also an artist and one of whom she had heard all manner of tales, struggled to her feet and held out her own hand, although not close enough for them to actually touch. After which neither of them seemed disposed to leave and Orion, lying back against his pillows, watched as Mrs Hemy guided his mother towards the door and her husband almost pushed Henry through it behind them.

"I'm sorry Ma'am. I din't ought to 'ave come. I'll go now if you don't mind."

Ida Goss was shaking. From the shock of seeing the state of Orion – and even more so from what he had told her. From Henry's sudden and startling entry. And from the discovery of who this man – who had called Orion his 'poor boy' – actually was.

The thought of sitting down to take tea with a lady and two gentlemen in the lady's sitting room was more than she could contemplate.

"I must go 'ome," she insisted as Mrs Hemy tried to dissuade her. "I'm sorry Ma'am and thank you, thank you so much for what you've done for my boy." And as Amy protested that she was only too glad… she hurried across the broad hallway, almost colliding with one of the Hemy boys coming in from the garden, and blundered out of the front door.

"Alfred! Where are you? You come down 'ere right now!"

By the time she reaches home Ida Goss's shock has turned to

fury and she hurtles through the back door yelling for her son as she has not done since he was ten years old. Certainly not since he has been old enough, and large enough, to make her afraid of him. So angry is she that it does not occur to her that he may not be in; it is almost as if her rage is sufficient to conjure him up, wherever he may be.

Although Alfred is in fact at home. Lying across his bed, as he generally does when he is not eating or drinking, attempting to sleep off the headache that a couple of hours in The Chain Locker have made worse rather than better, he answers his mother with a roar that would have unnerved her if she were not so angry.

"Wa' the 'ell is it? Yelling like a bleddy 'ooter."

But he shambles downstairs to the kitchen where his mother slams the iron kettle with a resounding crash onto the range.

"My bleddy 'ead!" Alfred flops down at the table and cradles it in his arms.

"*Your* bleddy 'ead! It's your brother's 'ead I'm talking about! What was you doin' Alfred? 'Alf killing the boy. What the blazin' 'ell was you doing?"

Ida Goss is a good Methodist and it is not her way to swear but she has been through a great deal today.

"What, Alfred?" she demands. "Tell me! I'm waiting to 'ear."

Alfred, head still in his hands, is thinking. For he has not yet worked out – not being the smartest of thinkers and having so sore a head – a suitable story for his mother. Last night it all made such sense. His pathetic apology of a brother with his pretty face has been seen – so he has been told on good authority – with that nancy boy artist who paints the dirty pictures. Not that Alfred has ever seen any of these but he knows that, whilst pictures of naked women are acceptable as 'art' and to be gawped and sniggered at by men, pictures of naked men are filthy, disgusting and as perverted as the men who paint them. Who are in turn as perverted as the seamen who hang about the dock gates and Market Strand and are willing to pay local boys to indulge their disgusting practices.

Last night after several pints of strong ale and especially after Mabel, who has kept him waiting far too long for his oats, told him very firmly to keep his filthy hands off her before departing with Will Anstey, it seemed exactly the right thing to do; to teach the dirty little blighter a lesson by kicking his guts to blazes. His mother, it would have seemed to him then, had he thought of her, would have felt the same.

Now, still suffering from last night's over–indulgence and in the face of the sort of fury he has not encountered for years, he is not so sure.

"I 'eard stories." He mumbles his first words into the scrubbed wooden table top and then, with belligerent confidence, raises his head. "I 'eard stories," he says, meeting his mother's crimson and hostile face straight on. "Stories wot made me see red. 'Bout your precious boy. Tha's all."

"What stories?"

Ida Goss subsides into the chair at the head of the table. On the range the water in her kettle is singing its way towards boiling point but, although she has been desperate for a cup of tea every since Mrs Hemy, back in what seems already to be another universe, offered to make her one, she doesn't even hear it. For ideas – and suspicions – have been whirling inside her head ever since that man, that artist, flung himself almost headlong into the bedroom, demanding to know who had done such a thing to his poor boy.

"What stories?" she repeats. "What 'ave you 'eard?"

"Stories 'bout Orion. An' that artist. That Mr Tuke. Going round 'is 'ouse, they d'say. Goin' out with 'im on bicycles. Orion, on a bicycle! Where did 'e ever get a bicycle? Tha's where 'e's been when you thought 'e were with some girl. The dirty little swine and if I get my 'ands on 'im again I'll kill 'im, I tell you Ma. I'll kill the dirty bugger."

"No you won't. Don' matter what 'e's done, *you* won't do

139

nothing."

His mother speaks slowly, trying to take in what he is saying. Trying to convince herself that it cannot possibly be true. That there is some other reason for the strange events of the past few hours.

"You'll leave 'im be," she says, still trying to order her thoughts and not succeeding. "Or you'll 'ave me to answer to."

"Awright. P'raps I'll leave 'im be." Alfred presses a red and swollen fist against his throbbing brow. "But I don' think Pa will."

"Alfred!" New horror smashes into his mother's head. "You never! You never told your father? Oh my good God, what in the world did you do that for?"

Most of the time, Ida manages to forget that Percy Goss, who walked out on her – perhaps 'staggered out' would be a better way of putting it – when Orion was a baby, still exists. Every so often she is, of course, forced to remember – when she bumps into in the street, for example, the man who is still, divorce not being something that ordinary working folk can possibly afford, her husband. This happens rarely enough, however, for Percy, when he is working, does rough labouring jobs on the waterfront and spends most of the rest of his time in one of the public houses or sleeping off the effects in the room he shares with Betty Angrove above Fish Strand Quay. As Ida rarely goes near the waterfront and never into a public house and would never go near the room he shares with Betty Angrove, who is well known for being no better than she should be, there is little chance of their meeting and it is easy enough to forget that they were ever of any significance to one another.

But Percy Goss does still exist. And is still physically strong, in spite of his overindulgence. And is a brutal man with a violent temper which has, more than once, landed him in trouble with the police, once earning him a spell of twelve months imprisonment with hard labour in Dartmoor prison.

What Percy Goss, in his cups, might do to Orion, for whom he has no affection but who is known to be his son, does not bear thinking about.

Chapter 22

It was several days before the swelling on Orion's face had gone down enough for Amy Hemy to see that she had been right about his good looks. By that time most of his cuts and scratches had healed to scabs and he was able to get out of bed although his broken ribs still hurt and Doctor Ellis said he must keep his wrist and ankle bandaged and not use them for at least a week.

"But I did oughter be back at work Sir, or I'll lose my job."

He was worried, in fact, that he might already have lost it. It was a busy time in the market garden, after all. Cabbages, spinach, onions, turnips, Brussels and cauliflowers needed sowing, potatoes, all the time, needed digging, the rest of the raspberry canes must be cut down now the crop was finished and the wall fruit netted to protect it from the birds. Mr Cyril would have no patience with him idling about and had very likely already taken on someone in his place.

He wasn't even sure if his employer knew he had been injured and had fretted about this, once he had recovered enough to remember where he should be, although Henry, who visited every day, told him not to worry.

"I'll send a message to say you've met with an accident," he said. "No blame can be attached to you. He can't dismiss you because of that."

But Henry was a gentleman and didn't understand – how could he? – how it was for someone like Orion. Jobs weren't so plentiful that he could afford to lose one – and if Mr Cyril did dismiss him it would be hard to get another. Certainly not another gardening job and what else could be do?

And how, exactly, was Henry intending to send his message? Mr Cyril was a suspicious man. If he was sent a message about Orion from Mr Henry Tuke heaven knew what he would think. It would be better, he insisted, for there to be no message at all.

He worried too how long he should stay here. In his own

home they had never had a visitor to stay even for one night. When his elder sister, Jane, came from her home over near Redruth every six months or so and then for only a few hours, it was an occasion demanding immense preparations. It was hard to imagine, even though Henry assured him that it made no difference to the Hemys, that he wasn't a burden.

"Don't be ridiculous!" Henry was perched on the edge of the bed. "Amy's only too glad to have someone to fuss over and Charles is so occupied with his prayers and his painting that it makes not the slightest difference to him. You concentrate on getting better," and he heaved himself off the bed, causing the mattress to rise up and making Orion wince at the sudden pain.

Although, as it happened, Henry was wrong about this. Orion's presence did make a difference to Charles, making it harder, at times, to concentrate on his painting and giving him a new theme for his prayers. It was no small matter, after all, to have a young man, unknown to him up to the early hours of Saturday morning, lying in his guest room. And disturbing that Henry was obviously so concerned about him. He had always worried – and prayed – about Henry's friendships with young men but had been reassured that they were simply subjects for his painting, and, although at least two had become trusted servants and closer friends than Charles might have felt fitting, they were both known to have lady friends and one of them was now a married man.

This time, Charles felt, was different and he was quite unable to forget the distracted passion his friend had found it impossible to conceal on the ride back from his house on Sunday afternoon.

And the boy was, of course, so very beautiful. No-one, especially an artist, could fail to see that.

The other worry was the boy's mother, who had hurried away that Sunday and had not been seen since. This did not particularly concern Charles, who tended to hold himself aloof from female, and household, matters but Amy had mentioned it several times.

"She must, surely, want to see her son. Should I send one of the boys with a message? She only lives a few minutes' walk away," she had said anxiously once again at the dinner table the previous evening.

"In which case, there is nothing to prevent her coming here without being sent for."

"I'm not 'sending for her', Charles! I want to reassure her that she's welcome. According to Cook she works for Mrs Trembath in Kimberly Park Road. She's a decent, hard–working woman, apparently. A Methodist." She glances across at her husband. "She may feel nervous about calling here," she says quietly.

But Charles, keen to return to his sketches of a trawler, finished his steak pie, declined dessert and prepared to leave the table.

Ida Goss was indeed anxious about her son but her anxiety was less about his present state – she had last seen him, after all, lying in linen sheets in a fine bedroom – than his state should his father get hold of him. For, although Percy Goss had not been to see her – since he had not been to the house for the past sixteen years this was not surprising – he had been to the market garden; Mr Rowse having, unusually, called in to tell her so.

"'E come in lunch time," he said, standing peevishly on her front doorstep. "'E was asking 'bout Orion. I thought you should know. I told 'im 'e was off work, poorly, an' 'e said when was I expecting 'im back. I said I din' know; I only knew what Doctor Ellis's boy told me and 'e din' say no more. When is 'e coming back?" he asked, reminded of his other grievance. "I got my sister's youngest 'elping but I don' 'ave the time to keep telling 'im everything and young Richie's as much use as a rat in a snow storm."

"I'm not sure. E's got broken ribs, Doctor says. An' a bad

wrist."

Mr Rowse's big mouth turned down further than usual.

"Well I can't be doin' without 'im much longer, you tell 'im. If 'e's not better by Monday, I shall 'ave to let 'im go."

He didn't ask to see Orion, which was as well, but turned away from the door with an irritable shrug. Then he turned back.

"'E 'ad another bloke with 'im, Percy did. Big chap. Evil lookin'. Not someone I knew." And then, about to turn away again, "'E asked what time we shut of an evening."

"Ave you 'eard anything? About my Orion? Or Percy? 'As Joe seen 'im?"

Although it was Friday Ida had not intended going on her weekly visit to Bea, being too anxious about Orion and too concerned about what she could say about him to her friend. But Mr Cyril's words had preyed on her mind and when Alfred came in from the pub the night before – the worse for wear, as always, now that Mabel would have no more to do with him – she had told him about his father's visit to the market garden.

"Percy 'ad a friend with 'im, Mr Rowse said. Big bloke. Evil looking. D'you know 'oo that could be?"

But Alfred had only shrugged.

"I don' know 'oo 'is friends are. Someone from down Fish Strand, p'raps."

"Well I don' like it."

Ida cut bread against her brawny chest, scraped dripping from the bowl across the cut slice and thumped it down in front of Alfred.

"Well it's not my fault is it? 'F your little nancy boy goes off with perverts 'e's got it coming to 'im. Where is 'e, anyways? Still lolling around up Churchfield?"

"If you d'see your pa, don't you dare go telling 'im that! Understand?"

With the bread knife still clenched in her fist Alfred was not

145

about to argue with his mother and, taking his bread and dripping, he went upstairs without answering.

Just as Bea Rogers did not, for some little while, answer her friend.

For she had – of course she had – heard things. About Orion and about Percy. For Joe Rogers, if he was not exactly bosom pals with his old friend, did occasionally frequent the same public house. His son, he had heard Percy bellow, was a filthy, perverted, young pup and he'd feel his boot up his backside – and worse – when he caught up with him.

And Bea had heard the rumours about Orion before this. For Kezia, always reliable at relaying the gossip from the Falmouth Hotel, had been told, some weeks before, by one of the waiters, of an overheard conversation between two gentlemen diners.

Harry Tuke, one of them had told the other, was no value these days. Not since he'd taken up with his new, pretty boy. There were none of his parties on the Piebox. He no longer took his painting groups round to Newporth beach. A waste of the fine summer weather, they agreed, and the sooner he bored of this Orion lad he was so obsessed with the better.

Kezia had remembered the name because it was such an unusual one.

"I did 'ear summin'."

Bea spoke carefully, not wanting to upset her friend, which was why she had said nothing before this. On the other hand, if what Kezia had said was true, she was going to be upset some time and it was best for it to be here in Bea's front bedroom with a friend to discuss her fears with and no–one else to witness.

"Go on." Ida leaned forwards in her chair. "What was it?"

"Just that…That 'e was friendly, if you know what I mean, with that Mr Tuke. Tha's all." Bea leaned back against her pillows, tucking her shawl against her neck as if she felt the cold, although it was so stuffy in the small room that this wasn't possible. "Friendly," she repeated. Nervously because of the intensity with which her friend was staring at her. "Just that. You d'know 'ow folk talk. Jealous, I 'pect." She went on speaking to cover the uncomfortable silence. "After all, 'e is a gentleman. Mr Tuke. 'E's got smart friends. I don't see as 'ow 'e'd do your Orion no 'arm."

Although this was not exactly what Bea thought. Mr Tuke certainly did have smart friends. He mixed, and dined, with some of Falmouth's most influential men and, perhaps more significantly, their wives. But there were others... Men who did not mix and dine with the most influential men in Falmouth or their wives. Men whose reputations were, to say the least of it, a little tarnished. Bea might never leave her house – or even her bedroom – but she still heard things. More, perhaps, than most.

And there were the boys. The son of one of Bea's neighbours had been out, several times, on Mr Tuke's painting parties around the coast from Swanpool. And had been painted, or so he said, stretched out flat on the sand, in his bare skin. There was nothing wrong with it, he had told his mother. Artists needed models, Mr Tuke had paid them well for their time and at least one of the paintings was now hanging in one of the famous galleries up London.

His mother had been less certain and so, when she had heard, was Bea, but the lad had insisted Mr Tuke was always polite and gentlemanly, which she took to mean that he didn't take liberties. It was still worrying, however, and, if she were in Ida Goss's place she would be more worried still.

"Don' you fret, midear," she said, nevertheless. "And pour us another cuppa. Your Orion's a good boy. 'E wouldn't do nothing wrong."

But Ida, as she poured the tea, could not help fretting and mostly about Percy Goss.

Orion, in bed between clean linen sheets up at Churchfield,

147

might be safe for the moment – and she felt almost angry with him for this – but he couldn't stay there for ever and there was no knowing what Percy and his evil-looking friend might do when they caught up with him.

Chapter 23

Orion went home on the Saturday morning. He would have gone days before – some of his scabs had already fallen off to show the new pink skin underneath and his bruises had faded from black and purple to green and yellow – if Henry had not insisted he stay where he was. His ribs still hurt when he moved and his wrist and ankle were still tightly bandaged but he could walk about the room without too much pain and it was dreary stuff sitting indoors when he wanted to be up and doing.

"You must come downstairs and join us. Sit in the lounge or the conservatory. Take some exercise in the garden. You're very welcome."

But Orion, Amy Hemy quickly realised, was shy and she did not press him. The thought of eating with them – he had heard the voices of several boys and the laughter and lighter tones of girls – terrified him and if it had not been for Henry he would have gone home as soon as he could walk.

"You can't possibly go until you're strong enough," Henry had told him. Strong enough to defend himself, he meant, for Orion had admitted, if only to stop him from going down to the police station and reporting the attack, that one of his assailants had been his brother. With no real idea of the lives of families like Orion's, Henry had made it his business one morning to walk past the row of cottages where he now knew he lived and saw that they were small and poorly maintained, with missing slates and rotting frames to doors and windows. The lives led inside them would, he imagined, be dark, cramped and quite possibly violent and he marvelled that someone so gentle as Orion should have emerged from such a place.

His mother and sister had been greatly perturbed by the Quaker Seebohm Rowntree's survey of poverty in the city of York, which he had published the previous year. They had spoken of it to Henry on his last visit and, although he no longer subscribed to Quaker beliefs, he cared very much about his fellow men and had also read it. Now, as he looked at the row of low and impoverished houses, he could not help but remember Rowntree's descriptions of what he called 'primary poverty' when the basic requirements of food, shelter, clothing and fuel could not be met from a family's income, no matter how carefully they budgeted.

Ida Goss would have been hurt in the extreme if she had been aware of Henry's opinion. In fact, from her wage as a general domestic and the contributions of Orion and, less regularly, Alfred, they managed well enough. A great deal better, certainly, than before Percy's defection. They might have little money for such luxuries as doctors but they were able to eat and dress adequately and maintain a warm and simply but sufficiently furnished home, which was as far as her ambitions reached and which placed them above Rowntree's lowest levels of deprivation.

Henry, with his well–nurtured and protected background, saw things differently and if he could have kept Orion safe inside the airy comfort of the Hemys' guest bedroom for ever he would have done so. It would be the next best alternative to the obvious impossibility of taking him to live at Pennance Cottage.

Keeping Orion in bed, however, was akin to keeping a bird in a cage, which was something of which Henry had never approved, since there was so little for him to do. It was not as if the boy read books – he could read but it was not something he was likely to do for pleasure and he did no more than glance at the copy of Tit Bits which Henry brought for him. Nor did he enjoy music. He did not even talk much and it was not until the Wednesday that it occurred to Henry that the gift of a sketch pad and pencils – he had too much respect for Amy's linen to bring charcoal – might keep him occupied. Then, propped against pillows in an easy chair, Orion – nervously at first at the thought of that other, so much more frightening, artist whose house this was and who might appear at any moment – embarked on a study of the view from his window – a Scots pine, a lawn fringed with shrubs and, in the distance, a strange–shaped monkey puzzle tree up the road in the Kimberley gardens. His grasp of perspective, Henry noticed, was improving and his work on the closer trees showed a pleasing sensitivity for detail.

Meanwhile he worked on sketches of his own, portraits of the boy, lit or in shadow as the sun moved across the sky, frowning with concentration as he bent over his drawing. That Wednesday, Thursday and Friday, he thought later, were three of the happiest he could remember, tinged as they were by the knowledge that they must soon end and that the ending would bring with it the possibility of unknown horrors.

And so, when he arrived at his friend's house on Saturday morning, he was distressed but not surprised to be told that Orion had gone home.

"Was he fit to walk, do you think? Will he be all right?"

"Of course he will. He's young and strong and it's no distance. You go down now and have a cup of tea with Charles."

Amy, overseeing the turning out of her now empty, guest bedroom, shooed Henry downstairs. Charles, she knew, wanted a serious talk with him.

His mother would be at work until midday and Alfred was busy on the pleasure boats at weekends so that the house was empty when Orion arrived home. After Churchfield it seemed very small and dark and the noise of the Blacker family next door where five young children ran about shrieking, seemed much closer and more intrusive than it had before. The walk, short though it had been, had tired him and he lowered himself cautiously against the pain in his ribs into his mother's wooden–armed chair in the empty kitchen. Her breakfast cup and saucer lay on the drainer and on the table the teapot, under its leather cosy, was still warm but, although he would have liked some tea, the effort of lifting it was too great and he sat staring out into the yard where his runner beans had grown long and would be tough and stringy and the outer leaves of his cabbages had been comprehensively chewed away by caterpillars.

His flowers were also suffering from neglect. The nasturtiums, whose bright trumpets of yellow, orange and deep scarlet had scrambled over the bean sticks, were tangled and overgrown and he could see even from here that they were thick with black fly. The carnations, which had let out a rich scent that almost masked the smells of the privy and the pig sty three doors up, were brittle from lack of watering and choked with looping stalks of bindweed and their few surviving flowers bent forwards over the flagstones, were dull and lacking in colour.

In the short time he had been from home his patch of garden had suffered badly.

Ida Goss was glad – she supposed she must be – to have him back. He looked pale, she noticed as she came in through the yard door. He also looked plumper in the face, from lying in bed, she supposed, and being fed rich food. But he moved awkwardly in his chair, as though he was still in pain, and it was hard to mask the feeling of irritation that this was one more thing to worry about.

"I'll make us a cuppa." She moved the kettle to the hotter part of the range and sat down at the table with a sigh. "Then we 'ave to talk about you and this Mr Tuke."

Chapter 24

Mr Cyril didn't seem over-pleased to see him back but then that wasn't his way. Not that there wasn't plenty for him to do and certainly more than he could manage when it still hurt to bend or to lift. Mr Cyril's nephew had been worse than useless, according to Ricky, and spent most of his time smoking behind the shed. He hadn't long been home from South Africa – although quite long enough to find himself a job if he'd set his mind to it – and when he wasn't hiding from his uncle he was going on about the bloody Boers and what a tricky bunch of rogues they were and the marvels of some place he called Joberg that Ricky just wished he'd go back to.

The nephew didn't come in the day Orion started back – too much drink the night before, Ricky reckoned – and the leeks and celery needed earthing up and there were no potatoes in the boxes, since the nephew had done as little digging as possible and Ricky had been busy with tidying the raspberry canes.

"I suppose you'll say you're too injured to dig," Mr Cyril snarled, so that Orion realised he wasn't going to get any sort of an easy ride and went off to do his best in spite of the scorching pain in his ribs. He was much slower than normal though and after a while Jacka appeared silently next to him, took his fork and gestured towards the spinach which needed cutting at the top end of the garden.

This brought him closer to Mr Cyril, glowering from the selling table, but it was easier work, if still painful, bending to gather and then bunch the thick growth of leaves and setting them in their boxes for the morning hotel round. Ricky meanwhile was harvesting early onions and, when cutting the spinach was too painful for him to continue, Orion sat on the bench by the potting shed, plaiting the stems for hanging. Mr Cyril, he noticed, went on glowering but onion plaiting was something Orion did more skilfully than any of them, even Jacka, so he said nothing and when his nephew did eventually turn up he told him to bugger off and not to come back.

"I can't afford to keep two of you idling about," Orion heard him say but it was something to know that Mr Cyril valued his 'idling' more than his nephew's.

In the afternoon he trimmed cabbages and set wasp traps amongst the plum trees but when Mr Cyril went off with the afternoon deliveries he felt too exhausted to do more than sit by the table to rest his throbbing ankle and wait for customers.

He was lucky, he thought afterwards, that several came in and he was needed there rather than down in the garden. Indeed, when Mr Cyril arrived back he was serving a lady with lettuce, chives and salad tomatoes and there was a boy waiting from one of the guest houses, wanting a couple of gallons of potatoes. Mr Cyril could hardly complain, he thought, that he was doing nothing.

And then Henry appeared and it was obvious from his fustian trousers, the navy blue jersey and the red scarf knotted at his neck, that he had been on his boat. He had missed being on the water, he had told Orion last week. He was working on a painting of a French barque in the harbour and was worried in case she might set sail before he had finished his detailed sketches of her masts and rigging.

He should go off and do his sketches while he could, Orion had said, but Henry had fixed his dark eyes on him and said it wasn't possible.

"I shan't leave you on your own any more than I have to. No matter if she sails. There'll be others."

"Where's Mr Rowse?" he asked now, frowning to see Orion lifting the gallon scoop to pour the potatoes into the bag the boy held open in front of him. "You shouldn't be doing that," and Orion saw the boy's mouth drop open as the tall gentleman, who wore rough clothes but spoke with an educated voice and had elegantly trimmed hair, seized the scoop and started to shovel the potatoes himself.

"'E's over there."

Terrified, Orion jerked his head in the direction of the little yard where Mr Cyril and Jacka would be undoing the pony from his traces. It was Jacka's job to give him his hay and water and sweep out the yard and Mr Cyril would be back here any moment, reluctant, as always, to leave customers to anyone else.

"There you are then lad," Henry put down the scoop, gently twisted the astonished boy's ear and wiped his hands on the side of his trousers. "I'll have a half pound of tomatoes and a bunch of parsley," he said as the boy scuttled off through the archway. "And you look pale. You should stop now. You've done enough for one day."

"I do 'ave to work." Orion put four tomatoes onto the scales. "Mr Cyril's been very good to leave me keep my job."

It was strange to see Henry out here. A customer. A gentleman, in spite of his clothes. An important man. When most of last week they had sat together in Mr Hemy's smart bedroom, sketching and talking as friends. Very strange indeed and harder to get used to than that older relationship, the evenings they had spent painting and sketching in Henry's studio, bicycling around the quiet lanes, or rowing around the headland to Newporth. Perhaps that had been strange too but somehow he had got used to it and he supposed the difference was that last week they had been in a bedroom. Some of the time he had been undressed and in bed. It was not the sort of thing he was used to and now, seeing Henry again, he felt as confused and awkward as he had felt all those months ago when they didn't know each other at all.

"Good afternoon Mr Rowse!" Henry's voice took on a new and public heartiness. "Another fine day, wouldn't you say? I'm glad to see you have your young assistant back. I understand he was beaten by a group of thugs on the night of the King's coronation." If he had been looking in Orion's direction he would have seen him start nervously but he kept his face turned away. "One of the boatmen was telling me," he went on blithely. "A terrible thing to happen, and on such a day too. But I hope you won't over-work him now he's back. I'm sure you can't afford to lose such an able employee."

Mr Cyril looked more toad-faced than usual. Yes, he agreed, it had been a terrible thing. He wondered what Falmouth was coming to. And he had been about to tell young Goss he'd done enough for the day. His mother, he added, rubbing his hands together, had been worried about the lad. He'd promised he'd watch out for him.

Which was more, Orion thought, than he knew. And more than he believed.

"I thought you might like to come out to the cottage." Henry looks both ways along Woodlane, as they come out of the gateway and cross the road. "I've instructed Mrs Fouracre to cook one of her ham and herbie pies. Then I'll order a trap to take you home so you don't have the long walk."

"Walking don' 'urt." Orion fixes on one thought at a time. "I c'n walk 'ome easy. I'll go now," he goes on, staring down at his boots now that he has come to the difficult part. "I'll walk 'ome now," he expands, as if he needs to make things completely clear. "I don' think… It wou'n be right…"

But it is impossible to explain to this not-so-familiar man; this customer; this gentleman, what he wants to say. That they cannot be seen together, him and Mr Tuke. That if Alfred or, worse, his father, hears that he has been seen with him again, far more terrible things will happen to him than have happened already. That the times spent sketching and painting in the studio or down at Sunny Cove, or cycling along the quiet evening lanes are over. None of these things can happen again.

"I'm goin' 'ome," he says firmly, setting off as he speaks in the direction of the town. "Thank you very much," he adds but without looking round and without being entirely sure what he is thanking him for.

And Henry, who left Piebox early this afternoon and although his fingers were desperate to go on working, in order to ensure that his boy got away from the garden safely and would get safely to Pennance Cottage, from where he would ensure that, much later in the evening, he would get safely home, stares after the determined figure, limping alongside the ancient grey stone wall, watches in helpless silence until he reaches the brow of the hill, silhouetted dark against the blue brilliance of a late summer sky and then turns unhappily away towards his own home.

Chapter 25

It was several weeks before his injuries were properly healed. Dull, miserable weeks in which he went to work, came home, went occasionally to the Queens Arms and every Sunday to chapel – morning and evening, to make up for all those Sundays when he had not gone at all.

This did not pass unnoticed and when a visiting preacher, credited with many hundreds of conversions, came to the chapel he made mention from the pulpit of 'a young man among you who had strayed from the path of the Lord but who has returned.' They should all give thanks, he instructed them, and Orion, realising with some embarrassment that he was the young man referred to, saw his mother, unusually, beaming across at him.

He was proud of him, Reverend Ogden told him afterwards, taking him by the hand as he tried to leave without being noticed. Proud that Orion had seen the error of his ways and had returned to the fold. He must feel great happiness, he went on. The inexpressible happiness of giving himself to the Lord.

Orion tugged at the hem of his Sunday jacket and hoped some other redeemed sinner might attract the minister's attention. For he could hardly disagree with Mr Ogden's words but he felt, at this moment, no happiness at all; certainly nothing to compare with the joy of those evenings in Henry's studio or bicycling with him along the quiet summer lanes. That might have been described as 'great', perhaps even 'inexpressible'. By contrast the dreary life he had been leading these past weeks had held no joy – or hope of future joy – for him at all.

Outside the chapel his fellow Wesleyans shook hands, congratulated each other on the continued warmth of the weather, shook heads over rumours of the new king's indiscretions and dispersed slowly across the Moor. Ida Goss moved off towards home where she had a meat pie in the oven for herself and Orion and, should he return from the Chain Locker in a fit state to eat it, Alfred.

"Don't you be long now," she told Orion. But a fellow worshipper claimed her attention and she failed to notice her son walk off, without answering, in the opposite direction.

From Market Street a number of narrow alleyways – they are called 'opes'– lead between shops and down to the harbour's edge. One of these – it is called Anstey's Ope, presumably after some long–dead seaman or fisherman or shopkeeper – is Orion's favourite. Here, between the blank walls of a tobacconist's and a butcher's, a damp passageway even in this warm weather leads to a narrow ledge built out from the harbour wall and a flight of stone steps into the water. Because the ledge is so narrow – less than two foot wide – it is protected by an iron railing against which Orion now leans, staring down at the clear water and the strands of brown seaweeds drifting gently with the currents.

The tide is rising. Each wavelet lapping against the harbour wall leaves its wet marking higher up and the green weed, dry and dull looking on the upper stones, is restored, minute by minute to bright and gleaming wetness. And two crabs, he notices as he stares downwards, are clambering up it, aspiring for some reason which Orion, and perhaps the crabs themselves, cannot understand, to heave themselves up the wall. It is quite obviously hopeless and each time one of them claws its way a few inches upwards it is knocked back down by a wave or possibly its own exhaustion and yet they persist. Flailing with tiny claws for a hold on the slippery weed. Determined, it seems, not to give up their pointless struggle.

Depressed, Orion turns away, stares out instead across the harbour, sees, moored off Trefusis Point, the converted yacht with the glass–roofed deck that he recognises as Henry's floating studio, although he has never been aboard like Henry's other boys – Harry and Bert, Johnny and the rest.

"They love it out there. You should come too," he used to say, until he realised this was something Orion would never do.

Which was when he stopped inviting the others.

But now...now that Orion no longer visits him...now that Orion has returned to the Lord... Henry is a man who loves company. He will not sit brooding alone in Pennance Cottage.

And then, as if Orion has somehow conjured him with his thoughts, he sees three raters, jibs and mainsails swelling in the breeze, making down river from the direction of the Falmouth Sailing Club. They make a beautiful sight – even to Orion, who has never sailed, such hobbies being beyond the reach of any working man – with their elegant lines and high peaked mainsails and Henry's Red Heart, he can see is in the lead. He recognises the red and white chequers of his racing flag flying from the mast, recognises the familiar figure of Henry himself in his dark jersey and yachting cap, sitting at the helm, and sees another figure, his crew, forward in the cockpit, leaning towards the jib.

It will be Bert White, he imagines, who often crews for him – and models for him as well. Who works in the foundry at the docks and has, according to Henry, 'beautiful, fine drawn features, almost as fine as yours, Orion.'

Slates have fallen from the roof of the tobacconist's shop and broken pieces lie along the narrow ledge. Angrily Orion kicks out, skittering several shards which splash into the water, disturbing the still–struggling crabs before he turns his back on the three yachts whose sails dip in unison to starboard in a sudden gust of wind and slouches back up the ope, hands pressed deep into his jacket pockets. The heavy scrape of his boots against the stone pavings echoes off the walls and beats despairingly against his ears.

His mother, when he arrived home late for his dinner, was in a rage. The fact that Alfred did not arrive at all made no difference, unless her anger at his absence made her still more angry with the present Orion.

"I come rushing 'ome to 'ave your dinner ready and what do you care?" She thumped a plate of pie and mash onto the table with such force that it might easily have broken. "Nothin', that's what! It don' matter one bit to you that I've been slaving 'ere. It don' matter to you that I might like a bit o' company. An don' you just sit there staring!" Changing tack with startling suddenness, she seized the pan of gravy and held it over his plate like a challenge. "Now you've come, get on an' eat. I don' 'ave all day to stand round watching you."

Tipping a stream of hot gravy over Orion's mash she slammed the pan onto the range, then snatched the water bucket from its place under the sink.

"Leave that. I'll do the dishes when I've finished."

But when Ida was this angry there was no appeasing her and Orion could only listen as she stamped across the yard, boots scraping violently on the flagstones, banged the pail onto the ground and started to pump so energetically that the water thundered against its metal sides. As she came back into the kitchen, her apron dark with splashed water, Orion bent his head over his plate and thrust into his mouth food he could hardly taste for misery.

It was well over an hour before Ida consented to stop banging about the kitchen, boiling water for the dishes, rubbing down the range, cleaning the sink, scrubbing the table, and she was about to start brushing the floor when Orion, hovering in the background, daring neither to leave her or attempt to help, lost control of his own temper.

"Leave it, Ma!" And, astonishing them both, he snatched the broom from her hand. "Go and sit down. It won' do no good to go wearing yourself out an' you're meant to rest Sundays. It says so in the bible."

"Tha's all very well…" But the fight went out of her as her son turned, broom held high as if he might be about to hit her.

"I said sit down. You keep saying you need a rest. Well darn well 'ave one."

This time, appalled by his swearing – and on a Sunday – Ida Goss did as she was told.

"I'm sorry I were late." Orion comes into the parlour with a tray of tea and a plate of scones and lardy cake. His mother, he rightly suspects, has had no dinner but is unlikely to admit it. "I… I 'ad things to think about."

But they know, both of them, although Ida, sitting upright in the best armchair, says nothing, that the fault is not really his. That the fault lies with the still absent Alfred who will be drinking in some ale house, who will return when he has no money left and will see no reason to apologise for his behaviour. And that the fault also lies, although neither of them will admit this even to themselves, with Ida, who should have long given up expecting him to behave otherwise.

"I worry." Ida swallows tea, considers the scone on her plate and allows herself, very slightly, to relax. "Ever since… what 'appened, I worry about you."

"There's no need. It won' 'appen again."

Orion stirs sugar into his own tea and stares across at his mother. Who looks worn out, as well she might after her bout of furious energy. Her full cheeks, always high-coloured, are a livid red and her heavy breathing, even after ten minutes, still causes her chest to rise and fall. Around them the parlour settles into its Sunday gloom. The small windows with their dark curtains let in very little light. Grandfather Goss's clock marks the passing seconds with its solemn tock. A brown and yellowed photograph of some grim-faced aunt glares from the wall.

As Henry races Red Heart across the sunlit waves of Falmouth bay, the wind pulling at his dark hair and the fair curls of the beautiful Bert White in the cockpit before him, Orion sits unhappily on the overstuffed leather of his mother's ancient couch and stares into a future that holds no promise of any pleasure.

"It won' 'appen again," he repeats. "Not never."

Alfred and his bullying friend beat him because he was a nancy boy – or so they said. Because of his friendship with Henry. But Henry has not visited the market garden for almost three weeks now. He is no longer Orion's friend, he must already have forgotten him and there will be no further beatings.

His mother, biting at last into her scone, looks back at him and says nothing.

Chapter 26

The weather that October, although still mild, turned wet. Day after day the rain beat in off the sea and Henry woke to the mourning bell of the St Antony's lighthouse, tolling across the bay.

It fitted, he thought, his mood.

The sun, which he had always seen as a life–giving force, was invisible most days behind low–hanging clouds. The sea, grey–green and tumultuous, beat against the rocks below his home, crashing in seething white foam up the gullies with a rumbling echo that made his head ache. Gulls shrieked and called, falling about the sky as if they were under attack, and made it ache still more.

Or was it, he wondered, not his head but his heart that ached? For had there not always been days, even weeks, like this? And had he not enjoyed such wild weather in the past? Striding across the beaches and around the cliffs, head on into the wind and rain, rejoicing in the violence of the elements. Sailing Red Heart when other, more cautious men, remained safely ashore. Sketching in turbulent seas and biting winds from the lurching deck of Piebox until even he felt so ill that he was forced to give in.

But not now. Not this October.

He works; of course he works, it is in his nature to work but only in the cottage, with the reluctant help of Mrs Fouracre, who insists she has better things to do than stand around while he sketches her. And, because he is a sociable man and has many invitations, he goes out, to the pleasure and relief of those friends whom he has neglected in the past months. Plays bridge with Charles Fox, meets other friends at the Falmouth Hotel, dines with the Bulls in Marlborough house and the Hemys at Churchfield.

The Hemys… Charles and Amy have been unusually generous this autumn with their invitations. Henry has always been a welcome guest but the sombre, devout Charles is not usually such an enthusiastic host. This September and October, however, he has allowed, even encouraged, Amy to arrange weekly dinner parties and Henry is always invited. One might almost imagine, Fox has commented over bridge, that Hemy is worried about him.

And so Henry has plenty to occupy his time. For, apart from these social engagements, he has done other things. He has watched his friend Johnny Jackett, returned safely, thank heavens, from the South African war, play rugby. He has played ping pong with Charlie Mitchell at the boys' club run by Charles Fox. He has been out in a racing rival's five ton sloop to see how she performs and is seriously considering commissioning a similar craft for himself. He has spent time overseeing the hanging of new paintings at the Falmouth Art Gallery of which he is one of the most distinguished patrons...

And yet... And yet it is not enough.

He needs an outlet for his energies, he tells Charles Fox, pacing restlessly about Fox's drawing room before dinner, immaculate in evening dress and yet somehow less... 'glossy' is the word that comes to Fox's mind, than he appeared only a couple of months before.

It is that wretched boy, of course. He has no doubt of this. Henry is missing his company, which is something Charles can understand. And yet the whole business is, quite obviously, impossible. Henry has allowed himself – as he has never done before – to become besotted. His enthusiasm has carried him beyond the bounds of common sense, although not, Fox feels quite sure, the bounds of propriety, and the boy's family have got wind of what appears to them to be an unnatural friendship.

He too has heard of the brutal attack on the night of the coronation and Henry, although reluctant to discuss the subject, has admitted that the injuries were inflicted by the boy's own brother and that he is terrified such a thing might happen again.

165

And so,

"Why not take a trip?" Fox suggests, attempting to divert his friend. "France. Or Italy. You love Italy. You often say you intend to go back."

"In October? " Henry snorts and turns away up the room. "November, by the time I make arrangements. What would I do in Italy in November?"

"Go to the South. Naples. Sicily even. It will be warm enough there. Go for a month or six weeks. You could be back in London before Christmas…"

"No." Henry stops pacing. Stares with some concentration at a painting on the wall opposite – it is one of his own – and frowns. "I would rather stay here."

"Is that wise?"

Even as he asks it his friend wonders if the question itself is a wise one and Henry, his attention still apparently fixed on the painting – two naked boys towelling themselves dry on a rocky shore – does not answer for some time.

"Probably not," he concedes, stepping back and, at last, smiling. "Probably not."

And Fox's manservant appears in the doorway to announce dinner and the conversation is allowed to lapse.

Nor would it be wise to visit Mr Rowse's market garden. He knows that as well. Not even to buy vegetables. Not that there are many of these at this time of year. Swede, of course. Cabbage. Potatoes. Onions. Nothing to get excited about. Summer fruits have long gone and Mrs Fouracre already has a store of apples, eaters and cookers, carefully wrapped in newspaper and placed in boxes in a cool outhouse and no need of any more.

And yet… And yet it is, in the end, impossible to resist. Impossible to occupy himself so fully that he can forget, towards the end of Orion's working day – earlier, at this time of year, when darkness comes early – that if he walks along Woodlane he may, quite by chance, meet him on his way home.

It has been another dreary day. Not especially cold but damp and grey with a thick drizzle gusting in off the bay from early morning and no point in going out on Piebox since there would be nothing to see. And so he has worked in his studio on his painting of Mrs Fouracre, whose figure is by now sketched in fully enough for her to no longer be needed as a model. 'The Widow', it is, provisionally, called and he has clothed her in black, placed a bible in her hand and spent most of his day, with the aid of a few draperies, working on the reflections of gaslight against her skirt and face.

By five thirty the drizzling rain has stopped and the sky cleared to a leaden grey–blue, lightening towards white at the horizon. This far south west the light has not yet completely faded but the hawthorn hedge outside his studio window stands out in dark and prickling silhouette against a paler sky and he can still see the redness of the few berries that the birds have not yet eaten.

Stepping back from his easel, Henry glares at the black yards of bombazine, stretches his aching back and flings down his brush. There is still enough light, he thinks; still enough time, for a walk. He needs air, after a day in this confined space, breathing in the smell of oil paints, of gas fumes, of the dusty material he has draped across the model's chair... And, after a day of relative inactivity, he is desperately in need of exercise.

The water fowl, as he passes Swanpool water, are already settling for the night. Small scuttlings and squeakings rise from the reed beds, an unseen duck disturbs the water as it lands further out and through a gap in the bushes he sees the bright whiteness of two swans against the dark water, making their unhurried way towards their nesting place.

A pony trap passes him on the road. The driver calls a greeting as he turns up the steep hill alongside the burial ground and Henry follows the hollow clip clop of the hooves, slowing as the animal tires on the gradient.

Perhaps one day, he thinks, trudging uphill past the overgrown cemetery wall, he may be buried here himself. It is peaceful enough, lined with elms and yew trees and overlooking the pool. One could have worse resting places. Although why in Heaven's name should he be thinking such thoughts? He, who is healthy and in his prime. Is it just the time of day – dusky evening, drawing towards night? Or the time of year? Or is this uncharacteristic morbidity simply the result of a gloomy day spent painting widow's weeds?

Mocking his melancholy with a bark of laughter, he strides out, taking the curving uphill slope at a speed that sets his heart thumping and causes him to pause, breathless, at the top. And who, he wonders, as he leans against the newly built granite wall of the bridge over the railway line, will visit his grave, wherever it may be? Who will keep warm his memory after his death? His sister and her sons, for his mother will, presumably, pre–decease him. His friends – probably not Hemy, who is twenty years his senior, but Fox and others. His boys – perhaps, but boys are fickle creatures and will not remember long and there will be no children of his own. He will not marry and will, therefore, leave no progeny.

In the distance he hears a train approaching down the line from Truro; the preparatory hum of the rails, the clatter of wheels, the sudden rush of steam preceding the appearance round a bend of the black, high–funnelled engine, sparks flying into the darkness, the sulphurous whiteness of its smoke engulfing him as he remains, unwisely, staring from the bridge. The dark engine, its footplate lit scarlet and orange from the fire, and the line of four carriages, their windows glowing yellow, clatter below him and Henry, thrilled, as always and in spite of the choking smoke that fills his throat and lungs, at the sight of such power, sets off again, striding towards the town.

Halfway along Woodlane, not far from Mr Rowse's market

garden, he slows his pace. It is almost dark by now, the sky a deep grey, although out over the bay long trails of cloud, tinged with pink and orange, promise a better day tomorrow and Henry, on a pavement that rises three feet above the muddy roadway, walks in the shadow of thick evergreen oaks and lime trees, planted at intervals on the outer edge, whose bushy stems, outgrowing from the base of their trunks, present a hazard to the unwary walker. Lights show in some of the large houses across the road but otherwise it is poorly lit and, it has been suggested in the Falmouth Packet, not always a safe place to walk.

This does not concern Henry, although, as an obvious gentleman, perhaps it should. But he is also a tall, well-built man and no easy prey for an assailant on what is, after all, a residential road. Pony traps – tradesmen making deliveries or gentlemen or ladies returning home – pass regularly and, once, one of the new motor cars which Henry dislikes so intensely. Business men pass on their way from town, who politely raise their hats, and roughly dressed dock-workers, clothes and faces black with grime, who ignore him. Two schoolboys weighed down with satchels come up from behind and pass him, chattering hard. A girl in uniform, some sort of nurse, he supposes, lets herself out of a front gate and closes it carefully behind her.

The market-garden, he tells himself, will not still be open and he pulls out his hunter, squints at it in the limited light and sees that it is well after six o'clock. The gates will be closed and Mr Rowse and his workers will have long gone home. There is no reason to pass it – and yet there is also no reason why he should not. He can turn down the narrow lane beyond the gates, which leads to a wooded dell and then out towards the sea front from where he can walk home along the cliff path and get some more of the fresh air he has been craving, even if the path will be in darkness.

But the gates, he sees as he comes closer, are still open. Indeed a flickering light glows out into the road as two women, heavy coats over their voluminous skirts, emerge with full baskets and go off in the direction of the town. Even this late there is trade, it seems, for vegetables.

The pavement opposite the gates is overhung with bushes from the gardens of the villas which line this side of the road. Henry pauses beside a thick laurel, reaches into his pocket for the cigarettes he sometimes keeps there and spends some moments opening the case. As he fumbles to light one a balding, bandy-legged man he recognises as Mr Rowse's silent assistant comes out into the road, looks up and down as if to check for customers and goes back inside. A moment or so later the tall gate, which is hooked back in the daytime against the inside of the wall, swings shut with a creak, followed by a clattering of bolts on the inside.

A couple of young clerks come chattering along the road towards Henry, who continues to make play of lighting his cigarette as they tip their hats and pass by. And he too should pass by, if he does not mean to arouse suspicion. Lurking, he tells himself with a grim smile, like some lovesick youth, standing well back now amongst the thickly-bunching laurel leaves so as not to be seen by the occupants of the trap that passes briskly along the roadway below.

The small doorway in the gate is pulled open from the inside and Mr Rowse steps cautiously over the threshold, followed by his silent assistant and then, after a moment of sickening anticipation, Orion. To whom Mr Rowse makes some comment as he pulls the door to and then bends to lock it.

"Yes Mr Cyril," he hears Orion say and, as the two older men turn away towards the town, he crosses the road to the high pavement where Henry is waiting.

"Good evening Orion. Imagine meeting you."

Henry, in the shadow of the laurels, startles the boy who steps suddenly sideways, his boots grating angrily against the pavings.

"My Gor! You din' 'alf make me jump. What you doin' 'ere?"

"I wanted to see how you were. Whether you'd recovered from your injuries."

The boy hesitates, looking down at the ground.

"I'm awright. My chest don' 'urt nor nothin'."

"Excellent news!" Henry winces inside himself at the boisterous vigour of his words. "I'm very glad to hear it," he says more quietly. "And your face? I can hardly see in this gloom. Are the cuts and bruises healed?"

"It's awright Sir... Mr Tuke."

So he is Sir Mr Tuke again Henry thinks sadly. And it will, almost certainly, take a long time to change matters – time that they may not have.

"You're late finishing, aren't you, Orion? Surely you don't work so late in the winter months?"

"At times we do 'ave to. There's a big lunch down the Royal tomorrow. They d' want the veg first thing so Mr Rowse said we should get boxed up tonight." The boy shifts on his feet, glancing nervously behind him. "Besides, we d'quite often get customers this time of day."

"In that case you must be thirsty. Why don't I treat you to a glass of ale?"

This is not what Henry has expected to say and as he speaks he sees his own anxiety mirrored in the boy's eyes. For where exactly does he intend taking him for this glass of ale? To one of the hotels on the sea front, where he meets his friends? To one of the alehouses in the town where Orion, perhaps, meets his friends?

"I dunno."

But neither of them knows what he means by this and for some moments they stand, each staring away from the other, saying nothing. Another car passes and this time Henry recognises it – there are few enough cars in Falmouth – as the vehicle owned by his friend and patron, Alfred de Pass. He has even ridden in it himself, although this is not an experience he wishes to repeat.

"I'll walk with you," he says, stung into action. Certainly not wanting Alfred, who is of uncertain temper but has fits of sociability, to see him and turn back. "Are you going home?"

Orion nods without speaking and Henry strides beside him up the side road.

This leads to a terrace of three-storied houses, fine buildings with stucco frontages, overlooking the harbour and the Carrick Roads, the broad area beyond the harbour mouth, guarded by the twin castles of St Mawes and Pendennis. On the far side of the harbour lights gleam in the little village of Flushing and in the large, sea–captains' houses that spread out along the waterfront, whilst below them boats rise and fall at their moorings, darker shadows on the liquid darkness.

As the road dips, the houses become smaller, just two stories now of unfaced granite, where children loiter in the narrow front yards, on the pavement and in the road. Three women stand gossiping across a low wall and neither Henry nor Orion speak as they pass, Henry wondering, nervously, if the boy knows any of them.

About halfway along the road they come to the gas lit windows of a public house. It is not one Henry has ever been inside but it looks decent enough with no louts lounging outside or sounds of rough behaviour coming from within.

"Why don't we go in here? I'll buy you that glass of ale?"

There is a narrow lobby and, to the left, the snug bar. Which is probably, he imagines, not the one Orion would have chosen if he were on his own. The boy, he notices, glances swiftly around the room but appears not to recognise the two elderly men playing cribbage by the window or the lanky clerk perched on a stool next to the narrow hatchway.

"So, have you been painting?"

Henry brings two glasses to the table by the wall where Orion, pale–faced in the half–light, sits on a wooden settle, eyes still

172

flickering nervously about the room.

"I don' 'ave no space…"

Nor, he might have added, any paints and Henry thumps his fist against his chin in annoyance at his own stupidity but persists.

"Or drawing. You used to draw in your bedroom, didn't you? I remember those sketches you showed me. The jacket on the chair, the window…"

But that was before. When Alfred had no suspicions. When Alfred could be relied on, at least on Friday nights, to be out of the way. Which is no longer the case.

For the Victoria, on which Alfred acts as crew for cruises up the river Fal, is laid up for the winter months and, although he picks up the occasional job rowing customers across to Flushing or up river to Penryn, his income is greatly reduced. At the same time his periods of idleness are greatly increased and it is not unusual for Orion to come home to find his brother snoring in bed, where he has obviously spent the entire day.

And where, in any case, with Alfred at home so often and so eager to poke his nose into his brother's affairs, could he hide a sketching pad and pencils; let alone paints?

Chapter 27

"Come out to the cottage again Orion. Come on Sunday. Your work's still there in the studio."

The snug was filling up and each time the door opened, with a creak of its hinges as if they resented the disturbance, Henry saw how the boy's glance moved instantly towards it. He was, it was obvious, increasingly uncomfortable.

"I d'go chapel Sundays."

"Surely, once in a while…" Henry forced the irritation from his voice but Orion, anxious as he was, did not miss the shadow of a frown which crossed his face. "You work so hard. Look at the time you finished work this evening. You deserve some recreation, lad. More than that, you need it."

And what sort of god would want to keep a seventeen year old already working six days of the week, imprisoned for – he had no idea how long Wesleyan services were but he had heard of hour–long sermons and compulsory Sunday schools – on the seventh? Why should the boy be trapped inside a chapel, listening to the sanctimonious words of some pompous little minister, when he could be opening his mind to the beauty of the world?

"I'm sorry sir…Henry… I d'in mean to make you angry."

"I'm not angry. Or not with you. Just with the system that…"

The system, he would have liked to say, that kept lads like Orion in their place. Lads who started at the bottom of the pile and were forced to stay there, with no chance to make something of their lives.

"It doesn't matter," he said instead. "Would you like another?" He indicated Orion's almost empty glass. "Or do you want to go?" For it was obvious the boy was getting no pleasure from the occasion and there was little point in prolonging it.

Outside it is almost completely dark. The gas lights give only a dull and flickering light and little comes from the neighbouring houses. On the blackness of the water below them and across three terraces of slate roofs, three small boats – fishing boats Henry imagines – make towards the harbour mouth, their mast-lights rising and falling on the swell, and the wind blows in, cold and salt–tasting, as he and Orion set off in the direction of Jacobs Ladder, the one hundred and eleven, granite steps that lead precipitously down to the Moor.

"I promised to drop in on the Hemys," Henry lies to give himself an excuse to continue walking in the opposite direction from his home and Orion, feeling that he should send greetings or at least thanks for their kindness but uncertain how to do this, says nothing.

And then everything changes and the evening, up to now merely awkward, becomes a nightmare…

Three men; big men with broad faces, wide shoulders and a hefty build; men in rough, workmen's clothing with caps pulled low over their faces; men whose breath… whose whole bodies… reek of ale, tobacco and other, less definable, filth, appear from a side alleyway and stand blocking the pavement in front of them. And, for a moment, neither Henry nor Orion think anything of it. The men have paused to wait for someone or to decide which direction to take. As Henry and Orion come nearer, they will move sideways to let them pass. They may mutter an apology or touch their caps, since Henry is so obviously a gentleman.

It is not until one of them – the tallest, broadest–shouldered of the three – moves forward with a speed that catches them off guard, seizes Orion's shoulder in his great paw and twists him so that he falls sideways against the low wall at the front of a house, that they realise their mistake.

"Hey you! Leave the boy alone!"

Henry reaches out to stop the boy falling, only to feel his arms grabbed from behind, wrenched upwards in a wrestling hold from which he is powerless to escape, as a hoarse voice – it is now he notices the stench of ale and tobacco – asks who is going to make him.

"You an' 'oos army?" it demands as the third man grasps Henry's head under his stinking arm pit, twisting it so that he stumbles sideways and falls to the ground, against which the two men pin him with their considerable weight.

His first thought – if the rush of images pelting through his mind can be given such a name – is that they are thieves; jobless men, of which there are many in the district, who have seen him take money from his wallet in the public house and have sneaked out to lie in wait. In which case they are welcome to it. To the wallet and the contents, which are insignificant to Henry but may satisfy them. They are welcome to the gold hunter watch in his coat pocket, inherited from his father and quite valuable, but not valuable enough to physically fight for, even if he were in a position to do so. They are welcome, if they want it, to the coat itself, which can be replaced…

And then he realises that these men are not thieves. They are not after his wallet, his watch or his coat. The hands that press him against the rough, hard ground are not searching his pockets; one man has, in fact, let go of him whilst the other, tightening his grip on his arms, places a knee in the small of his back, holding him down more helplessly than ever. Raising his head as best he can, he sees, through the blur of his watering eyes, Orion struggling and squealing in his assailant's arms; sees the man who has released him place a hand across the boy's mouth…

"You listen 'ere nancy-boy," he growls. "'F'you know wa's good for ee you'll make yerself scarce or you'll get worse'n this by a long ways. This 'ere's your warning see? You jus' take 'eed of 'n." And, shuffling backwards to take aim, he glances behind him, raises one leg to deliver a massive thump of his boot against Orion's slumping body and, with surprising speed for so big a man, thuds off in the direction of Jacob's Ladder, followed by his companions.

The woman who hurried from her house, towed by the small boy who had watched everything from the first floor window, was anxious to help – but not particularly helpful. Possibly, Henry thought afterwards, because she could think no further than summoning the police, which was not what he, or Orion, wanted.

"They din' ought to be allowed to get away with it," she kept saying, rubbing her hands, which had been wet but which must long since have dried, against the front of her overall. It was dreadful, she said several times, to think of respectable men being robbed, right outside her door.

"'Ow is 'ee, your son?" she asked, as Henry bent over Orion who lay hunched and moaning on the pavement. "Should I fetch 'im a cup of water? Then I'll get young Ernest to run down the police station."

"No thank you. I mean, some water would be welcome, if you wouldn't mind. In fact…" It was astonishing that no–one else had come past and yet perhaps the whole incident had lasted only seconds. "I wonder if you would be good enough to allow us to come inside for a few minutes?"

The house was shabby but decent enough, the boy Ernest seemed glad to substitute helping Henry support Orion for the drama of running to summon the police and his mother's attention was demanded by the howling of an unseen baby almost as soon as she had fetched their cups of water. Orion, leaning, eyes closed, against the back of his chair, looked pale and sick but was not, it appeared, badly hurt. Henry's arms ached from their wrenching, his knees were bruised, his face stung from being scraped against the ground and he was shaking from the shock of the assault but he was a strong man, used to the rigours of sailing his yacht, and had suffered no serious damage.

But he had not been able to protect Orion. That was what shook him. That he had been so helpless. And that it was all – he gulped the cold, earth–tasting water and forced himself to confront reality – his fault.

He had befriended the boy. He had waited for him tonight. He had insisted that they come to this public place, where obviously they had been seen together. And now the boy had been assaulted and threatened and was obviously terrified.

"I'll get us a cab. The boy can take a note."

But the cab rank at Market Strand might not be manned at this time on an October night or a cab man willing to come up the steep slope of Trelawney Hill to this address unless Henry signed the note with his own name, which was not something he wished to do.

"Or better still. He can take a note to Hemy. He can organise something." A note to Charles need only be signed with his Christian name. "Yes!" Taking action made him feel immediately better. "That's what I'll do."

He felt in his pocket for a pen and notebook.

"No!" Orion jerked forward in his seat, eyes wide open. "Not for me, anyways. I'll walk 'ome."

"Don't be ridiculous!" The thought of the boy, still shaken, walking back down Jacob's Ladder, with those three louts still abroad and, quite likely, with no compunction about flinging him down the steps in the darkness, made Henry forget completely his aching arms and battered knees. "I can't allow it. You can't possibly go anywhere on your own."

"Well, I can't go nowhere with you, can I?" The boy spoke quietly, sulkily even, and sat back in his chair. "I can't never go nowhere with you. Not ever again."

Chapter 28

"I'm desperate my dear man. You have to help me."

Henry had been forced to let Orion make his own way home, stipulating only that he should avoid Jacob's Ladder and stick to the more open roadway of Trelawney Hill, before instructing the driver of the trap sent by Charles in response to his note to take him home to Pennance Cottage.

Next morning, after a sleepless night and in some pain from his wrenched shoulders, he walked the two miles or so to Churchfield where his friend was obviously expecting him. It was equally obvious that he was in a sombre mood.

Amy was not at home. She had taken the girls to visit their cousins, Charles told him, and from the expression on his face Henry suspected him of arranging this so that they might talk without interruption.

It was hard to shake off the feeling of having been summoned to the headmaster's study – possibly, he felt, conscious of his damaged face and aching limbs, for fighting – although Charles' studio was far from intimidating. It was, in fact, the room Henry loved, in normal circumstances, more than any other. Enormous, divided by screens and flooded with light from the conservatory at the north end, it was a studio to envy. There was a music corner with an olive green grand piano, built to Charles' own design with a stool and music stands to match. There was a fine fireplace. There were rich and elegant window hangings. And there were, of course, pictures. Finished works on the walls, sketches and studies on frames and tables around the room and the painting on which he was working on the easel before which Charles was standing. A sea scene, naturally. A grey, lashing November sea and a cutter, flung sideways by the winds, making head–on towards the viewer, spume flying wildly. So vivid that Henry could almost feel the chill of the waves and admired, even envied, his friend's technical ability.

But this was not why he was here. And Charles, dressed in his drab painting jacket, put down his brush and palette as he came into the room as if he were turning to other business.

"What it is now?" He gestures towards a chair but Henry is too full of unease and nervous energy to sit.

"I'm desperate, my dear man," he says then. "You have to help me."

He paces the length of the room before turning to stare back at his friend. Who stands, bristling eyebrows raised, regarding him solemnly.

"I assume," he says at last, "that this is something to do with your wild request last night. And your, if I may say so, somewhat battered appearance. What have you been up to Harry? Have you fallen among thieves?"

If this is the case, his expression seems to suggest, Henry has only himself to blame.

"You could say so. These three… ruffians… set on us. On Wodehouse Terrace." He fingers his damaged cheek. "Two of them caught me by the arms and flung me to the ground…."

'Us'? But Charles pushes the thought, for the moment, to the back of his mind.

"You were robbed? Have you contacted the police? Did they take…"

But Henry shakes his head and resumes his pacing.

"No. That wasn't…" He pauses at the far end of the room, turns, contemplates, or so it seems, a study of a seagull staring into a rock pool, takes a deep breath, "They quite obviously did not intend to rob me," he says. He speaks quietly, causing Charles to lean forwards, frowning slightly. "It was a warning."

"A warning?"

Charles is not a man for melodrama, which is what this sounds like, but as he contemplates his friend, his handsome head bent forward, shoulders drooped, as though he is about to make a confession, he takes pity on him.

"My dear fellow…" He puts out a hand and leads Henry to the captain's chair in front of his easel. "Just tell me what has been going on," he says in a much gentler tone of voice. "I'm sure we can work out some sort of plan of action."

"Oh Charles!" Just for a moment the thought of his grave, severely clad friend working on a 'plan of action' causes Henry to smile and then the smile slips suddenly sideways and he presses his hand to his mouth as he starts, quite helplessly, to sob.

Charles, shocked, embarrassed and, for the first time for as long as he can remember, uncertain what he should do, retreats to the far end of the room, where he stands very still, head bowed, quite possibly in prayer.

"I'm so sorry." Henry feels for a handkerchief and wipes it across his face. "I feel so desperate." Which is what, Charles thinks, he has already said. "I have lain awake all night, trying to think what I should do. Well, I *know* what I should do. I know what you would tell me to do. I simply cannot do it, Charles. Forgive me, I cannot."

"And what is it? That you should do; that I would tell you to do and you cannot do?"

Charles stares out of the window. The elms are bare of leaves but the camellias below them are already, he notes, in bud. He is fairly confident that he knows the answer to his own question but stands quietly, waiting for Henry to confirm it.

"It's… the boy." Of course it is. But Charles has never heard his friend sound so … defeated, is the word that comes to mind, and this is something new. "I care for him, Charles. Very much. But…" He looks up as his friend turns towards him. His eyes, bloodshot and wet with tears, beseech him to believe. "There has been no impropriety," he insists. "You must believe that," and he reaches out a hand towards Charles. Whose instinct would be – he cannot help but glance towards a bible lying on a small, occasional table – to ask him to swear on it but, although Henry is no longer a practising Quaker, he knows this would be wrong.

181

For Quakers, he is well aware, do not swear oaths, since this implies double standards of truth. And perhaps Henry can read his thoughts because,

"I do not lie, Charles," he says quietly and Charles, believing him, nods his head.

"So tell me," he says instead, "about this boy." And pulling a chair towards him, sits down opposite Henry. "It is, of course, the boy who came here? The boy who was beaten on the night of the coronation?"

The boy whom he and Amy have discussed on several occasions. Whom Amy accepted unquestioningly into her house, into her best, guest bedroom, as a young protégé of Henry's who had met with a mishap. And Charles, seeing some of the sketches he produced under Henry's tutelage, has noted that the boy possesses some sort of raw talent. That his sketches, simple of line and lacking the inhibitions of so many 'taught' artists, show an energy, a truth of observation that may perhaps repay nurturing.

But who is also a handsome, well–built boy and Charles' thick brows knit, almost menacingly, in a frown, it being hard not to suspect that it may have been this, rather than his talent, that has attracted Henry. Who, he has to remember, has friends, mainly in London but also in Falmouth, with whom Charles, the pious, sober husband and father would never consort. (He has not, naturally, shared these thoughts with Amy. Although – the trial and subsequent imprisonment of Oscar Wilde having been widely, if circumspectly, reported in the newspapers – she is almost certainly more informed on these matters than he would prefer, or perhaps imagines, her to be.)

Henry stares down at the floor.

"I have been… encouraging him. He has talent you know. Untutored, of course, but he can draw, and paint, and, given the opportunity… I was hoping to sponsor him for some classes at the School of Art," he breaks into his own thoughts. "Fool that I was, I thought it might actually be possible!"

He thumps his hand against the wooden arm of the chair, shaking his head angrily, although whether this anger is directed at fate, his own stupidity or something else, Charles cannot imagine.

"I gave him lessons." He regains control and goes on in more measured tones. "Out at Pennance. Most evenings during the summer and at weekends. And we did other things. Bicycle rides. Swimming. That sort of thing. You understand?"

He looks up, despairingly, at Charles. Who nods. Understanding, he feels, all too well.

"I have become very fond of the boy. I feel for him as a father for his son." Charles sniffs and rubs at his moustache but Henry takes no notice. "I get pleasure from his company. From teaching him… But now…"

Henry stares down the room, seeing nothing of its charms. Staring into a distance which holds nothing but bleakness. For a long time – but Charles can maintain silences and does not interrupt this one – he says nothing and then,

"Others obviously see it differently," he says coldly. "These attacks… Both times, they've called him a nancy-boy." He speaks the words with distaste. "He's not, of course. I know – forgive me Charles – I know what… boys of that kind are like and Orion is not one of them. And nor, for that matter, am I," and now he looks across at his friend with an expression that, in spite of the red–rimmed eyes, is dignified. And open, Charles tells himself. The gaze of a man who is telling the truth.

Somewhere at the back of the house a door bangs. Footsteps – heavy steps that must come from one of his sons for no servant would be that careless – thump on the stairs, but Charles is not to be disturbed in his studio and no–one will come in.

"So this… attack. On yourself and the boy. You said it was a warning?"

Henry nods.

"The boy has a father," he says quietly.

"I see."

And for the first time in the conversation Charles feels that he does see. Quite clearly.

"He is estranged from the boy's mother. Apparently he lives down near Fish Strand with... some other woman. He drinks, according to Orion."

"I see."

"And is dangerous, in his cups."

"It was he who attacked you?"

"Oh no. These were younger men but set on, I suspect, by Goss. From what Orion has told me he has shown no interest in him since childhood but this does not prevent him..."

This does not prevent him, Charles imagines, from reacting with anger at the thought that his son has a reputation as a milksop. And a man who lives and frequents the public houses near Fish Strand will, no doubt, have plenty of not–particularly-desirable friends, willing, for a pint or so of ale, to set upon Henry and the boy.

The footsteps come crashing back down the stairs and across the hallway and Charles, irritating as he finds the interruption, cannot help but think how distressed and worried he would be if any of his sons were in the sort of situation his friend has described.

"Even if I never see him again... if I go abroad or to London, I am still afraid for him." Henry, who has paused while the noisy footsteps pass by, goes back to staring, hopelessly, at the floor. "Next time," he says miserably, "they could kill him."

Chapter 29

"Emigration." Charles turns onto Henry the full, forbidding force of his dark eyes. "It's the only option. You must buy the boy a passage to America – or one of the colonies. South Africa perhaps. Australia even."

He nods his head slowly, as if in agreement with himself.

Hours have passed and Henry, who is dining with the Hemys after spending most of the day disturbing Charles' work, looks up startled from his contemplation of the tablecloth. He has eaten little and has been a morose dinner companion, to the disappointment of the two youngest Hemy daughters who normally enjoy their uncle Henry's visits but on this occasion have been relieved rather than otherwise to leave the room with their mother.

"There is port in the decanter," Amy reminded her husband, whose abstemious habits often caused him to forget his visitors might be differently inclined but Henry shook his head and Charles did not fetch it from the sideboard.

"Australia! But it's an appalling country, surely? Full of flies and convicts. And America's little better. Besides, what would the boy do there?"

"Grow vegetables? Or fruit? Or I was reading only the other day of the need for young British farmers in South Africa."

"Which would delight the Boers, I'm sure. I think we've interfered quite enough in that country, don't you?"

"Well America then. It's the new world, Harry. Men make fortunes. Men who leave England with nothing can come back as millionaires."

Charles' enthusiasm is uncharacteristic and, very probably, insincere.

"Or die of cholera or malaria and do not come back at all."

"Unlikely." Having made up his mind, Charles holds to his argument. "He's young and healthy and will have no need to work in the mines or on the railways. If he sticks to the work he already knows he could do well enough. Men will always need fruit and vegetables." Charles reaches into the fruit bowl for a Worcester Pearmain. "It could be the making of the boy." He divides his apple into quarters with his dessert knife. "A chance to rise up the social scale in a way he could never do if he remained here. Surely that pleases you, of all men?"

"I would prefer that it were possible for men to rise up the social scale, as you put it, in this country as well. Certainly without facing the hazards of emigration."

"I agree." Charles removes a portion of core from one of his apple quarters and places it with some delicacy at the side of his plate. "But this is hardly a possibility for Orion Goss – if his father is attempting to have him killed…"

In any case, he thinks but does not say, the boy and Henry need to be kept apart. For, although he believes his friend when he says that there has been no impropriety between himself and the boy, Henry's feelings are obviously far stronger than mere friendship. They are – or appear to be, although it is a concept Charles finds hard to accept – closer to love. And he has never before seen Henry in love.

Just as he has never seen Henry in the state he is now – unless he counts that appalling half hour's journey with him the afternoon after Coronation Day, which he would prefer to forget.

If Orion remains in Falmouth – whether the threats of last night's assailants are to be taken seriously or not – Henry will have to leave, since he can obviously not be trusted to keep away from the boy and Falmouth is, in any case, too small a place for it to be certain they would never meet by accident.

Charles, the man and the artist, contemplates the thought of Henry leaving Falmouth. As a man – contented father and husband as he is and difficult friend as Henry can be – he would miss his company. As an artist and although Henry is twenty years the younger and the less experienced of the two of them, he would miss their discussions and disagreements as well as Henry's help and energy in the management of the art gallery. He has never resented the younger man or the fact that there are two successful artists in this small town and the loss of Henry, should he move away, would be quite hard for him to bear.

And the loss to Henry himself? How would he thrive without his lengthy stays every year? Without his early morning swims. His sailing. His floating studio. His local friends. His 'quay scamps', willing to pose for him aboard ship, on Newporth beach, in Sunny Bay…

All these, Charles supposes, could be replicated elsewhere. He could, for example, move down the coast to Newlyn, where he has lived before and where their friend Stanhope Forbes heads a school of painting which is more prestigious and better known than the Falmouth school. He could swim there and sail and, for he is nothing if not sociable, make new friends… But it would not be the same. Henry has been living eight months of the year in Falmouth for seventeen years. The pattern of his life is comfortably set.

Nor does he wish to be associated with a particular school of painting.

And his work – whatever are Charles's views on the naked boys – has never been better.

There is no alternative, he feels. For the boy's sake and for Henry's, Orion Goss must emigrate.

It is gone eleven before Henry leaves Churchfield, sets off briskly up the steep slope of Killigrew Street and turns onto Western Terrace, the main road into the town, which is, at this hour of the night, almost deserted. A closed cab passes, taking some gentleman home from cards or dinner, and the creaking of the reins and then the clop of the horse's hooves fade as it turns the corner. Two unknown men, but their clothes are respectable and they raise their hats politely, come towards him and pass by.

187

A dog wails from its kennel.

Ahead of him the road slopes downwards towards Falmouth Bay. Moonlight lays silver pathways across the dark surface of the water. Drawn–out streamers of cloud drift like smoke across the paler grey of the sky. Tall pine trees rise in cones of darkness until the white–stuccoed bulk of a house obscures the view.

The road is poorly lit. There are houses but the gardens are thick with foliage and the gas street lamps are widely placed so that the shadows between them, especially, around the trees that edge the roadway, are deep and, if one were of a nervous disposition, sinister.

Henry is not of a nervous disposition. Or was not, up to last evening. For years he has walked fearlessly around Falmouth, even when there have been rumours of foreign seamen with violent tendencies. He has walked equally fearlessly around London where there are plenty of thugs, felons and even murderers. It is not so many years since the unsolved murders of the man given the name Jack the Ripper and, although his victims, like those of the majority of attackers, were women, this did not prevent gentlemen like Henry from exercising greater than usual caution when walking the streets at night.

Gentlemen like Henry, but not Henry himself. Who has never believed in the innate evil of man and who, accepting as he does that some may be driven by need or greed to attack those with a greater share of wealth and property, has always been prepared to hand over whatever he has in the way of sovereigns or watches – and has felt besides that he presents too athletic a figure to be considered an easy prey.

Up to last evening.

Now he feels less sure of anything.

The three assailants, he cannot help remembering, easily overpowered both himself and Orion. Were obviously motivated by neither need nor greed. Were motivated, he suspects – and the suspicion causes him to shudder in spite of his warm overcoat –

by disgust...

And so when a stronger than usual gust of wind causes the bare branches of an elm to   creak and rattle he feels inside him a sensation that is quite new to him, that clutches across his chest and worms its way downwards to flutter uneasily somewhere in the pit of his stomach as he begins, in spite of himself, to walk faster, forcing himself not to give in to the impulse to look nervously around him. The sound of the last train from Truro chugging its way through the cutting is a comforting one. And the sight of the sudden head of steam, stained orange–gold and lit with engine sparks, which briefly envelopes the bridge as the train passes below is a cheering reminder of civilisation as he walks swiftly down the road towards the tall pines which mark the limit of the burial ground, chiding himself for giving in to foolish and unworthy fears.

He continues, nevertheless, to walk fast. Hearing with ears nervously alert to anything more sinister the sound and echo of his own footsteps and the clatter of the stones which he disturbs on the rough downhill track. And as he skirts the edge of the swan pool the sudden scuffle of a poolside rat, followed by the croak of a disturbed water bird catch at his breath and it is hard not to break into a run.

Even when he arrives at Swanpool cove he does not pause, as he does normally, to watch the waves breaking against the pebble shore but hurries up the hill and along the path to Pennance cottage.

Which is silent as he lets himself into the darkened lobby and stands, breathless, inside the door. In spite of the night chill his forehead is unpleasantly damp, he can feel the sweat slipping between his shoulder blades and his body is shaking – and not from the cold. As he feels his way upstairs in the darkness he forces himself, as Charles has been trying to persuade him all evening, to face the truth.

For if he, Henry, cushioned as he is by his confidence and

189

social status, feels fear, how much worse is it for poor Orion, who has very little confidence and no status at all?

And yet, has it come to this? That the threats of a drunken and no doubt feeble–minded father, who has shown no interest in the boy for years, will cause the boy to leave home – even to leave the country, probably for ever?

Chapter 30

"I have a proposal to put to you, Mrs Goss. It concerns your son."

Sunday afternoon, Charles had decided, would be the time to catch Mrs Goss at home and at leisure, since Sunday was not a day on which any work could be done. (It did not occur to him that Ida Goss might not have the luxury of 'leisure time' or that, having cooked and cleared away dinner, swept the kitchen and scullery and dusted the parlour, she would be more or less worn out by the time she did eventually sit down.) Sitting down, however, she was. Still wearing her Sunday dress and without her apron and when the knock sounded on her front door she was dozing in her front parlour, looking for all the world – apart from the duster lying forgotten on the mantel – like the leisured woman Charles might have been expecting.

She was flustered to see him, recognising him as the unnerving Mr Hemy in whose home Orion had spent several days back in the summer and who was still, however kind he may have been, a Roman Catholic and an artist. (Ida was still unsure which of these was the worse.) And why in the world, she wondered, as she ushered him indoors, too confused even to offer a cup of tea, had he called to see her?

Which was when Charles explained that he had come with a proposal.

"My son?" Ida stares at him as if the word is an unfamiliar one. "A proposal about my son?"

Her face, already warm and pink becomes hot and red and she can feel a trickle of sweat below the thick knot of her hair at the nape of her neck. Her son – one of her sons – has obviously done something wrong and her mind ranges from Orion, who, after eating his meal in the desultory way he does everything these days, has gone out for a walk, to Alfred who is upstairs sleeping off his dinner – and his pre-dinner session in the Queen's Arms.

"What's 'ee done?" she asks, without asking which son they are discussing.

"He's done nothing. I mean…" Charles has settled his long frame somewhat uncomfortably onto a leather–covered chair so stiffly stuffed with horsehair as to be totally unyielding. "Allow me to explain." The chair creaks below him as he sits forward and, as if to balance himself, he presses his hands together, almost, Ida notices in alarm, as if he is praying.

"Your son, young Orion, is…" He presses his palms together, opening and shutting his splayed fingers as he searches for the right words, fails to find them and starts again.

"My friend, Mr Henry Scott Tuke…" Using Henry's full name will, he hope, make what he is trying to say sound more respectable but he does not miss Mrs Goss's sudden intake of breath and wonders if he has done the right thing. "He takes a great interest in the boy. A paternal interest you might say." Mrs Goss continues to stare, her face redder and hotter–looking than ever and he wonders if she understands the meaning of the word 'paternal.' "He feels that the boy has talents that he will never have a chance to use while he stays in his present occupation…"

"'E's got a good job with Mr Rowse. 'E's done well."

Ida sits more upright than ever, her Sunday stays creaking with the action. For she is by no means a stupid woman and understands now where this is leading. Does she not know, only too well, about the boys Mr Henry Scott Tuke takes out with him on his boat? Boys who sail with him but who also model for his pictures.

Model for his pictures without their clothes.

There are women, she knows, who have no objection to such goings on, for Mr Tuke has asked their permission, the boys have been paid for their services and their mothers have been glad enough to allow this. But not Ida Goss. She is a decent woman, a strict mother and a good Methodist and, however little money they may have, she is not to be bought off. Oh no! Ida Goss is an altogether different proposition – which is presumably why Mr Tuke has sent his friend to see her, rather than come himself.

"E's a good boy, my Orion. A decent boy. An' 'e don' need no… no…" Ida pauses, having no idea how to word her suspicions. "'E's got a good job," she repeats, her stays creaking once more with her indignation.

"I realise that, my dear Mrs Goss. I realise that very well." Charles clasps his wrist, seeing that he has allowed things to get out of hand. "If I could just explain… My friend Mr Tuke would like to… sponsor the boy. Sponsor the boy," he repeats, thankful that God has, at last, put the appropriate word into his mouth, "to enable him to start a new life overseas. Australia, perhaps, or America…"

"America!" Ida subsides as if the air has been extracted from her body.

"He would pay his passage and give him an allowance to enable him to live until he finds acceptable work. Market gardeners are needed in America as anywhere else. It would be a new life for the boy. Men have made fortunes there. He could become rich. It is, they say, the land of opportunity."

Charles speaks with some difficulty, this sort of enthusiastic talk, particularly about America, which is not a country he particularly admires, not coming naturally to him. For Henry's sake, however, he is determined to do his best and when he has finished he looks across at Mrs Goss and smiles with what he hopes is conviction.

Although in fact his expression is irrelevant since Ida is too absorbed in her own thoughts to notice it.

"Am–er–ic–a." She sounds each syllable as if the word were foreign to her. "Mr Tuke… 'E'd pay for Orion to go 'Merica?"

"He would pay his passage and give him an allowance to live on while he sets himself up."

"America."

But it is not actually America of which Ida is thinking. She is thinking of South Africa, where Ivan Hart went, all those years before, to seek his fortune. And perhaps found it for he never sent for Ida and perhaps he also found himself another girl. Perhaps he became rich and, if Ida had been bold enough to go with him, she too would have had a new life. Which might well have been a great deal better than this one…

"Mrs Goss?" Charles leans uncomfortably forward in his chair. "I'm sure you would like time to think about it. To talk over the idea with Orion and with… your family. It's a big decision, I realise, which is why I… we thought I should speak to you before mentioning it to your son…"

"Oh no!" The exclamation startles Charles, who has been concentrating on rising from his slippery chair, preparatory to taking his leave. "It's a good plan. A very good plan. I think 'e should go."

"She doesn't *mind* him going? Did she understand what you were saying, do you think?"

Henry, who had been stalking nervously around the Moor, pounced on Charles as he came out of the house and the two men walked up the road together.

"She appeared to. She said 'America' several times, so she must have. Whether she realises how distant the country is…"

Unwilling to take Henry, in his excitable state, back to Churchfield, Charles led the way into the Kimberly Gardens, where they joined the crowds of Sunday–clad people enjoying the brief November sunshine. Here, as they paced the footpaths, he described as best he could his encounter with Mrs Goss, ending with her assurance that Orion would, if she told him to, go to America.

"Poor lad!" Head down, Henry almost walked into a boy chasing a ball along the path. "To be sent to the other side of the world. To have no choice in the matter."

"I'm sure if he really doesn't want to go…" Charles raised his hat to a smartly dressed couple, hurrying home out of the wind, "his mother would not force him. And it will be such an opportunity for the boy." He stopped, having no wish to go through the same arguments yet again, and tucked his scarf more firmly around his neck. "She says she will speak to him and I agreed that we would call next Sunday."

They reached the upper end of the park, where trees gave way to open grass and the wind was sharper than ever. The low winter sun, Charles noticed, as they turned along the perimeter path, shone a golden light which caught against the dark foliage of a group of pines. A young couple, he in black clothing, the girl in a paler dress beneath her dark coat, hastened, heads down, through the trees as if escaping from some danger, although they were probably just eager for their tea.

"Come back for tea," he told Henry, reminded, but his friend refused.

"I'm poor company at present," he said. "I'll walk it off on the way home."

As they moved towards the stone gatehouse neither of them saw Orion in his cap and Sunday suit come out from among the pine trees.

Henry and Mr Hemy, he thinks. Enjoying a Sunday walk. But soon Henry will go back to London – as he does every year – and perhaps this time he will not return.

Which leaves Orion… where?

Which leaves him exactly where he was before. Working for Mr Cyril. Which, at this time of year means mending the stone pathways, carting truck-loads of sea weed from the beach to spread in stinking heaps across the earth, scraping down and washing out in freezing water the clay pots in which they will plant their seedlings, wrapping sacking around the tender shoots of the early asparagus…

The cold, damp, miserable weeks between now and spring

stretch out before him in an unending line of knotted ropes of onions, rotting cabbage stalks, swedes which must be prised from the heavy earth and little or nothing to look forward to. No trips to Pennance Cottage. No rides on the bicycle that will remain unused in Henry's shed – until he passes it on to some other boy. To Bert White, perhaps. No more lessons in his studio. No chance, even, of drawing at home since his pencils and charcoal have vanished and earlier this week he found the torn pages of his sketchbook lying, filthy and sodden, in the yard. And there is, he knows, no point in replacing them.

"You keep yer nancy boy rubbish outer my room, yer little ponce." Alfred woke him only last night, bulging, wet lips hissing beer–stinking threats against his face. "An' if I see yer wi' your poncy friend you won't neither of you know what's 'appened. Not jus' me neither. There's plenty others waitin' ter get you!"

More followed, if less and less coherent, then a clumsy cuff against the head, a growled oath, the violent gush of urine into the chamber pot and the warm dribble of the final, stinking drops across Orion's half-muffled face…

It appears to Orion, watching from the distance as Henry and Mr Hemy disappear between the granite pillars of the lodge gates, that there is little enough for him to live for at this moment, let alone look forward to.

Chapter 31

Ida said nothing to Orion about Mr Hemy's visit until after her visit to Bea the following Friday.

It was a long walk on a dark and blustery evening and as she made her way up the main street the wind funnelled its way up the narrow opes from the harbour, catching her long coat and broad skirt and threatening to bowl her over in spite of her bulk. As she walked past the small ship yards and workshops along Bar Road, it was all she could do to hold onto her hat, let alone keep her hair from flying as the wind roared in across the harbour where the waves, whipped to a frenzy, broke against the retaining rocks and sent up fountains of foam which poured in places right out into the road.

"My Gor! It's some dreadful out!" she gasped, arriving breathless in Bea's bedroom doorway, attempting to push her dishevelled hair into some sort of order without the help of at least half of the hairpins she had left home with. "I shan't stay long. Not with this weather."

But the weather made no difference to Bea, other than shaking her window-frames and sending a stronger than usual draught into the room. Besides which she had information she was anxious to give her friend.

"You get your breath back an' I'll make us some tea," she told her, setting the kettle on the small spirit stove she now kept in her room. "An' don't you start talking about going when you've 'ardly got 'ere. Besides, I've something to tell you."

"Joe saw your Percy, night before last."

Ida had drunk two cups of tea, tidied her hair to her greater satisfaction and her bosom had at last stopped heaving up and down. It was time, Bea judged, to give her the news.

"He aint my Percy. Not no more." Ida's tea cup clattered against its saucer.

"'E's still your 'usband though. An' Orion's pa."

"W'as that got to do wi' anything?"

But Ida felt her heart thud above the constriction of her corset and, unconscious of the action, placed one hand against it as she stared across at her friend. For she knew quite well that these things mattered and felt herself breathing faster and more shallowly as the old uneasiness came flooding back.

"'E were making threats, Joe said. About your Orion an' 'is… 'is friend, Mr Tuke." Bea reached over the rug she wore tucked across her knees and gently touched Ida's hand. "It might be nothing. 'E were full of ale, Joe said, ranting an' not making no sense; not really," she added doubtfully. "You d'know what 'e's like."

Oh yes, Ida was thinking, she knew what he was like. A rough, drunken pig, who might make no sense but had little sense either and was quite likely, with enough drink inside him, to do real harm.

"What sort of threats?"

"The usual thing, Joe said. 'Ow 'e'd see to it the boy learned 'is lesson, whatever that might mean. An' 'is friend should watch isself too, 'e said. Case they might find theyselves pitched off the quay one night."

"'E's a fool. Always was." But Ida's heart went on thudding and the heat of her face was nothing to do with the heat of her tea, for she knew that, fool though Percy might be, he was well capable of violence; perhaps even of murder.

And people did fall from quays or boats or walkways and were not always rescued. The Packet regularly carried stories of men, usually stated to have been the worse for drink, who had drowned getting on or off a boat and, while these were always reported as 'tragedies', they attracted little speculation. And, while there might well be an outcry and some suspicion about the drowning of a well known artist, the police would be ready enough to believe that a seventeen-year-old youth, son of a notorious drunkard, had simply taken too much ale and fallen.

"Can't Joe talk no sense into 'im?"

Bea's eyes flickered towards the darkened road outside.

"'E din' like to say nothin'. 'E's got some rough friends, Percy. Joe don' like to get mixed up with 'em."

A gust of wind, blowing itself in under the guttering, wailed like a distracted sea bird, the pine trees along the railway line creaked unnervingly and Ida pulled her shawl closer around her neck, thinking already of the long walk home.

"There's only one answer," she said. "I can't see no other."

And, swearing Bea to secrecy, she told her about Mr Hemy's proposal…

After a wild night it rained all day Saturday and Orion arrived home soaked and coughing for his tea, which he ate in the gloomy silence that was normal to him these days. Alfred, having earned some money scraping down the hull of one of the Fal pleasure boats, had gone straight to the public house to drink it and Ida and Orion were on their own.

Watching her son pick at his tripe and onions, Ida couldn't help thinking back to those summer months when Alfred had spent his spare time with Mabel and Orion was off with his own, mysterious friend. If only the friend had been a young woman, as she had imagined! A decent young woman like Mabel with whom he might, in time, have set up home and started a family.

"I don' know wa's wrong wi' 'ee!" she snapped, irritated by her thoughts, as the boy put down his knife and started again to cough. "I went down Dunnings special to get tripe."

Coals dropped inside the range, which gusted tar–scented smoke into the room and Orion, giving up the effort of shovelling mashed potato, started to hack once more. Clicking her teeth in exasperation, Ida pulled open the yard door to let out some of the smoke, succeeding only in letting in a blast of cold, damp air.

"E'nt it never gonna stop?" she demanded. And then, reminded, "You should be grateful – going 'Merica. Blue seas and blazing sunshine all year round."

(Ida's view of the United States, taken from a story serialised in the Falmouth Packet and set in California, was not particularly accurate but neither she nor Orion were to know this.)

"What 'ee mean, goin' 'Merica?"

"What I say." Ida spoke crossly, pausing as Orion bent forward over his plate in another spate of coughing. "Your friend; your Mr Scott Tuke. 'E's paying for you to go 'Merica. Mr 'Emy come to see me last week. 'E told me."

"But I don' wan' go 'Merica. I don' know no-one there. I never said I wanted…" The cough overtook him again and he lurched across to the door, trying to hold back the little food he had managed to swallow. When he turned back his eyes were wet with tears but neither he nor his mother could have said whether they were from coughing or misery.

Ida took the kettle from the range and filled her teapot. Then she told him in more detail what Mr Hemy had said.

"It's a chance for you to make good," she ended up. "It's a new world. You could make your fortune." She stared at her son across the still smoky room, thinking again of Ivan Hart with his black hair and mocking smile, wondering if he had made his fortune in the new world or if it had turned out to be as harsh and unrewarding as the old one.

"I don' wan' go 'Merica. 'Ow would I go on over there?"

Henry pulls the boy through the door to Pennance Cottage and is unable to prevent himself from peering into the darkness of the garden in case he has been followed. And, in spite of everything – his fear, the fact that he is entertaining friends, the look of misery on the boy's face – he is delighted to see him.

"Come inside boy. It's a foul night. And you're soaked, for God's sake."

But Mrs Fouracre and her children are eating their supper in the kitchen and the dining room is filled with his friends, who, having reached the cheese, dessert and port stage, are loudly disputing the rival merits as batsmen of Tom Hayward and Victor Trumper.

"Come quietly." He tows the reluctant boy along the passage and into his study which is in darkness and is very little warmer than the front porch. "Wait there a minute"

He leaves him standing, bemused, in the middle of the room and goes back to his guests.

"You must excuse me." The three men stop arguing and stare towards him. Their faces, red from the heat of the fire, good food, wine and argument, look cheerful but puzzled. "A slight... problem..." Henry is aware that this is not how he wishes to describe Orion, and yet, what else is he? "I have a visitor – a neighbour, with a... a problem." That word again but how else can it be expressed? And why has he described him as a neighbour when they all know he has no-one living closer than half a mile? "Go on with your dessert. Help yourselves to more port. I won't be long."

His friends stare in some surprise as he closes the door on them, until one, Warren Goodall, a local writer with interests which often take him to the less salubrious parts of Falmouth, starts to guffaw.

"Poor old Harry! Some handsome young chicken come home to roost do you think?" He picks up the port bottle and re-fills his glass. "How about a hand or so of three-handed whist? I suspect our host may be some time."

Henry, leaning against the outside of the door, closes his eyes and winces. Tells himself that what Goodall says is of little consequence. Realises that his hands, for some reason, are shaking. Pulls himself together and goes back to the study...

Where Orion is a shadow, staring from the window. He holds his cap clenched in his hands and, even in the gloom, Henry sees that his hair stands out in windblown tufts.

"My dear boy!" There is a paraffin lamp on the table just inside the door and Henry lights it, adjusts the flame and watches as the light diffuses around the near side of the room. Orion, further away, remains in shadow. As Henry crosses to the window and pulls across the heavy curtains he starts to cough.

"Whatever are you doing, coming out on a night like this? Let me get you something. A drop of brandy to keep out the cold."

But the brandy is with the port in the other room and Orion, in any case, shakes his head.

"Ma told me…" He presses his hand against his mouth to prevent more coughing. " She said you'd pay for me to go to America." He looks across at Henry and then, quite slowly, around the room. Which, although only the one lamp is lit, becomes gradually more visible as his eyes adjust. Sees the confusion of objects – books, curios, binoculars, a model ship – which lie negligently along the shelves. The unlit fire in the hearth. The rocking chair lined with rugs. The paintings, along the mantel and around the walls, of rocks, ships, sea birds, youths… And one charcoal sketch – cruder and less masterful than the rest – pinned to the bottom of a shelf.

"I don' want to go away. I don' know why you d'want me to go."

"My dear boy!" Emotion wells up inside Henry so that he can hardly breathe, let alone speak. "My dear Orion, it's not…" His voice falters, he closes his eyes and presses one hand against his forehead, turns convulsively away and stands facing the wall and, although he cannot see it, a small water colour by Charles, a study of mackerel and whirling gulls. "I'm so sorry," he says at last. "But I fear for your life, Orion. Truly. Of course I don't want you to go but what alternative is there? What else," he demands angrily, turning to face him, "can we possibly do? "

The boy goes on standing quite still. His face, on the outskirts of the light, is pale but with the slightest tinge of gold. His eyes turn downwards, fixed, apparently on the faded pattern on the much-worn carpet.

"I dunno," he says slowly. "I dunno 't'all."

From the dining room comes a muffled curse, followed by a yell of masculine laughter. Obviously Henry's guests have found a way to amuse themselves in his absence but he can hardly leave them much longer. Apart from the incivility, he cannot trust them – cannot, certainly, trust Warren Goodall – not to come looking for him on some pretext. Or Mrs Fouracre may go in to offer tea or coffee and then seek out her employer to see if he wants the fire lit in here or more lamps brought…

"I din' ought to stay." Orion has also heard the voices. "I din' ought've come."

"Of course you should have! Although… are you sure no-one saw you? I'll have you driven home…"

There are two ponies here, waiting in the yard with their traps. They belong to his friends but Henry will face their curiosity and perhaps their mockery. It is more important that Orion gets home in safety.

"No!" The boy pushes his cap back onto his head and starts towards the door. "I don' need nothin' like that." And Henry, recognising the old obstinacy, follows him unhappily along the passage.

Outside the wind gusts more violently than ever. Below them waves crash against the rocks, boom hollowly against the base of the cliff and recede, dragging with them a trawl of rattling pebbles. Orion hesitates momentarily in the porch.

"I don' wanna go," he says in a low voice which, in spite of the wind which crashes through the cliff top trees, in spite of the waves smashing against the shore, is perfectly audible. And then, carefully, "I d'want things to be like they was. Coming 'ere. Drawing an' painting. Bicycling." He pauses. "An' bein' with you."

Henry hears his own intake of breath like the beginning of a sob.

"My dear boy… My dear, dear boy!"

He puts out a hand to clutch at his shoulder, draws him gently against him, feels within his own body the convulsive, thrilled awakening that he has trained himself, at all costs, to avoid, fights the impulse, loses and bends his head to press his lips against the warm but rapidly chilling face.

"How can I bear it?" he whispers, leaning back as if in exhaustion against the cold, wet wood of the door frame as the boy turns and walks rapidly away. "How can I possibly bear it?"

Chapter 32

Once started, arrangements for Orion's passage to America moved surprisingly fast. There was a steamer leaving Liverpool on December 5th with space available and assisted passages, so Charles discovered from the agency that arranged such things, were still available for healthy young men with experience of manual labour. Orion would not even need a medical examination, since he would be given one at the Ellis Island Reception Centre in New York, but Charles felt it would be unwise to wait until this late stage and arranged for Dr Ellis to check him over and, his cough having abated, write a letter certifying his fitness. All that was needed otherwise was Orion's certificate of birth, which Ida produced from a biscuit tin on her kitchen dresser, and his ticket, which duly arrived from the Cunard steamship company and which they examined with awe.

Not that Orion could believe it had anything to do with him. In fact everything about this new life on which he was supposed to be embarking was so unfamiliar that his mind seemed to have long ceased to take any of it in.

When Mr Cyril commented, as he and Ricky bent over the shallot drills, that it wouldn't matter to Orion whether they came up in straight lines or not since he wouldn't be there to see them, it was impossible to believe that this was so. For the past four years he had watched vegetables he had planted grow from the earth and there seemed no reason that this year should not be the same as last year and all the years before it.

When his mother took him to Goodings to buy new clothes, it was part of the same unreality. This new suit, this overcoat, these trousers, these shirts… they were not for him. They were for some other young man. A bolder, more ambitious young man setting out on some unimaginable journey. When one of Mr Hemy's sons appeared one evening with a leather valise and a canvas bag belonging to his father it was impossible to think that he, Orion, would be packing his own belongings into them.

And when Mr Ogden asked the congregation to pray for the safety and well being of 'one of our number, about to start a new life in a foreign land' he obediently prayed for this anonymous person without, at first, recognising himself...

Henry, meanwhile, left Falmouth for London, as was his custom at this time of year, leaving Charles to oversee arrangements for Orion's departure.

"I'm so sorry," he said as he handed him the considerable sum of money that would be needed for the boy's tickets, clothing and other expenses, "but I can't do it myself – for the boy's safety. Besides..." He turned away, staring out of Charles' studio window as if there were something of immense interest in his garden, "I don't think I could bear it."

"There's no need to apologise. I'm happy to help." Charles spoke hastily, anxious to forestall any outburst of emotion from his friend. He also did not entirely speak the truth. He was losing a great deal of time over this business and would be only too pleased when he could concentrate on his work again.

On the other hand he did not want Henry getting any more involved than he already was and had been pleased, if faintly surprised, when his friend announced that he would be leaving for London. He was well aware that the thought of the boy's emigration was making him miserable and, right up to the moment of his departure, did not entirely trust him not to change his mind.

Only when he had seen his friend onto the train at Falmouth station – he had never done this before and they both knew why he was there – did he start to feel safe. Henry was not going to change his mind. Apart from anything else, he had invested a great deal of money in the boy's new life.

He was comfortably off, of course, but by no means wealthy and the money he had given Charles, in addition to the boy's steamship ticket, the money the shipping agent had been instructed to bank for him in New York and the allowance he was making to Mrs Goss as recompense for the loss of her son's earnings, represented a considerable inroad into his capital.

Charles, turning out of the station towards his waiting trap, felt a mixture of relief that Henry was putting himself out of danger and irritation that his obsession should render this necessary.

He was to leave Falmouth, Mr Hemy had told him, by the nine twenty train on December 2nd, which connected with the London train at Truro. He would be met at Paddington station by a Mr Tebbutt, who would conduct him to his boarding house where he would stay the night and, next morning, would take him across London to Euston Station where he would catch the train to Liverpool. There the agent with whom Charles had been dealing had undertaken to meet him and see him through the process of embarkation.

"There will be nothing for you to worry about," he assured Orion. "Someone will meet you at each stage. You can simply enjoy the journey."

Which was, Orion felt, all very well. His travel up to now was limited to occasional visits to his sister five miles away in Mabe and one trip to Truro when the train ride had been exciting but had felt dangerously fast and they had crossed first the Penryn and then the Carnon Valley on viaducts so high that he had felt quite dizzy. And it was only a few years before – he and Will had walked out to see the wreckage slewed down the steep embankment – that a mail train had derailed at Hillhead near Penryn and Mr Cottrell, the driver, had lost his life. Trains, he couldn't help but feel, were dangerous things and they would reach even higher speeds between here and London and would cross many more viaducts – not to mention the great Royal Albert bridge across the River Tamar which separated Cornwall from the rest of the country.

It was no wonder fire–breathing engines careered through Orion's nightmares and that, one night, he found himself teetering on the edge of a sheer cliff at the bottom of which an immense fish waited with open, tooth–lined jaws.

And supposing this Mr Tebbutt was not waiting at Paddington Station? How would he find his way across the metropolis on his own? And even if he did, by some miracle, arrive to meet him, how would Orion, who had never spent so much as a night away from home, get on in a 'boarding house'? All this before he even began to think of the terrors of the sea voyage across the Atlantic Ocean and the unknown horror of this 'new life' he was expected to start in a vast new country.

His uncertainty was so great that when Mr Hemy, looking more than normally grim, his dark eyes glaring from under his heavy brows, lips invisible below his thick grey moustache, asked if there was anything worrying him, there was no possible way of putting all his fears into words and he could only shake his head.

December 2nd, he hoped, might never actually arrive.

But, and in spite of all his prayers, it did and he found himself, in his unfamiliar suit and the new boots which already pinched where he had laced them too tightly, on the station platform with Mr Hemy's valise and bag beside him and a newspaper package of his mother's pasties clutched in his hand. Inside his stomach it felt as if someone had drawn tight strands of string from side to side and top to bottom, the way they criss–crossed the nursery beds above the broccoli and the salad crops. And, having done this, that same someone was now pulling the strings so tight that he could scarcely breathe.

Mr Hemy was talking to the station master who stood, watch in hand, waiting the arrival of the down–train that would become the up–train to Truro for the first stage of Orion's long and unimaginable journey. Other passengers – smartly-dressed business men, two ladies with a small girl and a lady and gentleman who arrived in a cab with an immense amount of luggage – stood chatting and waiting. None of them, with the exception of the little girl, appeared to feel that there was anything unusual about their journey but perhaps none of them – with the possible exception of the couple with the luggage – were going as far as London. Let alone Liverpool. Let alone America.

It was probable, in fact, that only for Orion, apparently the least important of all these passengers, was this day of any significance.

His mother had not come to see him off. Mr Hemy had offered to drive her to station in the pony and trap with Orion but she had refused. The thought of the return journey on her own with a man she still found alarming was more than she could countenance, besides which Mrs Trembath had lunch guests expected and the fact that her son was leaving Falmouth, very possibly for ever, did not entitle her to let down her employer.

And so they had said their goodbyes, mother and son, before Ida left the house. She cross-questioned him for the last time as to how well he had secured the valise and checked, once again, that he had his birth certificate, his letter from Dr Ellis and the letters of introduction 'To Whom it May Concern' from Mr Hemy, Reverend Ogden and Mr Tuke, as well as his train tickets and his money, in his new pocket book in the inner pocket of his new jacket. Then, thrusting the pack of hot pasties into his hand, she hugged him briefly, stood back for a last look at his new finery and ordered him to be sure he didn't cause any trouble.

"You be sure you're ready when Mr 'Emy comes," she told him as she hurried out of the house. "Don't you go keeping 'im waitin'."

Which was why Orion had found himself standing by the parlour window, the package of pasties clutched in his hand and staring out at the roadway he would never see again, more than half an hour before the trap arrived.

The train was late. An unheard-of occurrence according to the station master, who stalked importantly to the far end of the platform to watch irritably as the incoming train was pushed out along the line and a new engine steamed noisily from the turntable to be linked onto what was now the first of the four carriages.

Perhaps, Orion thought, as these were shunted back towards the waiting passengers, they would miss their connection at Truro. Perhaps there would be no other train to Paddington. Perhaps...

"Right lad," Mr Hemy reached forward to grasp the handle of a third class compartment, pulling it open with a firm, downwards movement. The ladies with the little girl, the couple with the luggage and two of the business men were helped by porters into the superior, first class compartments and the station master, frowning with ever–deepening annoyance, motioned to the guard who stood waiting with his green flag and his whistle.

"Good luck, my boy. May the Lord be with you."

Mr Hemy's smile made his fierce eyes seem almost friendly as he shook Orion by the hand, then gestured to him to stand back as he slammed shut the heavy door. As steam forced its way from between the engine wheels, the pistons raced fast and violently and the funnel gave out a sudden and momentous exhalation Orion stood staring from a grimy window, pulled securely closed by its long, leather strap.

Mr Hemy lifted his broad–rimmed hat courteously in his direction and then, as the train jerked suddenly forwards, he disappeared, together with the station, the trucks in the coal yard and a pony and trap on the station road, in a suffocating cloud of steam.

And there was no point in looking out of the window, even after the cloud had cleared. If he was never coming back, what was the point in looking at this unfamiliar view of so familiar a place? If this were just a pleasure trip, it would have been interesting to see the back gardens of houses known to him from their frontages; to see the top end of the market garden, where, in what was already another world, Mr Cyril, Jacka and Ricky would be setting out the boxes of potatoes and onions and cutting the tall stalks of Brussels sprouts. It would have been exciting to look out from the other side of the carriage at the ships in Falmouth bay and perhaps even, between the tall pines above the graveyard, to get a glimpse of Stack Point and Henry's cliff top cottage.

But not when he was leaving them for ever and he stared instead at the dull, red upholstery of the seats and the small, gas lights on their brackets below the luggage rack where his bags were stowed. Then, standing, he examined the brown and off-white photographs on the compartment walls – St Michaels Mount, Restormel Castle, Shaldon and the Ness, the Winter Gardens at Torquay – and, finally, his own worried face, dwindling down through the reflections of opposing mirrors as if he, like his past life, might be disappearing for ever.

At Truro he followed with his bags the lady and gentleman with the luggage, now loaded by a porter onto a broad trolley which he pushed across the line to Platform Two where, he assured them, the up–train for London would arrive shortly.

Here were a lot more people waiting, some seeming almost as nervous as Orion. One family in particular, a father, mother and three small children, seemed especially worried, the woman several times asking her husband and once even asking Orion, if this was the right platform for the London train.

When it appeared, the black snout of an engine twice the size of the one that had pulled the train from Falmouth thrusting through a shroud of smoke, it became clear that the husband was not accompanying his family and Orion helped him stow their baggage onto the luggage rack in one of the third class compartments.

Being with someone even more nervous than he was made things seem momentarily more bearable, and as the train moved slowly across the high viaduct outside the station, he was able to look across the valley with awe towards the almost–completed structure of the great cathedral, which dwarfed the town, in its frame of scaffolding. Then, almost immediately, they were in a tunnel, the three children screamed and sobbed at the noise and sudden darkness and it seemed to Orion that he could quite easily do the same.

Chapter 33

The day which had started fair had turned to rain by the time the train passed through St Austell where Orion gazed out at the white mountains of waste from the clay pits of which he had heard but which he had never seen and the strange phenomenon of tongues of water, stained white by the clay, swirling outwards into the sea. Then the land closed in, rising up beside the line in steep fields bordered by walls of granite boulders, sometimes with a tall stone, or two stones like a long-abandoned doorway, standing inexplicably in the grass. Farm buildings appeared, the rain dripping like tears off dark slate roofs to form brown puddles in the surrounding yards, and were left behind. Woodlands – low oaks, bare-branched, their trunks jewelled with golden lichen – crowded so close to the line that twigs scraped against the side of the compartment and once a larger branch cracked loudly against the window, startling the children so that their mother pulled them against her, staring, wild-eyed, as if she too expected it to come through the glass.

"It won' break," Orion heard himself say, perhaps to convince himself as well as her. "They d'use special glass in these windows."

He had no idea if this was true but common sense told him it should be. Trains travelled along this line several times a day. If windows broke every time a branch hit them there'd be none left by the end of a week.

The train slowed as they crossed another viaduct, high over a valley studded with rhododendrons, some, even this late in the year, in blossom. The little girl, bolder than her brothers, crept across to sit opposite Orion, exclaiming in amazement at the bright red flowers.

"They're called ro–de–den–drums," he told her. "They come from foreign lands. Sailors d'bring them back for rich men to put in their gardens."

He thought of Henry's friend Mr Fox who had, Henry said, whole groves of them in his gardens on the Helford river. One day I'll take you to see them, Henry had promised and the old unhappiness came over him as he stared out at the blossoms glowing through the mist of rain above the valley and the dark and dripping leaves of their foliage. For he would never go there now. Perhaps he had never really thought he would but, like his idea of being an artist, it had been something to dream about.

The little girl squirmed in her seat, gazing across at him with wide, brown eyes.

"'How'd they bring them? Those great trees?" she asked. But she spoke softly and Orion was too deep in his own thoughts to realise she was talking to him and didn't answer.

"Don't pester the gentleman," her mother said but Orion, who might have been flattered to hear himself so described, did not hear that either.

At last they crossed the great iron bridge across the river Tamar, the boundary between Cornwall and Devon. Mr Brunel, its designer, Henry had told Orion, had only seen it completed once before his death and then he had been so ill he had to lie on a couch in the train as it crossed. Looking down–stream between the immense wrought iron tubes which formed the arches to the two main spans Orion could see in the estuary more steam ships than he would have imagined possible, naval vessels and alarmingly warlike in appearance. By comparison the more familiar fishing smacks on the grey waters of the Tamar and the rowing boats used as ferries looked like children's toys.

And now he had left Cornwall for the first time in his life and would, in all probability, never come back. The steep–pitched fields, the rain–soaked farms, the lush, wet valleys and lonely standing stones were lost to him for ever and it was hard not to think of all those other things and places he would never see again. The market garden with its steep–rising beds and the cosy potting shed where he and Jacka ate their croust, the smell of wet, rich earth mingled with the salt and iodine of seaweed and the dung and urine–soaked straw of the horse manure. Falmouth's narrow, twisting streets with their familiar shops and rowdy, beer–scented public houses. The quays and waterfront, littered with nets and ropes and wicker crab pots. Henry's studio, smelling of oil paints and canvas sizing, its walls almost invisible behind the hanging paintings. Even the granite mass of Wesley Chapel, its lines of dark–wood pews, its oppressive, overhanging gallery and great organ seemed, now that he would never see it again, a place of comfort.

Looking out at the grey terraces of the great city of Plymouth and, beyond these, the Devon hills which seemed, already, so different from their Cornish counterparts, it was hard to feel that he might ever find comfort anywhere else. Certainly not in the new world of America where, in New York where he was to land, there were buildings hundreds of feet tall and something called the Statue of Liberty which would be the first thing he would see when he arrived. All this was, however, impossible to imagine – and more impossible still to imagine himself in such surroundings.

At Plymouth North Road station the little family left the train. Orion got down to help with their baggage and was lifting down the little girl as a heavily–built, elderly man in gaiters who must be their grandfather came striding down the platform.

"Enid my love!" he bellowed, holding out his arms to the little girl who twisted from Orion's grasp and ran squealing towards him.

Getting back onto the train, Orion turned away as the mother and her children were folded into the man's embrace and stared instead at the confusion of activities on the station around him. At the young man in a smart GWR uniform who pulled a tall trolley laden with chrome–plated tea pots, trays of cups and saucers, plates of sandwiches and cakes piled high under glass domes. At a pair of lovers, locked in a tight embrace and

215

oblivious to other passengers attempting to push their way past. At a woman, muffled in furs and carrying a hat box and a long handled umbrella, who descended the broad steps from the bridge, looking haughtily around as if someone had, in some way, let her down. At a tall man hurrying along the platform, pausing at each compartment to peer inside. A tall man in a bowler hat, his long raincoat billowing behind him. A tall man with a dark moustache who looked almost like… but could not possibly be…..

"Orion! Thank God! I thought I must have missed you! Quickly! Quickly now. Where's your baggage? Porter! Over here! Hurry now. Hurry!"

And Orion found himself, breathless, capless and yet somehow still clutching the packet of his mother's pasties that he had felt too miserable to eat, standing on the platform whilst a tiny porter whose broad shoulders stretched tight the cloth of his jacket leapt onto the train and swung down the valise, the bag and Orion's new cap, touching his own cap at Henry in what appeared to be the same movement.

All along the train doors slammed shut. Goodbye Daddy, a woman shouted, a whistle blew, steam blasted in thick white clouds from between the carriage wheels, causing passengers leaning from windows to withdraw their heads and their friends and relatives on the platform to step smartly back as, with a hoarse whistle and a thunderous explosion from its funnels, the train – Orion's train – started slowly, and then faster, to move forwards up the line…

It was surprising how quickly the platform emptied. The man with the tea trolley moved down a ramp and across the line. The friends and relatives waved briefly and turned away towards the steps. Even the girl Orion recognised as one of the embracing lovers hurried off as if to another urgent assignation.

In no time, it seemed, Orion, Henry and the small, broad-shouldered porter, still clutching Mr Hemy's valise and carpet bag, had the entire, broad platform to themselves.

"Thank you my man. We can manage."

Henry, as if realising that any further action is, for the moment at least, impossible, reaches into his pocket for a coin. It is, judging from the man's reaction, an over-generous tip, after which he seems reluctant not to give further service and Henry has almost to prise his brown hands from Orion's luggage before he goes off, pulling at the peak of his cap.

"I don' understand. Why an't you in London? Mr 'Emy said…"

But whatever Mr Hemy has said makes no difference to the fact that Henry is here, in an unfamiliar hat and raincoat, and Orion, with his ticket for London in his pocket, is standing next to him on Plymouth station.

"My train," he says, pointlessly, as the back of the guard's van disappears up the line, and looks helplessly down at his new, uncomfortable boots as if they may tell him what is to happen next.

"I was." For a moment Orion has no idea what Henry is talking about. "I intended – I really did – to stay there until you were safely embarked at Liverpool. I… I even promised Charles I would not meet you at Paddington. I meant to stay in town until my usual time and then return to Falmouth when… when everything would be as it was before I knew you…"

His voice fades to a whisper and Orion strains to hear him over the clatter and rumble of a line of open goods wagons on the far side of the station.

"I could not do it! I could not bear the thought of you being forced… being forced into exile, because of me! The thought of you undertaking that long voyage on your own. Of starting a new life in a new continent on your own. Do you know…" He looks across at Orion and, for the first time since their meeting, his face lights in a smile. "I even thought of travelling to America myself. I made enquiries and they had several state rooms still vacant – I

217

doubt this is a time of year when people travel for pleasure – and then I thought… What would I do in that uncivilised place? How could I leave England, and especially Falmouth?

"And then I thought, how could I expect the same of you and I knew we must make different plans."

A down train draws into the opposite platform with a hiss of brakes and much opening and slamming of doors. Plymouth North Road, a voice shouts, this is Plymouth North Road, apparently reminding Henry where they are.

"Come along." He seizes Mr Hemy's valise. "I have a cab waiting outside."

And Orion, who has expected never to see Henry again, finds himself in a closed cab beside him trotting rapidly between terraces of tall white houses in the direction of Plymouth Hoe.

The boarding house is called 'Bay View' although in the gloom of a mid–December afternoon there is little to be seen but an inky stretch of what must be water where darker shadows move across the lesser darkness with lights that pitch and toss and sometimes, briefly, disappear.

Henry has been staying here, it appears, for the past two nights. And is known, to Orion's hastily concealed surprise, as Mr Scott. Orion, introduced as 'a young friend of the family', is obviously expected and is led upstairs to a room on the top floor.

"I hope you'll be comfortable, Mr Goss." Mrs Butchers, the landlady, turns, smiling, towards him. "There's a gas fire if it gets chilly." She indicates a black–leaded pillar with burners at the base. "Mabel will bring hot water for washing." She waves a hand towards the wash stand in the corner of the room and flicks with a duster, appearing in her hand as if by magic, at an invisible speck of dust. "Dinner is at eight. The… facilities," she adds delicately, "are across the landing. The door is marked."

She leaves him with the comment that dinner will be served at seven thirty and Orion, his bladder uncomfortably full and

218

hoping that the unfamiliar word 'facilities' means what he thinks it must, dares investigate the landing and finds, beyond a door marked 'Guests', the thrill of a flushing water closet.

Emerging, he meets Henry on the landing.

"I hope you're all right up here. It's a little…" he looks round at the lino-covered floor, the white distempered walls bare of any decoration beyond a sepia Crucifixion, "spartan."

Orion, beaming with the relief of an empty bladder, says it suits him fine.

"Do we 'ave to 'ave supp… dinner 'ere?" he asks. He is hungry enough but the thought of eating under Mrs Butchers' eye is nerve-wracking.

"Of course we do! Mrs Butchers is an excellent cook. She has promised Dover sole and I do not intend to miss it." Henry does miss, however, the reason for Orion's reluctance. "Meanwhile, how about a turn across the Hoe," he suggests, "as an appetiser."

He has been waiting, and fretting, all day and has energy to burn.

Chapter 34

The bed in Mrs Butchers' boarding house was the most comfortable Orion had ever slept in and next morning he lay revelling in its warmth and softness and the loss of the terrible burden he had carried with him these past weeks. For he was not, Henry had assured him last night, going to cross the Atlantic to start a new life in America. He was not going to Liverpool. Or even to London.

"Men do it, I know they do." Striding out across the windswept Hoe in a darkness broken only by the faltering glow of an occasional gas lamp, Henry gesticulated with his stick. "But these are miners. Men whose work here is falling away. Men without hope – except in the new world. And they go together. I have seen them. Great crowds of men, marching to the station in Camborne or Redruth. Like soldiers off to the war." He stopped suddenly and Orion, walking behind him, stepped sideways to avoid a collision. "I know Charles meant well. He was thinking of your safety, I know that. But the thought of you making that journey... The conditions in steerage – I know they have improved in recent times but they are still grim enough. And fending for yourself – in New York! I couldn't bear it for you, Orion. I really couldn't."

"Am I to go 'ome then?"

For, much as Orion had not wanted to go to America, he had understood the necessity. The men who had beaten him and Henry on Wodehouse Terrace that evening a few weeks back could easily have done them real harm. They might even have killed them. And Orion had no wish to be killed. Nor did he wish to be beaten again. The reminder of the pain of those broken ribs was still quite fresh.

And he knew that his father was not to be trusted. He had met him no more than a dozen times in his entire life and that had been more than enough. He was a brutal man, rough and coarsened by drink, and his friends were no doubt much the same. He was sure that if his father wanted him disposed of it would be perfectly possible.

And so, if he was not to go to America, where was he to go?

"Home? Of course not!" Henry's stick flew off into the darkness as he grabbed Orion's shoulders with both hands, his teeth, in the gloom, shining white below his moustache. "I have a far better idea. Far, far better."

Now, in his comfortable bed with its view out across the grey waters of Plymouth Sound, Orion contemplated Henry's far, far better idea.

There was a cottage, Henry had told him. A few miles round the coast from Pennance. Belonging to a farm owned by a friend of Henry's but the cowman who lived in it had died, the cottage was empty and the friend was happy to sell.

"It will cost me next to nothing. Less than the amount of money I had intended to start you in your new life in America and which I have wired the agent to return. You will have your own home, a place where you can live – and where you can paint! What do you say, Orion? Eh?"

He had said nothing. Not then. The idea being too immense, to take in. But all through dinner, when he was not worrying how he should manage Mrs Butcher's chicken broth without spilling any on her white linen cloth and how many of her crisply roasted potatoes he could take without appearing rude, he had thought about it. Tried to imagine himself, Orion, who had never had so much as a room to call his own, with an entire cottage.

It would work perfectly, Henry assured him each time the soberly-dressed little servant had left the room. There was a garden where Orion could grow his own vegetables, outhouses where he could keep chickens; even a pig if he wished. There were women on the farm nearby who would come in to cook and clean for him...

"More gravy Sur?" The servant girl reappeared with a

221

steaming jug and Henry started to talk about an item of news in that morning's Times. Watching the thick brown gravy stream fragrantly onto his plate Orion felt almost relieved at the interruption. Henry's enthusiasm could sometimes make it difficult to think.

"You must see it for yourself," he said as the girl closed the door behind her. "Then you can judge. We'll leave first thing in the morning."

It was strange to be travelling along the same tracks as yesterday but in the opposite direction. The sun, as if in recognition of his altered mood, shone brilliantly from a winter blue sky, its golden light slanting through the bare–branched woodlands, settling with a cosy glow on granite walls, farm buildings and the lonely standing stones in their empty fields and, as the train crossed the rhododendron valley that had so impressed the little girl the day before, the light caught the bright flower heads so that the white and scarlet blossoms shone out like lanterns strung among the greenery.

They must be careful, Henry said, not to be seen together – in fact Orion must not be seen at all and he produced one of his own sailing caps and a thick, grey scarf which he wound round Orion's neck and the bottom part of his face as if he had the toothache. Then he laughed and said he looked as if he were about to commit a robbery and since the cap hid his hair which was his most conspicuous feature he unwound the scarf, to Orion's relief, since he was already beginning to sweat.

At Plymouth station Henry bought two tickets, one First and one Third class, and they stood apart from one another on the platform, although Orion couldn't help feeling this was an unnecessary precaution. And when they reached Truro he followed some distance behind Henry and the porter who carried their luggage across the footbridge to the Bay platform where the Falmouth train was already waiting.

Here there was obviously more danger of their being recognised – many people travelled between Falmouth and Truro – but they reached the train in safety and it set off immediately, having waited only for passengers from the down train. Orion, by now a seasoned traveller, found a seat in a third class compartment with an elderly man in gaiters whose boots stank of the farmyard, until he lit a pipe of tobacco from which he blew out clouds of sickly–scented smoke which rose to the roof of the compartment and hung there like a captured fog.

They were to get out, Henry had instructed him, at Penryn, since someone at Falmouth station might easily recognise Orion as the young man Mr Hemy had seen off only the day before, and it was a relief to do so. Even Henry, more occupied in peering around as if he were expecting someone, noticed his greenish pallor.

"Not travel sick, surely?" he asked. Then, not waiting for an answer, "Ah! Excellent!" as a closed cab came up the hill and turned smartly into the station yard. "Come on lad! Climb up!" as the driver tipped his whip against his cap and jumped down to collect their baggage.

The journey took the better part of two hours, along the narrow lanes from Penryn to the sloping terraces of Budock Water, on to the village of Mawnan Smith and then out along a still narrower lane towards the coast. Exhausted from travel and the sideways lurching of the cab, Orion was asleep when Henry tapped loudly on the floor and startled him into wakefulness.

"Pull in here! By those trees," and the driver, also taken by surprise, brought his pony to a sudden stop, hooves sliding and grating against the stones.

"You sure, Sur?"

Orion would have echoed his question but Henry was already jumping down onto the grass verge.

"You won't get any closer with that thing. We must walk from here," he told the man and handed over what looked to Orion to be a considerable amount of money.

As the driver lifted down the bags and started to turn his equipage, Orion stared around him. It was only mid–afternoon but darkness, this late in the year, even this far South West, came early and the hedgerows, topped with brambles and thorn bushes, were already in deep shadow, the leafless briars standing out in vicious silhouettes against an evening sky of green and gold. On a stone platform beside the road two milk churns awaited collection by the dairy cart and from somewhere beyond the hedge a plume of smoke must come from the farm Henry had mentioned.

But no other signs of buildings and, apart from the hollow, receding clop of the horse's hooves and the creaking of the cab, no sounds other than faint squeaks among the bushes. Just once the dark shape of a small bird flitted across their sight and was, almost immediately, gone. Once a small creature, a weasel or stoat, dashed along the hedgerow and that too disappeared. It was the quietest place Orion had ever been and he felt suddenly quite afraid.

"Come on lad, let's get walking." Hefting his own bag and Mr Hemy's valise, Henry set off down a stony pathway beneath low–arching trees and bushes. His energy, as always, took Orion by surprise and he hurried to catch up with him, stumbling over exposed roots and doing his best to avoid the clawing briars.

It was an unpleasant walk. Brambles reached out to clutch at them. One dragged itself across the back of Orion's hand, tearing the skin and drawing blood; another caught in his hair, dislodging his cap so that he had to scrabble on the ground to retrieve it. The path itself was thick with fallen leaves, wet from the recent rains and easy to slip on, being laid underneath, as if it were cobbled, with broad pebbles, brought up presumably from the beach.

"A smugglers' path, I imagine – or even wreckers," Henry commented. "How wonderful."

Although Orion could see nothing wonderful about it. He didn't think there would be wreckers hereabouts, not any longer, but he knew that there was still plenty of smuggling. Cheap French wines and brandies and all sorts of exotic tobaccos were easily found in Falmouth and they certainly didn't come in through the port and under the eyes of the customs officers.

On the other hand the pathway was very overgrown and obviously rarely used and he tried to take comfort from this fact.

Coming out at the end was like emerging from a tunnel. The sea lay immediately before them, shining in the last of the light, white horses cresting the waves with bright white foam and, over towards the west, a pale green sky was streaked orange and gold from the setting sun, already sunk below the headland. There were rocks, Orion noticed, dark, wet and gleaming beyond an area of scrubby grassland dotted with gorse and brambles, and a dark bird – but, in this light, all birds except the gulls were dark – sat poised on the furthest rock.

And there was the cottage. His cottage. Set back from the sea and next to a strange, grassy mound that rose almost to roof height. A stone cottage – not that different from his old home except that it stood on its own. Four windows, a doorway, slate roof – a few slates had fallen and lay broken in the weed patch that must be the garden – and, behind it, a yard, surrounded by stone outbuildings.

"There you are. What do you think? Eh?" But Henry sounded less certain than he had the night before and did not wait for his answer. "Let's get inside," he said instead, and led the way to the front door. Which was locked but the key was easy to find even in the fading light, under a piece of broken slate on the window sill. It was less easy to turn and Henry had to push hard against the door which opened reluctantly, grating painfully against the flagstones, and the air that came out to meet them seemed even colder than the air outside.

It was also pitch dark and it was some time before they could see what the room was like. Bare, Henry was thinking, compared to Pennance Cottage and certainly compared to his mother's London home, although to Orion, gradually making out the shape of a table, two upright chairs and an armchair next to a fireplace surrounded by a tall mantel, it seemed well furnished. Beyond this room a narrow kitchen had a stone sink with a hanging drainer and a couple of shelves with pans, a couple of plates and a great number of mouse droppings. On the wall of the small building outside the window, which must be the privy, he could see the dark shape of a tin bathtub.

Just inside the main room a door led to a flight of stairs as steep as those in his old home but turning a corner and blocked by another door at the top. Beyond this a narrow landing led to two bedrooms, each containing an iron bedstead with a mattress but no bedding.

"Tch! They told me there were basic furnishings! I never considered bedclothes."

Henry looked into the second bedroom, strode hopefully across to a cupboard set into the wall and pulled it open to reveal… nothing. Turning, he peered through the gloom and banged his fist irritably against the side of his head.

"What a fool I am!"

"It don' matter."

Orion was still finding it hard to believe that this was to be his home. His home! A lack of bed linen, to one who had not even expected a bed, was of no consequence.

"But where will you sleep? Where, in fact, will *I* sleep – since there's no way I can get back to Pennance tonight. And what in the world," he banged his fist against his head once more, "are we going to eat?"

"I got pasties." His mother's pasties. Two days old now, which have travelled with him to Plymouth and back. "I c'n light the range. Heat 'em up there."

And now it seems to Henry that Orion has taken charge. He

appears to know, for a start, where candles will be stored – behind the frayed cotton curtain below the sink – produces a flame from a flint box to light them, fixes two onto enamel plates and one inside the lantern which he finds on the back doorstep. Then, lantern in hand, he disappears into the yard to return with straw, twigs and a battered willow basket filled with logs and, as Henry watches, lays a fire in the grate which burns, at first sulkily but eventually with more enthusiasm although it makes very little impact on the temperature of the room.

Henry, shivering, contemplates the thought of a night spent…where exactly? With little food, no bedding and only water to drink. Asks himself what he was expecting. A cosy cottage, already lit and warmed? A cheery Mrs Fouracre – or perhaps a Mrs Butchers – presiding over a roast dinner and a bottle of claret? Beds made up, aired and furnished with stone bottles creating comfortable pockets of warmth?

"Should we go see if we c'n find the farm? It can't be far off. I could see a light from the yard."

Orion is unused to taking control, but the sight of Henry huddled uncharacteristically into the shabby armchair emboldens him. "We c'n walk up the fields. The ground's not that muddy."

Although he is, as it turns out, wrong about this and they arrive some ten minutes later at the back door of the farmhouse, boots and trousers so covered in mud and cow dung that when the farmer's daughter, recognising a gentleman even in these circumstances, offers to show them into the parlour, Henry is constrained to refuse.

He does not, however, refuse her mother's offer of provisions and they return, muddier and more dung-covered than ever, to the cottage with a loaf, butter, a knuckle of ham and two jars of home brewed ale, while Orion, under his burden of woollen blankets, resembles a small, moving haystack.

And the fire, meanwhile has burned up, the room is warmer –
and certainly drier – than the fields outside and Ida Goss's
pasties, placed on the shelves on either side, give out a fragrant
smell of meat, swede and onion as their pastry starts to char.

Chapter 35

The farm–brewed ale was no substitute, to Henry's mind, to a good claret but went down well enough with the pasties and bread and ham. By which time the fire had burnt up sufficiently for them to move their chairs back and Orion, who knew nothing about claret, opened the second jar of ale.

"Proper job," he said, contemplating the foaming head on the cloudy liquid. "Better'n that dish slop they serve down the Seven Stars."

And a great deal stronger, Henry suspects, who is beginning to feel, in spite of everything, a pleasant blurring around the edges of his thoughts. Or perhaps it is just that his natural optimism is reasserting itself, now that the air is warmer and the pale light of fire and candles gives a glow even to this bare, unpromising room. Or perhaps it is the loosening of the taut and twisted strings of stress that wound themselves about his brain and body in the past few weeks, and especially these past few days when it has seemed increasingly unlikely that his insane plan might actually work.

For he is here with his boy. Who sits on the rag hearthrug, arms clutched around his knees, staring with apparent contentment into the fire. Who has agreed to all that Henry has suggested. Has not insisted on travelling on towards London and the new life in the new world that he has been expecting. Has allowed Henry to bring him instead to this grim and isolated place and has shown signs of an unexpected resilience and determination to cope.

And who is, at this moment, close enough for Henry to touch.

It would be the easiest thing in the world to reach out and stroke that untidy head of hair. To run his fingers through its ruffled waves, caught with fire–lit specks of gold. To slide them down to touch against the faint, illuminated down of that warm cheek. To trace the outline of those firm, red lips... But he cannot, he must not, think such thoughts and, creaking his chair as he shifts position, he sees Orion's head jerk suddenly upwards as if he has been falling asleep.

"Do you think…" The words catch in his throat. "Do you think you will… can be happy here? Will you manage, do you think, on your own?"

"I dunno." The boy speaks drowsily, reaching for his ale. "I an't seen it proper but… I reckon I c'n work the garden. Grow fruit an' veg. Did you mean it?" He turns to stare Henry in the face, his top lip fringed, like a blond moustache, with a thin line of foam. "That it's for me to live in? For good 'n all?"

"If it will suit you, yes. You'll be safe here. Falmouth men are unlikely to come out this far – at least not the sort of men you have to fear – and it's good land my friend tells me. You'll be able to grow what you fancy and sell it in the village. But I hope…" The old excitement takes over and he leans eagerly forwards. "This will be a chance for you, Orion, to…break away from your old life. You have talent, you know. I hope you will take the opportunity to nurture it. You enjoyed it, did you not," he explains, as Orion looks uncertain, "when we worked together in my studio? I hope you'll let me help you set up a studio here."

"Yes."

But he sounds doubtful, which is understandable. The boy has travelled a great distance, physically and mentally, in the past two days. It is unfair to expect more of him now.

"Tomorrow!" Henry speaks with a touch of his old heartiness. "Tomorrow we'll walk all round the place and you can make plans."

He takes another gulp of his ale, decides that yes, it is very strong and leans his head back against the chair. Orion goes on staring silently into the fire.

It is very quiet. Wood hisses damply, sending out occasional sparks. A burnt-out log falls apart, sparks dropping through the gratings to glow among the ashes, but no outdoor sounds penetrate the thick, granite walls. The boy's breathing becomes gradually louder and more regular, his head droops, his back slumps and slips slowly sideways towards Henry's chair until, hardly daring to breathe, he feels the warm weight of the sleeping body come to rest against his leg.

The sudden, blood-curdling cry of a barn owl startles him, the boy stirs, murmurs indistinguishable words and then his head rests back, more heavily, against Henry's thigh. And Henry, who has trained himself, all these years, to look, to admire but never, never, to touch, sits tense and still, looks down at the strands of curling hair, the long-lashed eyelids, thinks how he would love to paint the glow of firelight on those shadowed cheeks, does his best to repress those other, irrepressible, longings, gives in, strokes – but very gently so as not to wake him – the rough, untidy hair, then holds his arm around the boy's shoulders, drawing him in closer…

The damp chill that has possessed the inside of the cottage for so long reasserts itself as the fire begins to die. A draught blows across the stone floor and Henry, moving with caution, hunches himself further into the thick coat that hangs on the back of his chair. He should put more wood on the fire. He should find something to stop the draught. He should fetch a blanket to put around the boy who will catch cold with only the rag rug between him and the stone flags. But any of these activities will wake him, which is not what Henry wants. He would like, in fact, to sit like this all night. The boy's head heavy against his thigh, breathing gently and calmly, the two of them enclosed within the peace of the old cottage.

He would like to sit here, protecting him – for this is how it feels when he, the older man, watches over one who appears more than ever childlike in his sleep – from the cold, the darkness and whatever other dangers there may be beyond the walls.

In this mood, in fact, he might even welcome dangers beyond

the walls.

'I feel for him as I would a son' he has told Charles, and perhaps this is how it feels to be a father. And yet he cannot deny other feelings, that no father, no decent-minded father, would have for his child. For he has, he is forced to recognise, desires. The tumescence that stirs with an exquisite ache inside his trousers is inconvenient and shaming proof of this.

Sometimes, indeed, it has seemed unfair that a man so chaste and self-denying as Charles has been able to enjoy, with perfect morality, the pleasures of the flesh that have resulted in his many children when the cheery and sociable Henry is forced to deny them. For he spoke the truth, as always, when he assured Orion so many months before that he was no pederast. He is no Oscar, although he has always felt sympathy for him in his hounding and humiliation, and has never sought to satisfy his desires in such carnal ways. He may love the exuberance of youth and celebrate in his paintings the unselfconscious beauty of the adolescent male but his pleasure has never gone beyond friendship, whatever Charles may have feared.

Until now. This cold night in this cold, lonely cottage where he sits, tense with longing for this boy whom, he must admit to himself, he both loves and desires.

He has seen them – cold-eyed boys who lurk about the West End streets, especially those streets nearest to certain clubs frequented by Henry and some of his London friends. Boys in sharp waistcoats with sharp, ferret eyes to match who call after him and other lone men in their scornful, mocking voices. Come on yer lordship, yer know yer want it. Turning, if one is unwise enough to glance in that direction, to reveal a pertly rounded backside in tight-drawn trousers. Good enough for yer, Sir? Don't be shy then. Come an' get it, why doncher?.

In Falmouth too, along the road to the docks and around the opes and alleyways near the harbour. Roughly dressed, rough-voiced, altogether more homely boys, prepared for sixpence – or less – to satisfy briefly the urges of a lonely seaman – or any other man.

He has never been tempted, feeling only pity and an obscure sense of shame, although whether this is for what they have undoubtedly seen in him or because he feels, as a member of society, some portion of responsibility for their plight, he is not sure. What he is sure is that he has felt not the slightest vestige of desire. Certainly nothing to compare with what he feels at this moment.

Moving his hand from the boy's shoulders is like pulling it from the suction of sinking sands but he forces himself to do it. Perhaps it is the memory of those sharp-eyed boys and the shameful knowledge of what men with desires like his have made them. Or perhaps it is pride, in himself and in his family name, that helps him back into his familiar, ebullient self.

"Come on lad, you're falling asleep!" Shaking the boy's shoulder he jumps up to prevent him knowing how close they have been. "Take those blankets and get yourself upstairs. You're worn out and we have work to do in the morning."

He watches as Orion stumbles across the room and pulls open the staircase door.

"Take whichever room you prefer," he tells him. "I shall sleep down here."

Orion was not asleep when Henry first imagined him to be. With the warmth of the fire against his face, although he could still feel the chill of the stone floor through the thin hearthrug, he was drowsy but awake. Awake enough, certainly, to know that he was resting against Henry's legs. To feel the touch of Henry's hand against his hair. To feel his gentle grip across his shoulder and that slight tug that drew him closer.

Henry must not know he was awake or he would move away. He would let go of his shoulder; he would laugh or make some comment to cover the awkwardness and the moment would pass.

He did not want the moment to pass, in spite of his discomfort – the cold draught from the door, his legs cramping beneath him. The feeling of being held so close and so securely was a new experience and one he did not want to lose.

A sudden noise from outside the cottage – a sound like tearing metal which must have come from some bird or animal – startled him and then, feeling Henry's arm tighten protectively around him, he allowed himself to relax against it and went on feigning sleep.

His mother must have held him like this as a baby but it was not something he remembered and she had long ceased to show him any real signs of affection. His father would never have done so and Orion's early memories of him, like his memories of Alfred, were of the need to keep out of his way, especially when – which was most of the time – he had had too much to drink.

To be held affectionately and protectively by an adult was something entirely new for him and as he huddled into his blankets on the bare, damp mattress in the chilly bedroom, he could not help wishing that Henry had not stayed downstairs on his own.

Chapter 36

He knew there was no hope of getting to sleep, even if he followed Orion upstairs and lay down in whichever room the boy had chosen not to occupy. His brain was still too active, too full of nervous tension, and his body felt equally fraught and fine-stretched. His legs, as he huddled over the sulking fire, cramped and twitched with inactivity and he knew that relaxing into sleep, even in a warm, comfortable, well-aired bed – and the beds upstairs would be none of these things – was an impossibility.

A spider the size of a small mouse raced across the floor and disappeared into the log pile and Henry, who had never been able to rid himself of his fear of these crook-legged creatures, jumped to his feet and reached for his coat.

Outdoors seemed very little colder than inside the cottage. He stared both ways, left towards the mysterious mound and the tunnelled pathway down which he and Orion had come earlier and right towards the narrow footpath between bushes, mostly leafless by now, which led down the coast.

Choosing this route to walk off his agitation he found that, leafless or not, it was so overgrown that it was soon almost impossible to push through the trailing brambles thick with shrivelled blackberries, the viciously pointed blackthorn and the tangled chains of old man's beard and was about to turn back when he came upon a stone stile and, on the far side, an open field sloping to the cliff edge. It was a steep slope and the field was littered with granite boulders, mostly surrounded by a thick growth of thistles, but he scrambled his way down to sit on a convenient slab, regain his breath and gaze out over the darkened bay. Fast-moving banks of turbulent cloud bowled across the sky, lit by thin rays of silver moonlight and shredded by the wind to reveal an oily, blue-black backdrop. Below – but not so far below, it seemed, when the clouds hung so low – the sea heaved with black rollers, foam torn from their peaks as they moved inshore to break with a distant-sounding boom against the rocks. Such shading, Henry thought, in the darkness. Such blacks and greys and deepest blues. Such intensity in the lack of light.

And then towards the west, beyond the dark hulk of a long peninsular, a sudden flashing in the sky! Orange, blue and gold that at first he thought must be lightning except that no thunder followed. Instead more flashings lit the undersides of clouds and were, he realised at last, signals from Poldhu. The young Italian of whom he had heard. Who boasted that he could send wireless signals through the air, even across the Atlantic, to communicate faster and with less danger of interference than the transatlantic cable that already ran from Porthcurno further down the coast.

For some reason – perhaps it was because these unearthly flashes represented such optimism, determination and ambition – Henry, sitting alone on his rock, felt a sudden surge of hope within himself. Hope that he had done the right thing. That his mad plan of bringing Orion to live in this place might actually succeed.

The boy should have his chance in life, he told himself, jumping to his feet for the wind was blowing in under the thick collar of his coat and it was too cold to sit still for long. He should have his chance to become an artist and he, Henry, could have the satisfaction and reward of his protégé's success.

"I don't understand you, Henry. I haven't the remotest idea what you are talking about."

Four days have passed; it is Wednesday morning and Charles, who has hardly slept, stands in the front hall of Churchfield, still clothed in the dark, Dominican habit he has worn all night as he paced about his home. On his way to breakfast he has been startled by the sight of a pony and trap stopping at the gate and the familiar figure of Henry – who is in London; who is always in London at this time of year – striding towards the door.

And now is gabbling words that make no sense to Charles,

who can only note that something has happened to transform his friend from the miserable figure he saw off from Falmouth station less than three weeks ago to the exuberant, apparently irrepressible Henry he has known for so long.

He can hear Amy, who is always about early, talking to the housekeeper and two of his daughters laughing on the upstairs landing and he would prefer it if none of them meets Henry before he has established what in the world he is talking about and whether it is suitable for female ears.

"Come into the studio." He draws him across the hallway. "Do that later," he tells the girl who is in the process of laying the fire and, terrified, as always, by the sight of her master in his nasty, black cloak thing, scuttles back to the scullery to complain to cook.

"Now," Charles takes up his position in front of his easel, "tell me, for heavens sake, why you are here. Slowly, if you don't mind."

And looks increasingly appalled as Henry, slowly at first but, unable to restrain himself for long, describes his interception of Orion in Plymouth, their return, their journey to the coast, the state of the cottage, what they have done since…

"You would not believe, Charles, how hard that boy works! I've engaged a girl from the farm to do the cleaning but he's already done so much himself. Washing windows. Beating carpets. Clearing drains and gutterings. And the state of the earth closet! I've never seen anything like it but he just took it in his…"

"Stop!" Charles raises a hand. "Please stop it, Henry." Talk of drains and earth closets being more than he can take before breakfast. "Are you telling me that…the boy has not gone to America?" Even through Henry's ramblings he has made this out but the news is too astounding to accept without confirmation. "That you have… established him in a cottage along the coast? That…" And now he must take a deep breath. "That you have been… living there with him for the past several days?"

He closes his eyes as Henry nods his head.

"Who else knows about this?" Charles keeps his eyes tight shut. "His mother, for example?"

"No-one. That is the entire point, Charles. No-one must know. I have explained it to you. You know well enough, that it is too dangerous for him to remain here. Even out there, distant as it is from Falmouth, he would not be entirely safe…"

"Henry!" Charles feels behind him for his chair and sits down heavily, as if he has become, in the past few minutes, a much older man. "Henry, Henry, Henry… Can't you see what you have done? Effectively you have abducted this boy. All right…" He waves a hand as Henry goes to interrupt. "You say he came willingly but he is young, Henry. Young and poorly educated with no experience of life, whilst you are a mature man, a well-known man, well-educated, with a knowledge of the world which is far beyond his. Of course he did as you suggested. How could a boy like that stand out against a man like you?"

"It wasn't like that." Henry glares at his friend. His dark eyes are sullen and his nostrils flare as he attempts to contain his impatience. "There was no question of coercion. He hated the idea of going to America. That, if you like, he was too young for. And when I put an alternative suggestion he was only too happy…"

He stops, sighs, moves away to stare from Charles' window and tugs, a little nervously, at his moustache. For honesty – and Henry is, after all, an honest man – compels him to recognise that that he did rather more than 'put an alternative suggestion' when he intercepted Orion's train journey at Plymouth. That the boy had little or no choice in the matter.

"I couldn't bear it Charles, you know that. The thought of his going all that way. The dangers he would face. You said yourself; he is young and lacking in experience. How would he cope with life in that sort of world?"

He turns, gazing helplessly, begging his friend to understand.

"Others have. Young men like him. Children even. It might have been the making of him."

"But I couldn't bear…"

"Exactly!" Seizing the word, Charles strikes his hands against the arms of his chair and leaps to his feet. "You could not bear to lose him and so you concocted this foolish plan. You have consulted your own interests throughout this affair, Henry. I am disappointed in you. I did not imagine that even you would be so… unprincipled."

"*Even* me?" Henry looks for a moment as though his friend has hit him. "What does that mean?"

And Charles, stern, moral, steadfast Charles, is unable to answer him.

At which point the argument – for so it has become – might fracture their relationship for good. Bordering, as it does, on the conversation they have never had; the subject most of Henry's friends have never raised, either because it would embarrass them, or because they value his robust and cheery friendship too much or because they are themselves too innocent. The subject of his sexual tastes and proclivities. A subject which Henry himself has never mentioned either.

But he and Charles have been friends for years. And are, for all their differences, loyal to each other. And so,

"My dear Harry, I apologise." Charles steps forward, meeting Henry's hurt, unhappy eyes. "It was said in the heat of the moment. I simply meant…I meant…" He struggles, uncertain exactly what he did mean. "I am aware that we are very different people, you and I. Our… tastes are not the same but I have always thought of you as a man of principle. I have always valued our friendship…"

"Charles!"

It is to Charles' credit that he accepts and responds to Henry's enthusiastic bear–hug with welcoming arms.

"We should have breakfast," he says. "Then perhaps we can

talk more calmly. I am still worried that the boy's mother has no idea where he is. After all, it was I who introduced the idea to her in the first place."

"I'm not sure," Henry follows him towards the door, "that she cares a great deal. From what Orion has told me."

Chapter 37

But Ida Goss did, of course, care about her boy. Wondered, as she scrubbed Mrs Trembath's kitchen, prepared her meals and polished her silverware, how her Orion was coping on a journey she couldn't even begin to envisage.

Having no knowledge of Plymouth, London, Liverpool or transatlantic steam ships she could only hope he was, in the most general of ways, 'going on all right'. Hope and – every night before getting into bed and every Sunday in chapel – pray that her boy, who had never before been out of Falmouth on his own, would, in some unimaginable way, get himself safely to the other side of the world.

"You 'eard anything yet?" It was the first thing Bea Rogers asked every Friday when Ida arrived. Closely followed by, "Course not. 'Ow could you 'ave?"

For the first month at least. After that she ceased asking, since it was always obvious from Ida's face that there was no news to report.

And now it was almost two months and her friend's silence, as they sat on either side of her little tea table, was more than Bea could bear.

"It's bound to take time. Finding 'is feet in a new country," she ventured. "Do they 'ave a postal service over there even, d'you know?"

Ida held her sewing closer to the lamp and shook her head.

"I don' know," she admitted. "People must write letters though, mustn't they? Like they do 'ere."

She ponders on these unknown people called Americans. About whom she knows only that they fought a War of Independence against one of the King Georges and a Civil War against themselves, neither of which snippets of history offer her much comfort.

"But they'd take time to get 'ere." Bea brightened at the

thought. "Coming all that way. Weeks, I shouldn't wonder." And was rewarded by the faint shadow of a smile on Ida's face.

"An' we've never been a family for writing letters." (Or writing anything, she might have added, her entire output for a year generally consisting of no more than the occasional scribbled message to Mrs Trembath and two or three cards at Christmas.) And Orion, she thought, knowing nothing of his notes taken at the lectures at the Polytechnic Hall or copied from books in the library, had never needed to do even that. "I don't suppose it'll even enter 'is head."

Her face saddened again as she drew a length of thread through her material – she was embroidering a cushion cover for the chapel sale of work. For if it never entered Orion's head to write to her how was she ever to get news of him? Like Ivan Hart he might have disappeared into the vast darkness known as 'overseas', never to be heard of again. She might as well never have given birth to him and she felt the sides of her mouth draw themselves unhappily downwards at the thought.

For she was missing her younger son more, much more, than she had expected. Alfred had never been much company and now he was courting Edie Rusco she saw less of him than ever – and good riddance to bad rubbish was all she could say about that. But Orion, even if he had never had much to say for himself, was at least a good natured lad. Now, when she came home worn out after her exhausting day, there was no-one to talk to, no-one to complain at, most of the time no-one in the house at all.

"You could ask that Mr 'Emy if 'e's heard. 'E must 'ave friends over there."

A man like Mr Hemy, Bea was thinking, must have friends everywhere. Friends who did write letters to each other. "You should go up 'is place and ask."

She stared hopefully across at her friend and Ida, knowing that she would never dare do such a thing, nodded her head and started to pack away her sewing. The train from Truro, rattling across the railway bridge outside, let out a breathless sounding hoot, its brakes hissing as it slowed for the station.

"I should be getting off 'ome," she said. "It's a rough night and I don't want to be out late."

The wind, as if in agreement, gusted against the window and rattled the sash. The draught through the frames shifted the curtains and Ida pulled her shawl closer about her shoulders. She was not looking forward to the long walk home. She was not, if the truth be known, looking forward to anything any more.

"You must make some proper arrangement, Henry. Suppose I should meet the boy's mother about the town? Or if she should call here? She must be anxious about her son and I feel responsible. It was I who persuaded her that he should emigrate, after all. I can't tell you how much this business disturbs me."

It is the following evening. Henry, who has been on his, much delayed, visit to his mother and sister in London, has arrived back in Falmouth and has called in at Churchfield to see his friend.

Who is determined to make his point.

"If you do not go and see the poor woman while you are here this week I shall do so myself," he says firmly. "I have been on the verge of doing so for some time. The way things stand I am colluding in an untruth and I can't continue to do so any longer."

He turns the full force of his severity on his friend, who looks abashed and agrees that he will give the matter some thought.

"I'm going out tomorrow to see him," he admits, "and on Monday I am coming back to Jackett's yard to see how my new boat is coming on..."

This is the first that Charles, a keen sailor himself, has heard of a new boat and, just for a moment, Orion and his anxious mother slip from his mind.

"I had no idea... You haven't mentioned it."

"Oh yes. I placed an order a month or so ago. A sloop, like

Norton's 'Daphne'. After my problems with 'Red Heart' last season, I'm ready for a change and 'Daphne' impressed me greatly."

"Hm." They are sailing rivals, after all, and Charles is not sure that he wants Henry to have a still-faster boat. And then he remembers his point.

"And then you must go and see the boy's mother," he says. "Or I will do so for you."

Chapter 38

The cottage garden had been neglected, Orion reckoned, for years but it was good soil and a few days' heavy digging had got rid of the weeds. A day's digging before Christmas was worth a week's in spring, Mr Cyril always said, and as he laboured through the short, damp days of mid December Orion had hoped he was right.

Most of the dug-over soil at the front of the cottage he had left to be broken up by the frost – if they got any; if not he would break it up himself in spring – but he had risked planting a few rows of peas, sprouts and broad beans in the more sheltered area at the back, making sure he planted them, as Mr Cyril had always done, under a waxing moon to give them the best chance of growth. The peas had vanished, in spite of the moon, eaten, he suspected, by the mice, but the beans were sprouting well and now, under a waning moon because these were underground plants, he had sown his carrots, the seeds mixed with ash from the bonfire, and turnips and had several rows of seed potatoes set out for chitting along the outhouse windowsills. When he had dug over the remaining area again, he would make sowing of cabbages and onions, kale and beetroot; then he would start on his flower garden at the front of the house.

Meanwhile, following several days of gales and heavy seas, there was a harvest too good to resist and he spent the better part of a day hauling barrow–loads of seaweed from the little cove as manure for his empty beds.

"You're some 'ard worker, an't you?" Mary, daughter of the herdsman at the farm, who was being paid by Henry to keep the cottage clean and to cook Orion a hot supper, paused by the back door to watch as he dug in the still–glistening bladder wrack.

"Mind you, I'll be glad when that whiff's gone."

She smiled, picked up her broom and went back indoors.

She was a hard worker herself Orion thought, pushing his hair from his eyes as he watched her go. The flagstones in the living room and kitchen shone now, freed from ground–in mud so that he was obliged to leave his muddy boots on the doorstep. The shelves were washed clean and there were no more mouse-droppings. (Indeed no more mice since Mrs Roscrow had sent over a supply of mouse traps.) The sink was scrubbed clean, the range glowed from Mary's vigorous black-leading and the brown dado had been thoroughly washed down.

Nor was she a bad cook. Her pastry might not be as light as his mother's but she made an excellent stew and Orion found himself looking forward every day to five o'clock, although the fact that she went off home after dishing up his tea made it, he began to realise, a little less enjoyable. Some days he found himself thinking up comments, about the food, the weather or the state of the sea, that might cause her to linger a bit longer but conversation had never been his strong point and, now he was alone most of the time, had become more difficult than ever. Also just seeing her neat, busy figure made him feel tongue–tied and clumsy. It was easier, he found, simply to busy himself with his work and his plans for the future – a new experience for someone whose life up to now had involved simply acting as others instructed him.

He had been several times to Helston market with farmer Roscrow and was already preparing for the pullets he intended to buy there later in the year. When the weather was too wet to work outside he spent the time clearing the larger outhouse where they would roost and preparing the laying boxes for their eggs. He had never kept poultry but there were plenty who did and it couldn't, he reckoned, be that difficult.

And, as well as being cleaner, his cottage was more comfortable inside. There was a second arm chair, donated by Mrs Roscrow who said her own parlour was over-crowded. Heavy curtains kept out the draughts from the front door and the flagstones had two more rugs to cover them, one purchased in

Helston by Henry and the second, a rag rug, brought across from the farm by a blushing Mary who insisted that she had no use for it.

Orion dared not ask but the pink flush on her pretty cheeks suggested that it was one she had made herself.

He was not entirely sure how he felt about this. It was made by the same method his mother used, cutting old clothing into strips along the parts that were least worn, sewing them together, plaiting them and then winding the plaited strips round and round like the shell of a snail. The trick, he remembered, from watching his mother, was not to pull the plaits too tightly together or the outer edges of the rug would lift and trip the unwary walker and he noticed how flat this rug lay and thought how cleverly Mary had managed.

It was an odd feeling, as he sat in front of his fire in the evenings, staring down at her rug which he had laid in pride of place in front of it, to think that the pieces of material it was made of might have been part of her clothing. Not all of them, of course. Some would be bed linen – although he was not sure what he felt about this either – and some would have been swapped with friends or relatives, from their rag bags, in the way he remembered his mother doing. But the outer strip of plaiting – a mixture of deep green and paler green cottons – was Mary's he was sure. The dress she wore most often when she came to clean for him was green, with a white flower pattern, and it was, he was also sure, her favourite colour. Certainly it suited her dark brown hair and her almost black eyes, although he would never, he was sure, dare to tell her this.

In any case there was an 'understanding' Mr Roscrow had told him on one of their trips to market, between Mary and Tacker Chegwidden, the farmer's nephew, who had a nice little poultry business in the village and a temper, Orion had already heard, that did not bear crossing. Having escaped – after two months he felt sure of this now – from one dangerous situation he had no intentions of running headlong into another.

"You are happy here, aren't you?" It is nine miles, mainly up and down steep, coastal hills, from Pennance but Henry has cycled out on this dry Sunday morning. "You don't miss your home?"

After his talk with Charles he has to raise the subject, although he has still no idea what he should do about it.

"No. I don' miss it 't'all."

Orion is struggling with a lump of granite which will form part of the border for his flower bed and has little attention to spare. But as he stands back, wiping his grubby hands against the back of his trousers, he thinks he may have sounded ungrateful.

"P'raps me ma…"

Who will be, at this time on a Sunday morning, in Chapel. Praying, possibly, for Orion in his new life on the other side of the world. And who may well miss him.

But maybe not. He has never been sure what feelings she has for him. And out here, in such different surroundings and away, apart from Henry, from everyone he knew in Falmouth, it is quite hard to remember the life he led less than three two months before. In some ways it seems as distant as if he had really crossed the Atlantic.

"Will she be expecting to hear from you? To say you've arrived safely?"

Henry has been pondering how this might be managed. A letter, written by Orion, posted in, say Plymouth, apparently by a returning traveller? Saying that he has arrived in America and is well and happy? The idea, too close to a lie for his fastidious mind, makes him uncomfortable and he is fairly sure that Charles would not approve either but perhaps he may agree if he thinks it would put the boy's mother's mind at rest…

Orion shrugs. Reaches for another lump of granite.

"We're not much for writing in our family."

"Perhaps a postcard…"

It might, he thinks, be worked. He has London acquaintances who travel, occasionally, to America. It would be easy enough to acquire a postcard – of the statue of Liberty perhaps – for Orion to write a message, which the acquaintance might post on his next trip… It would take some months, however, and is still unlikely to meet with Charles' approval.

"I don' think she'll expect nothing."

And the whole business is too complex – and too deceitful. And Orion does not appear to think it matters. Henry, too delighted to see him again to want to spoil the occasion, shelves the problem.

"Right then, stop messing around with those stones and show me the rest of the place. And surely you can't have spent all your time out here. Have you done any sketching? Or painting? Come along. I want to see everything."

But Orion has nothing new for him to see, which is not surprising when he has spent so much time on his garden. And without Henry to encourage him – he does not tell him this – and although he no longer has to worry about Alfred finding his work, it is hard to convince himself that drawing and painting are activities he is permitted to do. It is different for Henry – he does not tell him this either. He has been to art school and art is his job. He is skilled at it. He is praised for it. He is *paid* to do it. Orion, however hard Henry has tried to convince him otherwise, is only a gardener and, having been given this extraordinary opportunity, should spend all the hours he has making the best of it.

"I bin busy." He stares at the lumps of granite that are starting to border his path and the other lumps that lie around, waiting to be placed. "I 'aven't 'ad no time."

"Well today you have. In any case, it's Sunday. Your day of rest. And…" Henry slaps his forehead at his own forgetfulness. "I brought you a present. From London. A Christmas present if you like," and, delving into the canvas bag he carries strapped to the back of his bicycle, he pulls out a small box with a picture of a large, many–windowed building with smoking chimneys on the front. "These are the latest thing. They're called oil sticks. Invented by a chap called Raffaelli. You rub away the film on the outside and – like magic! – you've got oil paint. Here, try them," and he thrusts the box in Orion's direction. "You can use them like crayons, or you can mix the paints on your palette or on your canvas. You can…"

But Orion, he can see, has his blank, uncertain expression on his face and his hands firmly in his trouser pockets. And Henry is forgetting that this is not one of the students he meets and mentors in South Kensington. This is Orion, whose hands are grubby from digging and handling rocks. Who has not yet progressed beyond sketching and water colours. Who has no idea about oil paints or, for that matter, canvases.

And then a gap appears in what has appeared to be an impenetrable ceiling of cloud and the sun, which has been lurking behind it all morning, pushes through a tentative, milky golden ray, lighting an area of dull grey sea into sudden, shifting patterns of green and white and blue…

"Come on! The cloud's lifting." Henry seizes Orion's shoulder and thrusts him towards the cottage. "Leave your wretched rocks for another day. We'll go and play with oil sticks!"

It is one of those glorious afternoons that come occasionally very early in the year and are all the more precious for being brief and unexpected. When rare sunlight brings unexpected warmth, the damp earth gives up its scent of roots and last year's rotting leaves and this year's tenuous growth, new buds are suddenly visible on what have seemed to be bare branches, one tiny, opening flower lights an entire hedgerow and it is impossible, for an hour or so at least, not to be conscious of life beginning again. And Henry, always the optimist, tows the reluctant Orion along the path and away from the house. Look, he keeps telling him, pointing to a robin opening its tiny beak on a tangled briar, a clump of dry grasses lit to gold by the sun, an impossibly early celandine glowing at the bottom of the hedge. Look at that. Isn't it wonderful? And Orion, trudging behind him, has, eventually, to agree that it is.

They stop at the point where the path opens out onto a bare headland with a view down the coast in the direction of Newlyn. Henry unpacks his bag, takes out his sketch book and one he has brought for Orion and his two boxes of the miraculous new oil sticks.

"This is where they can be so useful," he says, beaming. "You can just carry them with you without needing a pack horse."

Taking off his jacket and laying it on the still damp grass he sits down, resting his back against the granite stile they have just clambered over, selects one of his oil sticks, wipes the end with a rag and starts to sketch the opposite headland and the rocks below it. Orion, ignored, watches as he uses the sticks to draw his outlines, his fingers and his rag to blur the lines, a brush to add different shades and depths so that the cliff, the rocks, the sulky green grey sea below and the deeper green of the damp winter grass above appear, almost as if by magic, on the paper.

He couldn't do that, he thinks, as he has thought before. Not in a million years. And then, looking inshore, he sees a stone building, not much more than a hut – perhaps used by a famer for storing tools or cattle feed. Squatting next to Henry he picks up the second sketch book and the second, unopened, box of oil sticks…

251

Chapter 39

On the Monday Henry went, as he had explained to Charles, to Jackett's boat yard. It was the first time he had seen the boat that was being built for him and he was pleased with its progress, although Thomas Jackett may have felt, as he showed off her features, that his customer was perhaps not concentrating as hard as he might have expected.

"Excellent work," Henry told him. "I'm delighted with her. Well done."

Which was all very well but Jackett had known Mr Tuke show a great deal more interest in the details of a new craft and he was, after all, paying out a great deal of money for her.

Mrs Fouracre was also puzzled. She had been expecting her tenant and had stocked her larder accordingly, assuming that he would entertain as many guests as he usually did at this time of year, only to be told that he would be spending very little time at Pennance. Friends down near Helford had invited him to stay, he said, and it would make a change to do some painting in that, more sheltered, area.

She did not, she told her husband irritably that evening, believe a word of it. Something was going on, she said. Mark her words. She even wondered if they had done something to upset him.

But Henry was, as always, telling the truth. He had been invited by a young couple, Amber and Fearnley Robertshaw, who were renting a house not far from Mawnan Smith, to stay with them as long as he would like and the circumstances suited him perfectly.

"We're rather Bohemian in our arrangements," Amber, whose thick, wiry and intensely black hair fell untidily from a thick pile on top of her head and who seemed always to wear the same black, paint-spattered smock, even when shopping in the village, told him when he arrived. "We are rather frugal in our eating habits – I hope you won't find it a problem."

"I'm afraid poor Daphne does! I keep expecting her to give notice." Fearnley, who had, by contrast, more or less no hair and the cadaverous cheeks of someone who ate little but nuts and pulses, gave an unnerving bark of laughter and led Henry up to a bleak little bedroom which reminded him of his boarding school days. "Amber's delighted that you've agreed to come and stay with us," he added. "The thought of an artist of your stature, staying in our home! We're overwhelmed, I can tell you."

"Please don't be." Henry felt acutely embarrassed. "And please don't alter any of your arrangements for me. I intend to be out, painting, every day – even bad weather doesn't deter me. All I need is somewhere to lay my head at night."

Although, as he looked down at the narrow bed with its thin mattress and a pillow which, from its look and smell, must be stuffed with herbs from the garden, he couldn't help wondering if just a little more comfort might have been desirable.

"They are quite extraordinary," he told Orion next morning, after a breakfast of Daphne's not unpalatable porridge and a cup of bramble leaf and nettle tea, made, Amber assured him and it was easy to believe, by herself. "They entertained me last night with a recital of Fearnley's poetry. Arrhythmic and without form, was how he described it, and that was certainly how it sounded."

Orion, more concerned with turning his chitting potatoes, nodded, although he had no idea what Henry was talking about, but was more interested in the herb and potato pie Henry pulled out of his knapsack – lunch, provided by the long–suffering Daphne. Who had promised, he said, to slip a nice piece of rabbit brawn alongside the lentil bake she was preparing for tonight's supper.

"I d'like to see a man enjoy 'is meat," she had whispered to him when he came into the kitchen that morning. "All they nuts and beans is all very well but it's not proper food, is it now?"

Henry agreed with her and, although he felt slightly guilty, told himself that feeding him was probably encouraging Daphne to stay with his hosts, at least for the moment and, since he had insisted, as they refused to take any payment from him, on paying her wages while he was with them, he felt justified in living, at least partially, by his own diet.

And they were, he decided, a harmless, even an engaging couple. The arrhythmic, formless poetry could be tedious but in the semi darkness of the candlelit drawing room it was easy enough to doze off, although he hoped he managed to avoid snoring. Just as it was possible to listen to Amber's earnest pontificating on the subject of art and what she called the 'dead hand' of the Royal Academy, although, as an associate of that body, with hopes of being elected as a Fellow, he did not entirely agree with her. Certainly it was hard to find a great deal of merit in her dark and swirling paintings of what she called 'the reality beyond the life we see' but his vague comments on their 'verve and energy' seemed to please her enough. More importantly the two of them were so absorbed in their own, weird world that they showed no interest in what Henry was doing and he was able to spend his days the mile and a half down the coast at Orion's cottage.

Where he had set up a studio in the larger of the two bedrooms with its view down the coast where the strange flashes still lit up the night sky. With one of his own old easels and another which he and Orion fashioned between them from wood found in one of the outhouses in the centre of the room, a table brought from a Helston junk shop to hold their jars and brushes and other paraphernalia and an ancient dust sheet of Mrs Roscrow's to protect the floor boards it was at least possible to work there, which was what they did when the weather was too bad to paint outdoors.

Although the weather continued, for the most part, unseasonably fair and they spent at least part of most days out on the coast, where Henry used Raffaelli's oil sticks to produce small-scale paintings of the rocky coves and winter sea. He had pictures back at Pennance, he kept reminding himself, that needed attention before the Royal Academy exhibition but for now it was enough to hike along the coastal pathways, to find a sheltered spot and tuck oneself in beside a hedge or against a rock and work on these small, experimental paintings.

And Orion appeared equally happy. The new medium suited him well, both the small scale of the pictures and the ease with which he could manage the almost, it seemed, magical sticks of oil paint. Which worked, he discovered, equally well on the thin pieces of board – sides of an old crate – which he had found in an outhouse. His simple paintings – a grass-topped headland, a few trees, a sloop out near the horizon – looked more satisfactory, it seemed to him, against this rougher surface and framed by the poorly cut, almost ragged edges.

These days reminded Henry of the previous summer, before everything had started to go so wrong. Except that Orion no longer spent his days working in Mr Rowse's garden. Except that he lived in his own little cottage where, when it rained or was too cold to be outdoors, they could work together in his own studio. Except that they had no need to fear being seen by any of Henry's friends.

Whose company, he realised, he did not even miss. The evenings of bridge or whist or billiards, the convivial meals and intense discussions – even his rather quieter but no less enjoyable evenings with Charles and Amy – were pleasant enough to look back on but no, he did not miss them. He missed his sailing – but he would not have been sailing at this time of year in any case. Nor would he be painting his boys sprawled across the deck of the Piebox or on the rocks or sand of Newporth.

For now it was enough – more than enough – to spend his days comfortably painting with Orion, sometimes helping him to clear the rubbish from his outhouses, building tall bonfires, when the wind was right, to rid themselves of it or simply sitting, talking peacefully in the little downstairs room before he cycled home to an evening of Amber's rambling discourses and Fearnley's poetry.

"In the summer – or perhaps autumn would be better – I want to go back to Italy." They are sitting together in front of the fire which Orion has just lit to warm them after a day spent painting on the rocky outcrop that forms one side of the small cove. "And this time you must come with me. You'll love it. The warmth…" He rubs his still–numb fingers and holds them out towards the hissing logs. "The light. The colours of the sea and sky. The glorious plants. You can't imagine what it's like until you've seen it."

"It sounds nice." Orion pokes at a log with his foot and watches as the bark disintegrates and pieces drop, crackling and sparking, into the hearth. They grow lemons, he is thinking, in Italy. And oranges. Figs. Pomegranates even. "I'd dearly like to go there."

Henry, leaning back in his armchair, visualises Orion in Italy. His muscular limbs bronzed by the sun. His fair hair bleached white. His whole being released from its natural awkwardness and anxieties by the uninhibited, easygoing way of life under the warmth of southern skies.

Already he imagines the painting he might persuade the boy to model for. Something, perhaps, in the classical style. Orion below date palms or framed by bougainvillea, raising his bare arms to the sun god or, like a more innocent Dionysus, reaching in a vineyard for a bunch of grapes….

"We'll go then." He slaps his hands against his thighs as though the decision has been made. "Next September we'll spend a month – perhaps even two months – in Italy."

He cycles cheerfully back towards Mawnan Smith, owl-eyed

in the dark, along lanes with which he has become so familiar, while Orion sits, still thinking, in front of his fire. In September, he is thinking, he should be lifting and storing his onions and potatoes for the winter market. He should be harvesting his main crops of spinach, beets and carrots. He will need to be planting his spring greens and next year's onions as well as taking care of his winter cabbages and the cauliflowers which he has intended to go in for and which should be sown at the end of the month. And who, if he is in Italy for a month, let alone two, will see to the pullets he plans to buy? Not to mention, if he sells enough produce to afford one, his pig.

"The boy is happily settled."

Henry, in Falmouth for the night, is having dinner at the Hemys'. Or rather, he has had dinner and he and Charles are standing in Charles' studio. Talk of Henry's new boat has moved on – inevitably – to their other shared interest and Henry, who should be, at this moment, back in London working on one of the portraits which so comfortably boost his income, is enthusing about a portrait by the American Whistler, whose work he admires. Meanwhile he leafs through Charles' sketch book, stopping at a page of sketches of his yacht 'Barbara'.

When Charles, who has been waiting his moment, asks if he has yet spoken to Mrs Goss he at first feigns absorption and then admits that he has not.

"Please Charles…" as his friend makes an irritable growling sound deep in his throat, "allow me a little longer. The boy is happily settled. He is making a comfortable home for himself, planting vegetables in his garden, which he will soon be able to sell. He is safe and contented. But if I tell his mother where he is, his brother, and then his father, are bound to find out and then who knows what may happen? He is not completely beyond their reach, out in his cottage."

Which is precisely, Charles reminds him, why the boy was

257

supposed to emigrate.

"I know." Henry turns his dark eyes on him. "But what is done is done and, as far as the boy is concerned, has turned out for the best. And – his face brightens as he remembers – I have asked my contact at the shipping line to write to Mrs Goss, informing her of the ship's safe arrival in New York. Surely that will have reassured her?"

Charles sniffs reproachfully, pulling at his moustache. It is, he supposes, better than nothing.

Chapter 40

He returned to London, fully intending to stay until Easter. With a new boat to pay for as well as his projected trip to Italy he certainly needed the money he would earn from the portraits he had been commissioned to paint. And yet, even amongst the social bustle of the city, he found he was missing Orion even more than he had expected. At home with his mother, at dinners with friends, even in the theatre or concert hall, he was powerless to prevent his thoughts from drifting back to that first night in the little cottage and the memory of Orion's sleeping head against his thighs or their more recent, comfortable days, spent painting together along the coast. One evening, during a performance of a play which he would have said, if asked, was absorbing his interest completely, he found himself taking a pencil from his pocket and sketching on his programme and in the dimmest of light that rounded, lovingly remembered face and wide–set, uncertain–looking eyes. Later, in his bedroom, he spent a long time gazing at it before undressing and getting into bed.

And so it was, perhaps, not surprising that by the middle of March he could not bear to stay away any longer. He would just 'dash down to Falmouth' for a week, he told his astonished mother, to check on the progress of the boat and the following morning he left Paddington on the Cornish Riviera Express.

Orion, plodding with his dibber and a handful of turnip seeds along the rows of his well–dug vegetable garden, pauses and looks up. He gets few enough visitors. Mary, of course, but it is too early for her. Farmer Roscrow, occasionally, or one of his hands. Rarely anyone else.

He certainly does not expect Henry, who is in London and not returning until next month.

"Still busy I see. And look at all this!"

Henry waves a hand to indicate the sprouting greens, the

259

beans, the fluffy carrot tops and upturned tips of several rows of onions and they are both reminded of his visits, back in another world, to Mr Rowse's garden.

"'S coming on." Orion straightens and looks around at his work. "I shall need to get my bean sticks in next week."

"So I can see. And you've got raspberry canes."

"An' a couple o' black currants." Orion remembers the box of raspberries Henry once gave him, that his mother flung onto the kitchen floor. "From 'Elston market," he says. "I d'go in with Mr Roscrow most weeks now. I got a bit o' paid work too," he adds. "Digging an old lady's garden up Mawnan Smith."

And there is a silence. Orion has always found it hard to adapt to Henry's sudden arrival, especially now, when he spends so much time on his own, or with Mary's quiet and unobtrusive presence. Perhaps now more than ever when… But he does not even dare frame the thought in his mind. Something has changed in the few weeks since Henry has been gone and it is not just the arrival of raspberry canes and blackcurrant bushes. It is something far more important – possibly.

And now he is back – and nothing about him is unobtrusive. As Orion watches warily, fingering the tiny seeds he still clutches in the palm of his hand, he strides about the yard, bending to sniff at the clumps of rosemary, pulling a leaf from one of the sprouting raspberry canes, peering into the nearest outhouse…

"You have been busy," he says, turning back and smiling. He pulls off his cap and thrusts his hand through his hair so that it stands up thick and glossy.

And then, "But what about your art?" he asks. "Have you been just as busy in the studio? Or have you been spending all your time out here? You must show me what you've been doing."

"Who's this?"

A sea mist has rolled in, in the unpredictable way of sea mists, and they have left the broad beans, the seedling carrots, the raspberries and the sprouting greens and retreated indoors. But this last month the weather has been dull and wet and it has not been a good time for painting or drawing – Henry would have said it was not a good time for gardening either – and Orion appears to have done very little since he has been gone. Leafing through the sketchbook Henry sees very little new work – a few, not very successful, attempts at the view from his window, one quite decent drawing of his garden fork leaning against the shed wall – and then he pauses at a simple line sketch of a figure. A female figure, drawn from the back, neat–waisted, with one arm reaching downwards.

"Where?" But it is obvious from the dark flush on Orion's neck as he fiddles with the pencils laid out on his table, that he knows quite well what Henry means. "Oh… Tha's nothing. Tha's Mary. You know. Comes to clean."

"I know."

The girl he himself engaged to look after the cottage and make sure the boy has at least one decent meal a day. The girl who has left, he has already noticed, and although it is Sunday when she is not expected, a pie for Orion to heat up for his supper.

"Pretty girl," he comments, although this is impossible to tell from the sketch but now he remembers a pair of dark eyes and a shy but charming smile, glimpsed briefly and occasionally when he was here earlier in the spring. Orion says nothing but the red stain, Henry notes, rises from his neck and into his cheeks and he busies himself unnecessarily, sharpening a pencil that appears already quite sharp enough.

He will lose him, he thinks, as wood shavings flutter to the ground from Orion's uncharacteristically clumsy hacking. He stares at the drawing of the garden fork, indicates with a few strokes of his own pencil where Orion has got the perspective wrong and hears next to him the faint crack of the breaking lead. He will lose him, either to this girl or another, and he can do nothing about it.

He feels a tightening in his throat and finds it, for a few moments, almost impossible to breathe naturally let alone speak. And, if he could speak, what could he say? The boy is almost eighteen and many are married at his age. And he is strong, good–looking and a hard worker. Even in this remote place girls will find him and do their best to attract his interest and what can Henry do to prevent them?

After all he has done, all the risks he has taken, he is going to lose him.

"I don't remember her. I must meet her some time," he says after a long pause. He keeps his eyes fixed on Orion's drawing and forces his voice to remain firmly under control.

Hearts, he tells himself, do not actually break and yet, as he drives his hired trap back along lanes where overhanging trees weep mist, there is so much pain inside him that he can visualise the jagged wound and leaking drops of blood.

No, he tells Mrs Fouracre, who was not expecting him and is fretting about her lack of provisions, he will not be entertaining this week. He has come down to check on the progress of his new boat. He will be busy in Falmouth most days and may well be away overnight, staying with friends. She gives him a look which he finds hard to interpret and returns it with one that is similarly ambiguous. Then he goes outside, making his way through the shadows of the old mine building that adjoins his house to his studio, where, in the flickering light of the paraffin lamp, he sits huddled into his chair. When Mrs Fouracre appears in the doorway, a black shawl pulled over her head against the wind, and asks if she should light the stove he hears himself give an abrupt no but is incapable of doing anything about such uncharacteristic lack of courtesy.

It is the shock, he tells himself, that has caused this...numbness. These past weeks in London, and all the way down here on the train, he has looked forward to returning to

Orion's cottage, to seeing what progress he has made, in his studio and in his garden; to being with him again, as they were before. Just as they were before. With nothing changed between them.

He has imagined them working together in the little studio. Helping the boy improve his technique. Nurturing his talent, as they did that summer they worked together at Pennance. He has imagined them walking, when the weather allowed, around the cliff paths, cycling along the lanes – everything as it was before, but with the security of knowing that Orion is out of reach of his violent relations.

He has, above all, looked forward to taking him away in September. To watching him blossom in the warmth of the Italian sun.

And now... And now it appears that everything is different. Everything has changed in a way he has not anticipated.

It has happened before; of course it has. Boys – young men – with whom he has been friendly, whom he has cared for, have found themselves sweethearts and the sweethearts have become wives. But these were different boys. Noisy, sociable boys, with gangs of friends, eager to boast of their sexual exploits – exaggerated, more than likely. Always before he has seen it coming and has been happy for them.

But Orion. Shy, awkward, serious Orion. Who loves his plants, who loves drawing and painting. Who found his way, on his own, to the lectures at the Polytechnic Hall. Who has educated himself, in a small way, at least, through the public library. Orion, who has never seemed to have any friends besides himself and has never so much as mentioned a girl's name.

Until now.

It is bitterly cold out here without the stove and he drags off the rug that hangs over the back of his chair and pulls it around his shoulders. Through the wooden walls of the studio he can hear the sound of the sea below his cliff, a sound he normally loves – and misses when he is in London – but now the hollow thud of water against rock, the sad withdrawing flow of foam, serve only to emphasize the loneliness that seems to wind itself about his soul. He shivers, huddles further into his rug, which feels too cold and damp to offer any comfort, and tells himself he is a fool.

If he feels lonely, here, in the home he loves and with dozens of dear friends within easy reach, how can he have expected Orion to cope in his isolated cottage in a place where he knows hardly anyone? It was wrong to have left him on his own and now he begins to plan how he can alter his arrangements for the next few weeks so that he can spend more time with the boy when he needs him.

Orion is, after all, his pupil. It is only fair that he should give him more attention. Left to his own devices, he has done little enough drawing or painting this past month. He is still, after all, very young and still lacks confidence in his talent. It is up to Henry to rekindle his enthusiasm. To show the lad what he might, with application, achieve. To encourage him to broaden his horizons.

He is a good teacher, after all, and quite probably when Orion has other ideas, other ambitions, to fill his mind, his interest in this Mary will not last.

Throwing off the rug – which has still not warmed him in the slightest – he jumps up, stamping his feet and rubbing his hands to try to restore the circulation.

And it is still early – he peers at the clock to establish that it is not yet eight o'clock. He will walk across to Marlborough House and drop in on the Bulls, who will be happy to give him supper even if his visit is unexpected. Tomorrow he will see how the building of his new boat is progressing and then he will take the trap and drive out to visit Orion again.

Chapter 41

In this mild climate the daffodils were in already full bloom but Orion had found a few shooting bulbs in the back of one of his out houses and was unable to resist planting them, along with a border of primroses taken from the hundreds of clumps in the nearby woodland. He had also taken some roots of the montbretia which grew wild in the hedgerows and Mrs Roscrow had promised cuttings from her carnations. By next year his flower garden would have plenty of colour he told Mary as he paused after digging in the last of his bulbs.

"I do dearly love a flower garden." Mary looked at the line of wilting shoots that bordered the front pathway. "Da let me 'ave my own little patch when I was a little girl. I planted it with primroses too but I forgot to water 'em and they all died."

"They d'need taking care of." Orion poured water from his can carefully over his new plants and then stood staring out towards the cove and the glinting waters of the bay as Mary shook her dusting cloth and went back inside the cottage.

It was so hard to think of things to say, he thought as he heard the door shut behind her and dared to look round. And yet, as he sat on his own in front of the fire at night, or as he lay in bed, waiting for sleep, he thought of so much. Comments about the sea or the formations of cloud in the sky. Questions about Mrs Roscrow's chickens. Compliments even, about the new ribbon Mary had worn in her hair a few days ago or the way she had decorated the lamb pie she made for his supper yesterday, with a neatly plaited pastry O around the steam holes in the centre of the crust.

It was when she was actually there in front of him that all his clever ideas seemed to fly from his head, leaving him tongue-tied and feeling like an idiot.

She was so pretty, that was the trouble, with her brown hair pulled back from her face into a sort of shining knot at the nape of her neck and her large, brown eyes – so dark as to be almost black – that lit up so brightly when she smiled. And her slim waist, so noticeable when she tied her white apron around it. And her – he felt his face flush just at the thought – her full, firm breasts pushing out from under her dress like some comfortably ripening fruit...

No wonder he was struck dumb as Jacka every time he looked at her. No wonder, in bed at night and every night, his hand found its way down to his John Thomas and refused, however much he wished it otherwise, to leave it alone. And no wonder, remembering this, he found himself blushing like a girl when Mary arrived in the afternoons. Especially since Mrs Roscrow had confided in him that the 'understanding' between Mary and Tucker Chegwidden was at an end. Tucker, she said, had been seeing paying attention to a Helston girl who was well known for being no better than she should be.

"I'm not sure our Mary was ever that keen on 'im anyway," she said, throwing a handful of dried corn in the direction of her chickens. "Tucker never were that nice a man really. I reckons it was just she 'adn't seen anyone she liked better."

Wiping her hands across the front of her apron, she gave Orion a look he found hard to interpret.

At least Henry's return, even if it was a surprise, diverted him from the confusion of his thoughts and most days now he appeared, striding across the fields from the farm where he left the pony and trap he had hired for the duration of his stay, the weather being too unpredictable to make cycling from Pennance a comfortable option.

Some days they took their sketch pads and walked down the coastal path but mostly they worked in the bedroom–studio, Orion on what Henry called his 'exercises' – still life arrangements or detailed drawings or paintings of plants – and Henry on a series of sketches of Orion himself.

Who was not sure – in the midst of all his other uncertainties

– what he thought of this either.

The pictures were not posed. 'Just carry on with your work and take no notice of me' Henry instructed him when he first started them. 'Pretend I'm not here'. But that was easier said than done when, as he did his best to concentrate on the arrangement of shells and stones and a jar of last year's straggling Old Man's Beard, he could hear in the background the gentle movement of Henry's pencil against his sketching pad, the shuffle of shading, the crisp, firmer strokes of the stronger lines. How could he, so uncomfortably conscious of Henry's focussed eye, pretend he was not there?

It reminded him of the time he had stood in the shadows of the kitchen one afternoon just after Christmas as Mary stood at the mangle in the yard, the water pouring from his sheets and shirts as she turned the heavy handle. Then, sketchbook in hand, he had tried, with what Henry had once called 'a few swift strokes' to get onto paper the lines of her neck, her shoulders, her waist… He had not thought much of the result, although Henry, when he found it, had seemed oddly interested.

But then Henry liked drawing and painting people's backs. Boys' backs of course – he insisted that only boys would pose for him without their clothes. They were, he said, particularly fascinating. You could tell from the muscles and sinews of someone's back so much about the life they led and the sort of physical activities they enjoyed.

"You, for example." He had waved his brush, alarmingly, in Orion's direction. "You have strong, well-developed shoulders, from all your digging. Even through your shirt I can see that. The prominence of the shoulder blades. The deep cleft down the centre of your back…" A dreamy look had come into his dark eyes as though he were picturing in his mind something he could not see. "You can learn so much," he said, speaking in a different, more teacher-like tone of voice, "from the naked body. That's why colleges of art place such emphasis on life-drawing."

But this is just one more thing about which Orion is, at the moment, uncertain.

Is she, the policeman at Ida's door wants to know, Mrs Ida Goss? Wife of Percy Goss.

"Why? Wa's 'e done?" For policemen – and Percy Goss, for that matter – can mean only bad news.

He has died, the policeman tells her. He is young and not very experienced and somewhat intimidated by this large, crimson-faced woman who stands head and shoulders above him on her doorstep, wiping her wet hands, almost angrily, against her canvas apron.

"Of a seizure. Couple of hours ago. Down Market Street."

Going to or from The Grapes, Ida tells herself as she takes in the news. And drunk, as usual, no doubt. As the young man stutters his way through an account of how Mr Hosking was called from his chemist's shop to confirm that Percy was, as he formally expressed it, 'deceased' and how the men he describes as 'his companions' carried him back to his 'residence' she wonders why she is being told all this. She has hardly set eyes on Percy for almost eighteen years, most of which he has spent in the rat hole of a 'residence' he shared with Betty Angrove off Fish Strand Quay. If anyone is to be expected to mourn Percy Goss it is Betty Angrove, not Ida.

"Mr Hosking said it was only right you should be told. Being his lawful wife."

The young man answers her unspoken question.

"Yes. Well… thank-ee." And Ida, unable to think of anything else to say, closes her door.

Back in her kitchen she feels suddenly quite strange. Her head feels heavy, too heavy for her to keep holding it up, and her legs are correspondingly weak. Is this, she wonders as she sinks down onto her chair, what it is like to faint?

Mrs Trembath has frequent attacks of what she calls

giddiness, when she has to lie on her couch with the curtains drawn shut, smelling salts in her hand, and be given cups of tea, but Ida has never had the time for such elegant behaviour – nor has she ever felt the need. Now, faced with the reality of Percy's death, and much as she has despised and feared the man, she can see its attraction and, if she had a comfortable couch to lie on, she would probably do so. Instead she reaches the metal tea pot from the stove to pour herself a cup of, undoubtedly stewed, tea. Her hands, she notices, as she does this, are shaking and she wishes, more than ever, that Orion were here with her to discuss this startling, if not unwelcome, news.

It was two days before she plucked up the courage to walk up the road to Churchfield and ring at the front door.

"I'd like to see Mr 'Emy," she told the maid who answered her ring and followed her into the morning room where she stood, not daring to sit on any of the pale, upholstered chairs, and stared around her. It was, she couldn't help but notice, an attractive room, broad and sunny with pale green silk on the walls, darker green curtains at the windows and an abundance of cushions on the chairs and couches. Not at all the sort of room she would associate with the terrifying Mr Hemy – which, since it was his wife's sitting room, was perhaps not surprising.

And it was some time before Charles appeared. Told only by the maid, who was too flustered by the visitor's nervous ferocity to remember to ask her name, that 'a lady' wanted to see him and cross at being interrupted at his work, he took his time in cleaning the paint from his hands and removing his painting overall. Recognizing Mrs Goss – he had, after all, met her several times when they were settling Orion's emigration plans – his normal equilibrium was unusually disturbed.

"My dear Mrs Goss..." He held out his hand. "How very pleasant..."

Ida, unused to shaking hands, stood for a moment staring, forgetting completely the words she had been practising most of the two previous, sleepless nights, and Charles, conscious that he had intended, long before this, to tell her the truth about Orion's whereabouts, could only stare back.

"Please…" He made an effort to recover his composure. "Do sit down. May I offer you some tea?"

"My 'usband's dead. Percy Goss. 'E dropped dead in the street, day before yesterday. 'Alfway down Market Street," she added, as if the details were important. "A seizure, they said."

"Ah! I'm so sorry. Requiescat in pace." Forgetting for a moment that this man had been the cause of a great deal of pain and inconvenience, Charles stood completely still for several unnerving seconds, eyes closed. "My dear Mrs Goss…" He opened them again, "Please accept my condolences…"

"Oh no. Tha's all right. It don' matter. I mean… we an't… not for years…" Ida clenched her hands more tightly than ever around the handles of her shopping bag. "I come 'ere because I thought you'd know where my Orion's to. It's 'is father, after all. 'E should be told."

Charles nodded. Certainly if he should die he would want his sons to know.

Ida took a deep breath.

"After all," she said firmly, "There's no reason why 'e can't come 'ome now. Is there?"

Summoned by Charles' telegram, Henry went straight to Churchfield where his friend, irritated at having his work interrupted yet again, gave him short shift.

"You must go down immediately and make a complete confession to this poor woman. I can't tell you how upset and disturbed this whole business has made me and I want it to end at once." He brought down his hand on the back of a chair with a thump that made them both wince. "Go now, Henry," he said, in a tone of voice he had not used, even to his sons, for some years. "I want no more procrastination."

And Henry, uncharacteristically at a loss for words, went.

"I'm so sorry, Mrs Goss." He has intended starting with condolences until he realises how inappropriate this would be and switches to an apology. "I should have come to see you long ago."

Ida, standing in her front parlour – where else can she take a gentleman like Mr Tuke, even a gentleman of whom, for all his generosity, she is still deeply suspicious?– looks nervous. Has something, she wonders, happened to Orion that he should have told her about? There was that letter on fine, official notepaper that she received not that long ago from some man she had never heard of, telling her the ship Orion had sailed on had 'docked safely' in New York. She had assumed this meant that Orion too was safe but perhaps she had got this wrong. Or perhaps Orion has met with an accident in this dangerous country where they have fought wars against each other and where, as someone was telling her only the other day, Red Indians chop off the scalps of white men and hang them around their waists as prizes. Is some Red Indian at this very moment dancing outside his wigwam with her son's scalp tied to his waist by its fair curls?

"It's all right, Mrs Goss."

Henry, who has not been invited to sit down, stands uncomfortably between a high–backed chair and a table with a plant on it that appears to be dying, although in this shadowy room it is hard to tell. He peers worriedly at Mrs Goss, whose full cheeks seem to be an unnaturally deep shade of red.

"Nothing has happened to Orion. Nothing bad, I mean. He is well and happy. Very well indeed."

He pauses, hoping that what he is about to tell her is not going to cause her to fall into hysterics or faint or have some sort of nervous attack. Perhaps he should have brought a woman with him, he thinks, now that it is too late. Amy Hemy would have been a suitable person – although Charles might well have accused him of procrastinating still further if he had suggested

271

this.

If Mrs Goss collapses, what in the world should he do, he wonders, imagining himself fanning her with his hand, pressing a damp handkerchief against her brow, loosening her dress – heaven forefend! – or attempting to heave her bulky form onto her not very substantial–looking couch…

"Would you like to sit down?" He is well aware that, as the visitor, it is not his place to do this but is driven by desperation. "What I have to say is good news, I assure you – but it will surprise you…"

And, as Ida Goss sits, bolt upright and gripping onto the arms of her chair as if it might otherwise tip her off, he 'confesses', as Charles would have put it, everything.

"Why?"

The room is very quiet when he has finished. One hand on the clock in the corner marks off the seconds with an asthmatic wheezing. Carts squeak and rumble on the road outside. Boys run past, yelling incomprehensible words. A door slams in a nearby house… And Mrs Goss breathes heavily – but, Henry is relieved to hear, regularly – in and out for almost a minute before she speaks.

"Why did you do that? You was meant… You was paying for 'im to go America to start a new life. To give 'im a chance to better 'imself. Tha's what Mr 'Emy said."

"And that was my intention… What I meant to do. Sincerely. I assure you." Henry sinks down, uninvited, onto the overstuffed leather couch and holds out his hands. "But when it came to the point I…" But he can hardly tell the boy's mother that he could not bear to be without him. That he could not bear for him to cross the Atlantic and be lost to him for ever… "I felt I could help him more if he stayed in this country," he says instead. "He has talent, Mrs Goss. As an artist. And I wanted to go on teaching him. I do know what I'm talking about." For she is staring at him as if he is insane. "I am an established artist. I am an associate of the Royal Academy. My paintings have been exhibited, and praised, in galleries all over... I apologise," for she looks more bemused than ever. "All this means nothing to you. What matters is Orion. To you and to me!"

"My Orion? An *artist*. 'E don' know nothin' 'bout art!"

"Oh but he does, Mrs Goss. I assure you!" Henry balls his fist and thumps it against his other hand. "He has a real eye for detail. Have you never seen any of his work? The drawing of his washstand, for example?"

Ida Goss's mouth, already loose with astonishment, falls open still further.

"'Is *wash*stand?"

"Yes. The one here, up in his bedroom. You should see the drawing! You can see the scratches, the flaking wood..."

He waves a hand in the direction of the open door and the steep stairs leading up from the narrow hallway and then realises that he is making things worse. Mention of the bedroom – and then of the scratches and flaking woodwork of her washstand – is causing Ida's cheeks to flame more violently than ever.

"Can I take you to see him?" he asks instead. "Tomorrow. Or the day after. I can hire a pony and trap and we could be there in less than an hour."

"No!" Ida pulls herself upright from her chair and Henry, as if the same impulse rules them both, stands up as well. "You c'n tell 'im 'is da's dead. Tell 'im if 'e wants to come back 'ere 'e can. I don' know 'bout nothin' else I'm sure."

Now that Percy Goss is dead and no longer a threat, her only thought is that her Orion can come home. This does not mean that she is risking a journey miles up the coast with this strange, intense man whose motives – and most of whose words – she still does not understand.

Chapter 42

He had never felt so contented. Staring out over his growing vegetables, fenced off now from the yard where the pullets Henry had taken him to collect only days before scraped happily in the compacted earth, he felt as if this place had always been, in some strange way, his home. As though he had always known it and this was where he was meant to be. Now, looking up at the thin threads of cloud which drifted across the great bowl of the sky and the swooping, weaving shapes of the gulls that stood out, bright white against its blue, he knew already that he would stay here for the rest of his life.

And then Henry appeared – unexpectedly, for he had said he had work he must be doing in his own studio for a couple of days – with news that his father had died and his mother wanted him to come home.

"'Ow come 'e's dead?"

Percy Goss had never been a present figure in his life – he had left home long before Orion was conscious of his surroundings – but he had always existed, like some sort of shadow, or blight, on the edge of it. People had talked about Percy – drunk, abusive, violent and, on at least one occasion, in prison – lowering their voices if they happened to notice that Orion was nearby. He had occasionally read about Percy in the Falmouth Packet, when he was brought up before the magistrates. He had sometimes even seen Percy, although this was something he tried hard to avoid, around Fish Strand Quay or in one of Falmouth's many public houses.

In these ways his father had hovered over his life like a dark rain cloud – one that had become more than ever threatening after Alf had told Percy about Orion's friendship with Henry – and it had never occurred to him that anything about this would change.

Percy was a fact of his life and that was all there was to it.

And now he was dead, dropped dead, according to Henry, in Market Street, and it was hard to know what he was meant to say – or even what he was meant to think – about it.

"All right boy?"

Henry spoke gently but with the faintest touch of irony in his use of so Cornish an expression and put out a hand to touch his shoulder. Orion turned away, staring across his back yard where his chickens, disturbed by Henry's arrival, were venturing back out of their shed to peck irritably at the ground. In one hand he held the ball of twine with which he had been marking out the line of the seedlings he was about to plant. It hung loosely from his fingers as if he had forgotten it was there.

A gull landed on the roof of one of the outhouses, settled its wings noisily into place, and set up a loud squalling. The chickens, disturbed again, scuttled back into the shadowy safety of their shed.

"'E weren't a nice man." Orion picked his words with care. Ministers said you must honour your father as well as your mother but also that it was wrong to lie. Which made any statement about Percy Goss a little difficult. "I can't be sorry 'e's dead but it's strange to think of."

"Of course it is."

In a sense Henry would have liked Orion to be upset by the news so that he could, like a proper father, have comforted him. Pushing the unworthy thought from his mind, he forced himself to deliver the second part of his message.

"I went to see your mother when I heard the news." Orion turned, frowning. "I felt – Charles Hemy and I felt – that she must know where you are – especially now your father is no longer a… a threat to your safety," he explained hastily. "In fact she… she had been to see Charles, to ask if there was news of you."

The gull gave an even louder squawk and sprang from the roof into the air, dropping a splatter of white shit onto the slates as it took off. The young cockerel, peering from the outhouse, jerked backwards into the shadows and a stronger than usual gust of wind set the newly green leaves of the surrounding oak trees rustling as if in agitation.

"Did you tell 'er? Where I was?"

Orion watched the gull wheel across the cottage roof towards the sea, then looked back at Henry, who nodded.

"Of course. I had to. She has a right to know." He took a breath. "She asked me to tell you that you could come home now, if you'd like to."

"I don' wanna go 'ome. I d'like it 'ere."

Time had passed. Henry had shared Orion's bread and cheese lunch and they were up in his studio, Orion sprawling, uncharacteristically idle, on his chair, staring out of the window, while Henry sketched his untidy curls and worried expression.

"If I go 'ome I'll 'ave to go back to work for Mr Cyril, if 'e'll 'ave me, or for someone else. An' I won' be able to draw or paint no more. And," he move his head so that he was facing away from Henry, who put down his pencil, "we still won' be able to go on being friends. Not back in Falmouth. It'd still be no good."

He turned back, cheeks flaming, with a nervous half–smile.

"My dear boy!" The day had clouded over but, as Orion spoke, it seemed to Henry that the room was lit in sudden gold. "My dear, dear boy!" He reached across to press his arm – and then, with a supreme effort, "So, let's get back to work," he said hastily, covering his confusion. "I will explain to your mother how happily settled you are here and perhaps in the summer, when she's had time to get used to the idea, I will be able to bring her out here to visit you."

As he trotted the pony and trap home in the shadows of early evening, he couldn't remember when he had last felt so happy. Stones skittered from under the pony's hoofs as he pulled her up at the crossing where he would turn towards Maenporth and then Swanpool. A crepuscular blackbird sung joyously in the top branches of a wayside oak. A small creature – a stoat, perhaps, or weasel – diced with death as it raced across the dirt track in front of him and Henry laughed as it disappeared into the primrose leaves at the bottom of the bank.

Orion wanted to stay in his cottage. He wanted to go on with his art. And, most importantly – or so, at this moment, it seemed – he had chosen his friendship with Henry over returning to Falmouth and his mother.

Just for a moment, as he tugged gently on the right hand rein, turning the pony in the direction of home, he felt almost guilty about this. And then he remembered the futility and lack of opportunity of the boy's life in Falmouth – and his mother's unwillingness to come out and visit him in his cottage. Allowing the pony its head on the slight downward slope, he thought of the summer months that lay ahead and the long, happy, threat–free days he would spend with his pupil.

Chapter 43

So, his father was dead and no longer to be worried about. And his mother knew where he was and that he intended to stay here and what had seemed like some sort of dream, from which he would wake to find that everything was as it had been before, turned out to be real. The cottage, Henry had told him, was his for as long as he wanted it. He would be here to harvest his vegetables and sow more for next year and the year after and all the years to come. He would see his chickens become full-grown, lay eggs and produce their own successors. He would go, every week, to market, not just to buy but to sell and start to earn an independent living in his own home.

His own home…and all he needed was the right person to share it with.

The right person… and it was hard to feel that he hadn't found her. If only he could bring himself to tell her how he felt.

Every afternoon – she worked in the farm kitchen in the mornings and came to him when she had finished her chores – he found himself looking out for Mary's little figure – she was slightly built and several inches shorter than him – coming down the field. She would be wearing one of her light, cotton blouses and a long, dark skirt, her brown hair would be blowing either behind her back or across her face, according to the wind, and the hand that wasn't holding her basket would be doing its best to keep it in place.

He liked the way she did this. It was a part of her general neatness and once or twice he had found her in the scullery, head leaning forwards, busily brushing her hair so that she could pull it back tidily into its ribbon. She kept a hair brush, he had discovered quite by accident, on the little shelf under the stone sink, hidden behind the curtain she had hung there and sometimes in the evenings he would take it out and sit holding it, remembering its horsehair bristles pulling their way through her lovely hair. Mostly, he realised, she must clean it after she had used it but, just occasionally – perhaps she had been disturbed – she forgot and then he was able to pull out for himself the long, silken hairs, winding them round his finger into a fragile hoop which he could hold against his nose and breathe in their imagined fragrance.

It had become the highlight of his day, watching for Mary, rehearsing in his head what he would say to her as she came round the corner of the outhouse and into the yard.

Not that he was any nearer saying what he really wanted to say. Instead he would hear himself growl some comment about the wind or the muddiness of the yard or the excitability of the chickens before turning quickly away to his digging or wood–chopping in the hope that she wouldn't see the foolish crimson of his cheeks.

And then, one day just after Henry had left to resume his interrupted stay in London, it seemed that she was much later than usual and, tired of waiting, Orion gave up pretending to hoe among his growing crops and started up the field to meet her.

It was a still day for once and her hair hung neatly over her shoulders, which didn't stop her putting up a hand as if to tidy it as she saw him coming towards her.

"You coming to see Mr Roscrow?" She smiled as she spoke and Orion, daringly, said no, he was coming to see her.

"You can do that when I get down your place." She raised her chin and gave him what was quite a challenging look for a girl who had not long passed her sixteenth birthday.

"I din' wan' wait that long."

Orion held out his arm and, after the briefest of pauses, she took it.

They were walking out together, he thought, as they turned towards the house. She was his girl. It was as simple as that.

"I see." Henry, back for Easter, has noticed the change in his boy – even before Orion blurts out that he and Mary have 'an understanding'. "Isn't this rather sudden?"

"Not really."

He and Mary have known each other getting on for five months. Long enough for him to be sure that he… likes her more than any other girl he has ever known. Long enough to feel safe and comfortable with her.

"Are you saying…" Henry keeps his voice deliberately expressionless, "you want to marry her?"

"I dunno 'bout that!"

Marriage is a serious step and one that, much as he likes… loves Mary, he is not sure he is ready for. Besides which he would need his mother's consent if he is to marry. His mother whom he has not seen for almost the same amount of time – and who may have a great deal to say, when they do meet, about the fact that he has not, as she expected started a new life in America.

"I jus' thought…" But he is not sure what he thought. Except that it involves Mary making her home with him in the cottage. That things should be much as they are now – only more so. The 'more so' meaning that she will not go home every day at five o'clock and he will no longer have to spend his evenings contemplating her hair brush – or his nights trying to persuade John Thomas to settle himself down.

"I see."

And Henry does see, he supposes, as he feels the misery gather once more in the pit of his stomach. Certainly he knows that many people of Orion's class in society do not go through a formal marriage ceremony. That many so called husbands and wives have never had this fact legally recognised. He also sees that he might have anticipated such an outcome. That he was foolish to imagine that their friendship, however close, when he is so often away, is enough for the boy, who must be lonely out here on his own.

It is not surprising, he tells himself, that he should fall for a pretty face.

Assuming that this Mary has a pretty face. Henry, who has met her only once, with her rather more forceful mother, and has seen her since at a distance and busy with her duties, cannot remember and later, making the excuse of visiting the privy, he leaves Orion in his studio and goes out into the yard.

She is pegging Orion's freshly washed shirts on a line strung across the yard and as she lifts them from the tub the water runs down her bare arms. When the wind gusts across the yard the billowing clothes splatter her face with drops and she steps back laughing, putting up her hand to her hair.

And she is a pretty thing, Henry thinks, with dark brown hair pulled back into a knot at the nape of her neck and large, dark eyes that light her face as she smiles. And, although women's bodies hold no great interest for him personally, he can see that she is neat-waisted under her white pinafore and the arms which reach up again to the clothes line are slender and shapely.

"Allow me." He crosses the yard and takes up the forked pole that will lift the clothes higher into the air. As the girl goes to pick up the tub he takes that from her as well.

"I do throw it on Ori...on Mr Goss's veg. Coming on well, an't they?" She points towards the bed under the kitchen window.

"Indeed." Henry deposits the water where she has shown him, then hangs the tub on its hook. "I could do with a cup of tea. Would you have time to make me one?"

"Are you happy here?" he asks her, sitting at the table that she has scrubbed, he notices, to a state of which even Mrs Fouracre would probably approve.

He is, after all, her employer and there is no reason not to ask.

"Very 'appy, thank you Sir."

She puts the leaves in the pot and fills it from a kettle already humming on the range in the parlour. She has set in front of Henry an unfamiliar cup and saucer with dark blue stripes at the rim and now she pours milk from the metal container beneath the sink into a matching jug.

"It's a set we 'ad down 'ome." The girl sees him looking at the cup. "My aunty give it me. Not a full set but I thought Ori… Mr Goss might like it for when he 'as company."

She sets down a matching plate and Henry wonders what else she has brought to the cottage from 'down 'ome'. Thinks that the gift of unbroken china, even if it is not a full set, is no small thing. Considers this view of himself as 'company.' Notices a stone jar with a bunch of bluebells on the window sill. Jars of what appear to be bottled damsons on the shelf…

"Would 'ee like a fruit bun, Sir? They're fresh made."

She speaks politely and with composure and yet the look she gives Henry is a determined one. Almost defiant.

"You're a good cook," he tells her, biting into a bun.

"Ori… Mr Goss says I d'cook better'n his ma. But 'e's just being kind."

Henry cannot prevent himself from smiling.

"I think, if you normally call Mr Goss Orion, you should perhaps go on doing so. How old are you Mary?"

"Sixteen, Sir. An' almost two months." The dark eyes flicker towards him and then down to the floor.

How young, he thinks, who will be forty five in June.

He drinks his tea in silence. Eats another fruit bun and the girl, without asking, refills his cup. Then, apparently assuming from his silence that their conversation is over, goes across to the sink, pumps water which splashes noisily into the enamel bowl and starts to peel potatoes.

Henry watches. Is this, he wonders, why he brought Orion here? Why he took him away from his home, his family, his job, his friends…

"Have you seen any of Orion's work?" he asks the girl's back. "I mean, his drawing and painting. Not his swedes and carrots."

"Oh yes." She turns, smiling, he is pleased to see, at his small joke. "I think 'e's very… clever. I d'like the ones 'e's done of the back yard the best. Although it d'seem a strange thing to draw."

"Artists do sometimes choose strange subjects."

But Henry has seen no pictures of the back yard.

"Yes sir. And p'raps it don' matter. So long as e's 'appy with what 'e does." The girl wipes her hands on her apron as if her words are too important to be spoken with wet fingers. "Seems to me 'e's more 'appy when 'e's painting than any other time," she says firmly. "I wouldn't want to stop 'im doing that."

It is a declaration of love and he has lost him, Henry thinks, as he forces himself to finish his cup of tea, thanks her politely and gets up to go back upstairs.

Halfway up, where the widest, shallow stair bends round, and almost in darkness because the door onto the landing is closed, he pauses, leaning his head against the wall as if the weight of grief inside it has become too heavy to bear. She is not just a pretty girl; she is also a bright one and the good thing is that she will – if she means what she has just said – encourage Orion to continue with his work. The bad thing is that he, Henry, will – perhaps he already has – become redundant. He pulls at his moustache, allows himself one brief sigh of disappointment and then carries on slowly up the stairs.

Orion, concentrating on the earthenware jug Henry has set him to draw, looks up as he comes in.

"I've been talking to your young lady," Henry tells him. "She said something about drawings of the back yard. You haven't shown them to me."

His disappointment, he realises, causes him to speak gruffly, almost as if something has made him angry.

Orion looks guilty.

"I din' think… I mean to say, they're nothing like the stuff you give me to draw. Nor like your pictures. The sea and that…"

Henry thinks of his paintings of youths bathing or lying on the shore. Sailors working amongst the complex rigging of their ships. Jack Rolling, standing moodily in the bow of the Lily. 'The sea and that' could, he supposes, encompass these.

"You must draw, and paint, what attracts you. I thought I had made that clear." He still sounds as if he is reproaching the boy. "Draw what you want to draw. Not what you think will please me."

Orion, a red flush rising from his neck, pulls out from behind a wooden box – as if he may have been concealing it – a roughly bound sketchbook.

"I don' think they're no good but Mary…" He flushes a deeper scarlet. "She says she d'like them best of all."

And the girl, Henry thinks, looking at the sketches – part of a broken wall, a gull perched on the slate roof, Orion's garden spade leaning against the half–rotting door of one of the outhouses, the two wash-tubs on their hooks – is right. The pictures have the honesty he has always admired in Orion's work, a simplicity and attention to detail, but they have something else as well. There is love here and affection for this neglected place where he has made his home. These are not simply sketches of objects; they are infused with the artist's soul.

These, at long last, are pictures which will set him apart.

"Forget the jug," he says, and his voice is rougher than he would wish it to be. "I think you should concentrate on the subjects you most enjoy. Why don't we go down to the yard?" He makes a supreme effort. "You can draw Mary's washing blowing on the line."

Orion's face, he thinks, as he settles himself on a stool where he can sketch him at work, is altering. It is losing its roundness, his nose is strengthening, he is developing, along with the blond whiskers on his chin and upper lip, the look of a man, rather than a boy. And his blue eyes, he notices, as Orion goes past him into the kitchen to refill his water jar, no longer have their wistful, longing look, as if something is missing in his life.

"Don' fret…" His hearing is acute and Orion is only just

inside the open back door. "'E won' stay long. 'E's going out to dinner with friends, 'e says. 'E'll ave to leave soon."

The words twist like a knife in Henry's chest and the lines of his drawing blur in front of him.

"I shall be off to London again next week," he says as, later, he prepares to leave. "Is there anything I can send out from Falmouth before I go?"

This time last year he was reluctant to go. This year... This year he has no idea what he feels.

In one sense the leaving is more than he can bear. In another he is desperate now to put distance between them. The sight of Orion's new happiness – even if happiness is all he has ever wanted for him – is unbearably painful and he is afraid that, if he should stay longer, he will say, or do, something undignified.

And perhaps his dignity is all he has left.

"Let me know for certain when I come out at the weekend," he tells him. "It will be my last visit before I go. There are a lot of arrangements to be made first."

"Cratin' your pictures?"

"What? Oh yes. Of course. I have to get them to the Academy before April 22nd. This year's varnishing day. Not that I'll be able to varnish either of them. The paint won't be dry enough."

Beyond them in the cove the waves of the incoming tide splash and splatter against the rocks. A cormorant dives under water, disappears for several seconds and bobs to the surface unexpectedly close to the shore as Orion and Henry stare towards him.

They are both conscious that they have had this conversation before.

Afterword.

They have never been upstairs in this house before – Mary Bullen, née Goss, and her sister Elaine. They have visited many times, of course, especially as children, with their cousins, when they enjoyed feeding Grandpa's chickens, playing hide and seek in his rambling, stone outbuildings and swimming from the little cove in front of the cottage.

Their parents – and their aunts and uncles – had always complained bitterly, they remembered. About the cold that seeped from the stone floor, in spite of the rugs Grandma had put down, the rough stone walls that seeped dust onto every surface, the draughts from the doors and windows and the great, wide chimney. The next winter, they were always saying, would kill off the both of them but Grandma had lived to eighty nine and Grandpa had only just died, aged ninety two, so they had been wrong about that.

Although, once Mary and Elaine were grown up and were wives and mothers with homes of their own, they could see what a nightmare of a place it was. There had been improvements, of course, over the years. Gas and electricity and mains water had been laid on, none of which had been there, Granny Goss used to tell them, when she and Grandpa first married. The kitchen had been extended at the back of the house. And there was a small bathroom leading off it which, even though there was only a septic tank for the sewerage, at least it meant not having to go outside to the lavatory in its stone shed with the horrid possibility of spiders lurking under the corrugated iron roof.

Most of this had been paid for by their father, Henry, who was the eldest son and by far the wealthiest, having built up his market garden in the fields not far from the cottage into a thriving garden centre which he had just sold on to a national chain for a sum of money that would keep him and Mum in cars and cruises for the rest of their lives. He would happily have paid for his parents to move into a better house as well – a well–built, modern bungalow near their home in Falmouth, he kept saying – but Grandpa Goss was 'obstinate as they come' and there was no shifting the old man until he went out in his coffin.

Two weeks ago, that had been and it had taken Mary and Elaine this long to work themselves up to coming out here again. Mainly, although neither of them would admit it, because they dreaded the thought of going upstairs.

They were funny old stairs in that cottage. Leading up from the sitting room, from behind a door in the corner, and twisting sharply half way up. They knew this because this was as far as either of them had ever been.

"No need to go up there," Granny Goss would say, when they visited. "Nothing up there for prying eyes."

Which fixed it into their young heads that there must be something. Some secret that they mustn't know about.

And there had been stories about Grandpa. About how he had first come out here, to this odd little cottage half a mile from the road and two miles from the nearest village. He'd worked in a market garden in Falmouth, apparently – which made sense as he'd grown fruit and veg as long as he'd been here – and this famous artist, whose name neither Mary nor Elaine, who had no interest in art, could ever remember except that it was an odd one, had given him the cottage to live in.

Which was also odd and even odder was the story that Grandpa, a silent, lumbering old man with dirty nails and great, red fingers with calluses from all his digging, had been some sort of artist himself. Aunty Ida, who was the eldest child, had even talked of his having had an exhibition of his work in a gallery in Falmouth, but no-one took much notice of Aunty Ida, who was always a bit daft and had gone completely do-lally by the time she eventually died. The thought of Grandpa Goss in his old corduroy trousers and collarless shirt standing at an easel, clenching a paintbrush in his horny hands, was enough to make the rest of them giggle.

The key was where it had been left after the funeral – where Grandpa always left it, although he rarely bothered to lock the door – under a broken slate on the front window sill. The air that came out as Elaine thrust it open was cold – several degrees colder than the temperature outside – and smelt of musty carpeting, old pipe tobacco and something else that Mary said was 'mice'. And the living room looked as it had always looked – except that their mother, their remaining aunt and their Uncle Charles' wife Anna had removed all Granny Goss's ornaments and the few family photographs that had hung on the walls. No-one had wanted the furniture – not even the charity shops would take it, Elaine said, as none of the upholstered chairs were fireproof and most of the rest had woodworm – but her eldest daughter who was off to university had taken everything of value from the kitchen.

No-one had yet been upstairs and the estate agent was due this afternoon.

"It feels wrong somehow, doesn't it?"

The stairs were difficult in the dark and neither of them had thought to look for a light switch at the bottom and when Elaine pushed open the door at the top it was almost as dark up there. They were on a very small landing with one door in front of them and one to the right, both closed.

Mary nodded, although she was behind her sister who wouldn't see. She just hoped they weren't going to find anything really horrible up there. A pile of dirty bed linen, perhaps. More evidence of the mice they had smelled downstairs… or even rats. Or a stinking, forgotten chamber pot – Grandpa was very old after all; surely he wouldn't have staggered down those stairs to the bathroom if he'd needed to go in the night?

"Perhaps we'll find the decomposing body of the famous artist?" she giggled nervously.

But there was nothing out of place in their grandfather's bedroom. The bed was neatly made. His pyjamas lay folded on the bedside chair next to a Dick Francis paperback and the top of the chest of drawers held only his hair brush, a few tubes of ointment and some packets of pills with details of Boots Pharmacy on the labels.

The door to the other bedroom was locked.

"Leave it." Mary was already turning away. "Let the estate agent find his way in."

Elaine, always the more assertive one, wasn't having that.

"Suppose there *is* something in there? Something we wouldn't want outsiders to see."

"Then I wouldn't want to see it either."

But Elaine, as always, got her way and five minutes later, the key being in the obvious place in the knife drawer in the kitchen, she was turning it, with some difficulty, in the lock.

It was a sunny afternoon and the light flooded into this room which faced south westerly down the coast in spite of the salt residue that had built up on the glass over goodness knew how many years. And goodness knew how many years it was since anyone had come in here, thought Mary, the proud housekeeper, judging from the dust on the floor, on the table and the various filthy jars, rags and dried-up brushes that covered it, on the easel in the centre of the room and floating, in the way of dust mites, like tiny insects with no will of their own, in the air their unexpected entrance had brought in with them. And on the pictures, hundreds of them, it seemed, stacked against the wall.

"So he *was* an artist. Grandpa Goss. The stories were true."

Elaine, not noticing it seemed, the accumulated dirt that caught on her sleeve, drifted down the front of her coat and was starting to cover her shoes and form small piles on the floor beside her, pulled out picture after picture, holding them up for her sister to see. Some were quite small – painted on pieces of wood and showing sea scenes that reminded Mary of the paintings her daughters had brought home from primary school. Others were larger and more confident looking, framed, most of them as though they might have been part of the exhibition which they had been told about but never believed in. Not sea scenes this time but pictures of stone walls, of sheds, fences, bare hedgerows and stone stiles. One showed a young girl in a wind-blown dress pegging washing on a line. Others showed chickens pecking among rows of vegetables. Still more were of gardening implements – spades, hoes and forks, a wheelbarrow full of winter swedes… Others, on card or paper had been so chewed by mice that there was nothing left to see.

Against the far wall, next to the window, was a large, canvas-wrapped package. It would be more pictures, Mary thought, and she'd seen enough of them. And what in heaven's name, she wondered, were they meant to do with this lot? Were they worth anything? Should they try to sell them or give them to Oxfam? Or take them to the recycling yard? Or just burn them?

"Let's leave it for now. Hadn't we better just tell Father and Uncle Charles?"

But Elaine was already pulling at the string that held the canvas in place.

It must have been particularly tough canvas, Mary thought, because the mice hadn't got through it and none of the sketches, which slid out and across the floor until they were halted by the accumulated dirt and dust, were the slightest bit damaged.

"Who in the world…?"

The two sisters stared at the sheets of paper that stood out so clear and white against the filthy floor. And at the drawings, all of the same young man, a beautiful young man with wide-set, innocent, slightly puzzled-looking eyes.

"It can't be?"

But they had seen photos of their father and their uncle as

young men. And although neither Henry or Charles Goss had been as handsome as the boy in the picture, who must be their grandfather, there was no doubting the resemblance.

"Are they self–portraits? Or did someone else…?" And then Mary's eyes shifted to the painting that remained, propped against the wall and still half covered by its wrapping. A proper, framed painting on proper canvas and much larger than any they had seen so far.

It was also, even their inexperienced eyes could tell, the work of a much more accomplished artist.

It was a beach scene – Mary almost felt it might be a beach she'd visited – sand ridged from the outgoing tide, its left–over pools sparkling in the sunlight. A sea of shifting greens, blues, turquoise and points of gold, merged in the distance into paler, opaque blues and whites and a shimmering silver heat mist under a sky littered with fragile, scudding clouds.

Oddly, for what appeared to be a perfect summer day, there were no boats on the water but, in front of a rocky outcrop on the beach, lay an upturned dinghy and, leaning against it – Mary forced herself at last to fix her eyes on this, the focal point of the whole painting and the one she had been doing her best to avoid – a young man, the same, beautiful young man with those same innocent-looking, wide-set eyes, smiling uncertainly, his naked body seeming almost to glow in the summer light.

'For Orion from Henry' said the handwritten label in the bottom, left hand corner. 'August 1902. Coronation Day. With love.'